3.95

GUILTY UNTIL PROVEN INNOCENT

"You think homicide is *funny*? What's *funny* about death? What's *funny* about Murder One? What's *funny* about me?"

Renie leaped from the sofa and spun around the room. "Oh, good grief!"

Judith intervened. "Is that all? I can't think of anything else we can tell you that would be helpful."

Undersheriff Costello chortled nastily, then swung back to face the cousins. "How about the deceased's plans for the afternoon? How about all those empty beer cans? How about *grand theft*? What does the suspect have to say about *that*?"

"*Theft? Suspect?*" It was Judith's turn to be annoyed. "Now just a minute, Mr. Costello. My cousin and I aren't suspects. In fact, my husband is a policeman."

Undersheriff Costello refused to be impressed. "You think that people related to law enforcement officers never commit murder? Don't make *me* laugh!"

Bed-and-Breakfast Mysteries by
Mary Daheim
from Avon Books

FOWL PREY
JUST DESSERTS
HOLY TERRORS
DUNE TO DEATH
BANTAM OF THE OPERA
A FIT OF TEMPERA
MAJOR VICES
MURDER, MY SUITE
AUNTIE MAYHEM
NUTTY AS A FRUITCAKE
SEPTEMBER MOURN
WED AND BURIED
LEGS BENEDICT
CREEPS SUZETTE
A STREETCAR NAMED EXPIRE
SUTURE SELF

And in Hardcover

SILVER SCREAM

ATTENTION: ORGANIZATIONS AND CORPORATIONS
Most Avon Books paperbacks are available at special quantity discounts for bulk purchases for sales promotions, premiums, or fund-raising. For information, please call or write:

Special Markets Department, HarperCollins Publishers, Inc., 10 East 53rd Street, New York, New York 10022-5299. Telephone: (212) 207-7528. Fax: (212) 207-7222.

MARY DAHEIM

A Fit of Tempera

A BED-AND-BREAKFAST MYSTERY

AVON BOOKS
An Imprint of HarperCollins*Publishers*

This is a work of fiction. Names, characters, places, and incidents are products of the author's imagination or are used fictitiously and are not to be construed as real. Any resemblance to actual events, locales, organizations, or persons, living or dead, is entirely coincidental.

AVON BOOKS
An Imprint of HarperCollins*Publishers*
10 East 53rd Street
New York, New York 10022-5299

Copyright © 1994 by Mary Daheim
Library of Congress Catalog Card Number: 93-91032
ISBN: 0-380-77490-9
www.avonbooks.com

All rights reserved. No part of this book may be used or reproduced in any manner whatsoever without written permission, except in the case of brief quotations embodied in critical articles and reviews. For information address Avon Books, an imprint of HarperCollins Publishers.

First Avon Books printing: August 1994

Avon Trademark Reg. U.S. Pat. Off. and in Other Countries, Marca Registrada, Hecho en U.S.A.
HarperCollins® is a trademark of HarperCollins Publishers Inc.

Printed in the U.S.A.

10 9 8

If you purchased this book without a cover, you should be aware that this book is stolen property. It was reported as "unsold and destroyed" to the publisher, and neither the author nor the publisher has received any payment for this "stripped book."

ONE

JUDITH GROVER MCMONIGLE Flynn scooped up a handful of dirt, tossed it onto the bootbox, and bowed her head. At her side, Cousin Renie intoned the prayers for the dead.

" 'Out of the depths I have cried unto Thee, O Lord . . .' "

The words echoed in Judith's ears as she gazed down at the sturdy cardboard box that held her first husband's remains. Dan McMonigle had been dead for five years, but, Judith reflected, he had traveled more since his early demise at age forty-nine than in the last decade of his sedentary life. From the squalid rental house on Thurlow Street to the Grover home on Heraldsgate Hill, from the old toolshed in the backyard to the commodious Edwardian basement, he'd finally come to rest under the evergreens at the family cabin.

" 'From the morning watch even until night let Israel hope in the Lord . . .' "

Dan had enjoyed the cabin, as much as he had enjoyed anything other than stuffing his face, guzzling booze, and making Judith's life miserable. His business schemes had ruined their finances, his disposition had soured their marriage, and eventually, his gluttony had destroyed him. As Judith was wont to put it, when Dan hit over four hundred pounds, he blew up. It wasn't precisely true, but it was close enough.

"May he rest in peace. Even if he was the biggest jerk I ever met. Amen." Renie closed the prayer book and grabbed a shovel. "We did it, coz. Mike will be pleased. And Joe ought to feel relieved."

Judith, however, was still standing motionless at the other side of the shallow grave. There were tears in her black eyes. For whom? she wondered. For Dan, who had sympathy only for himself and strangers? For Mike, who had loved Dan as a father, but resented the harsh treatment of his mother? For herself, she who had been more relieved than grief-stricken when Dan died? Or for the eighteen years they had wasted, with Judith struggling to keep their travesty of a family together and Dan losing the fight against his self-destructive demons? Judith saw that Renie was looking at her, half-smiling, half-frowning.

"Well?" Renie demanded, shoveling dirt over the bootbox. Judith didn't say anything. Renie shrugged and kept shoveling. "That's okay. Go ahead and cry. You never did much when Dan was alive. At least not around me. If Joe were here, he wouldn't blame you, either."

Joe. Her second husband's name stopped the tears and brought a smile to Judith's face. She squared her wide shoulders, forced her statuesque figure to stand erect, and picked up the other shovel. The May sun filtered through the vine maples. Fallen branches covered with moss crisscrossed the dark earth. New ferns, budding trilliums, wood violets, and wild ginger grew around the little hollow. It was so peaceful in the forest, Judith thought, with the sound of the river rolling past and the spring air tinged with the lush scent of new growth. Across the river, above the cottonwood, Douglas fir, and alder trees, Mount Woodchuck sat comfortably with its winter crown of snow.

Renie threw out more dirt, then began stomping about, evening off her handiwork. She grasped a small vine maple branch and snapped it in two. "I'll make a cross to put on top," she said. "Or should I form a 'D' for Dink?"

Judith's expression was wry. "It'll work either way." She waited for Renie to complete her task, crossed herself, and collected both shovels. The cousins headed back up the little rise to the cabin.

For over half a century, the rustic summer home had sheltered the Grover clan. Only in the past few years had the younger generation developed other interests, and in the process, become weaned away from the verdant forest and outdoor plumbing. The cabin had suffered neglect. Moss covered the shingles; the front-porch floorboards were rotting; the downspouts, blown away in a winter windstorm, lay rusting among the salmonberry bushes.

Still, the interior provided a snug retreat. No one could have guessed by looking at the exterior that the little cabin could sleep at least ten without resorting to sleeping bags. The living room contained a fold-out couch and a Murphy bed; the two bedrooms next to the kitchen held a double and two twins, respectively; the loft had yet another double bed. The furniture was old and inexpensive, an eclectic grouping of cast-off wooden chairs and tables. Grandma Grover's homemade curtains hung at the windows, their serviceable blue-and-white plaid faded by the sun. Linoleum covered the floor, cracked and patched, worn away by four generations of work shoes, wedgies, bedroom slippers, sandals, sneakers, combat boots, hiking boots, fishing boots, and, in high summer, bare feet.

Though the world had changed in over fifty years, the cabin had not. The kitchen's wood stove remained, as did the sink with no running water. The cousins had stopped nine miles down the highway in Glacier Falls to pick up ice for the icebox. There was no electricity, and the outhouse was a good twenty yards from the back door. While the younger generation of Grover-McMonigle-Jones *et al.* found it a bore to rely on Coleman lanterns for light and on their own devices for entertainment, Judith and Renie enjoyed getting back to Nature, at least occasionally.

"I'll start a fire," said Judith, delving into the wood box. "It may be spring, but it's still cool."

"I suppose we can't haul water from the river like we used to before we learned about germs," mused Renie. "Do you think The Artist will mind if we dip into his well?"

Judith was crumpling old newspaper. "He never has. Of course, it's been a while since we've been over there."

"And he wasn't world-famous when we used to trot our buckets to his place ten years ago," Renie noted. "Riley Tobias has done very well for himself. I saw in the paper the other day that his paintings command a fifty-grand minimum."

"Wow!" Judith raised her dark eyebrows. "Think of all the customers I'd have to run through the Bed & Breakfast to earn that much! I'm lucky if I take in three grand a week during the height of the tourist season. And that's gross."

"It's gross, all right," Renie replied, getting down on her haunches to wrest the water bucket and the metal five-gallon milk container from under the sink. "My last graphic design project brought me a niggardly four grand, and it took six weeks. Maybe I should call myself a real artist and pretend I can paint. Some of Riley's recent stuff looks like he sat on it."

The newspaper flamed; the kindling crackled. Judith replaced the heavy round stove lid, then opened the vent on the chimney. "This stretch of river has always attracted artists and such. Is that how you got inspired, coz?"

Renie snorted. "You know what happened. My college profs got sick of me doodling instead of taking notes. Dr. Putz in the History Department told me to get the hell out and hie myself over to the Art Department. I took him seriously." Her round face grew ingenuous. "And thus was a career in graphic arts launched. Wasn't it lucky I knew what I was doing?"

"It's more than I did," said Judith, waiting to make sure the old stove wasn't likely to blow up. "Oh, I enjoyed being a librarian, but I would have liked it more if I hadn't had to make extra money tending bar at the Meat & Mingle while Dan lay around like a lump and ate us out of house and home. Running the B&B is much better. Especially now that I have a husband who—imagine!—actually *works!*"

Renie grinned at her cousin. Judith's elation over her second marriage had not yet worn off. Their first anniversary was coming up in late June, and if Joe Flynn could get away from his duties as a big-city homicide detective, they planned a long weekend in San Francisco. Judith beamed in anticipation, then suddenly pulled a long face.

"I shouldn't have come here for three days," she declared, grabbing the big galvanized water bucket. "If I'm going to take off in June when the guests start pouring in, I should have stayed home now."

Renie gave an impatient shake of her short chestnut curls. "You haven't had a break since your honeymoon. Relax. It's Tuesday of the first week of May. You only have four guests coming in while you're away, and Arlene can take care of them. She's done it before; she knows the drill like the back of her hand."

Judith had to admit that Renie was right. Besides being a longtime friend and neighbor, Arlene Rankers was well versed in the hospitality business. Still, Judith had qualms. "It's not the B & B that bothers me so much as . . . Mother. This is the first time I've left her alone with Joe. Or should I say, left Joe alone with her."

Renie pushed open both halves of the Dutch door. "Don't worry about it. Your mother has her apartment in the old toolshed, and Joe will be in the house—when he's not at work, sorting out mass murderers."

Judith remained dubious as she and Renie trudged through the trees to the meadow that fronted Riley Tobias's house and studio. The clearing, which had probably been part of a farm in an earlier era, provided an untrammeled view of the mountain. Long grasses, clover, wild strawberries, and vetch sprawled from the riverbank to the fence, from evergreens at one side to birch and alder on the other. The setting provided a favorite foreground for Tobias, who was also keen on cloudscapes. His one-story house was considerably newer but only slightly more sophisticated than the Grover cabin. The studio, however, was dazzlingly different, with huge panes of glass, two skylights, and a stone fireplace.

It was there that the cousins first spotted Riley Tobias, his back turned to them as he tossed some crumpled paper onto the empty grate. Judith wondered if it was a discarded sketch; she marveled that he didn't try to sell those, too. Riley Tobias seemed to have reached a point in his career where he could have sold his doodles in the Yellow Pages.

Since Tobias wasn't actively painting, the cousins had no trepidation about knocking on the knotty pine door. The artist opened it almost at once, beaming in welcome.

"Judith! Serena! It's been years! Come in!" He stepped aside and made a courtly bow. The big smile stayed in place, emphasized by the graying brown beard and tangled mane of curly hair. Riley Tobias was a big man, well over six feet, broad of shoulder, wide of chest, with huge hands that could apply paint to canvas in the most delicate ways.

He offered chairs; he proffered beer. The cousins accepted both. The studio was remarkably uncluttered, with only a few paintings tucked away under cloths and a large but empty easel. There was no sign of paints or palettes or brushes at the ready. Judith guessed that they had caught Riley between works. After the initial catching up, she posed that very question.

Tobias laughed, his big body vibrating with amusement. "I'm between periods, actually," he replied. "You know my landscapes—the mountains, the sky, the forest, the river. That was the seventies and most of the eighties. Then came people—my own version, what I call neonerdism. Not in public, of course." He laughed some more. "But people are such . . . silly creatures. They're so *average.* And that's what I wanted to capture, the ordinariness of the human race." He got up, causing his cane-backed chair to rock on its legs. Tobias bounded over to the covered paintings. "Look here—is this or is this not a nerd?" He whipped off the cover to reveal a five-by-seven-foot acrylic of what looked to Judith like a plate of cole slaw.

She blinked. "Ahhh . . ." She darted an appealing glance at Renie.

"Mm-mmm," murmured Renie.

Tobias tapped the orange part of the canvas. "See those eyes? No expression. He isn't perceiving. His body language"—Riley pointed to what looked like a blob of mayonnaise—"is timorous, ineffectual. He's caught in life's trap, destined to live out his days in vain." With his knuckles, the artist rapped on a zigzag pattern of bright green tinged with brown. "That's his soul—fresh, untried, yet withering around the edges. Painters, like writers and poets, seek Truth. You can paint a lie. In fact, you can do it without knowing you lie. But the measure of greatness," Riley went on without the least nuance of self-consciousness, "is in capturing what is true. That's what my nerd is all about. I'm not quite finished exploring the spiritual side. Does it dismay you?"

Judith was indeed dismayed, but not for the reason Riley Tobias thought. All she could think of was cabbage, left by her mother in the refrigerator until it spoiled along with the mauve baloney and the blue horseradish. "Gee, Riley," she said, trying to sound enthused, "it's certainly a change from your earlier style."

"Yeah," agreed Renie, never as strong on tact as her cousin, "we used to be able to tell what you'd painted. At least we knew the difference between animal, vegetable, and mineral. Are you sure you haven't enrolled in the Twenty Questions School of Art?"

Briefly, Riley Tobias looked annoyed. Then the big smile again spread through his beard. "Serena Grover Jones, you are, as ever, too tart. If I were to ask why you put a castle on the cover of a real estate company brochure, what would you say?"

Renie looked only a bit taken aback. "That the company I was working for wanted to project an image of palatial properties, of affluence, maybe even security." She gave a little shrug.

Tobias had set his nerd up on the easel and returned to his chair. "Exactly! But that company is *not* selling castles. I'm not painting portraits." He leaned forward, his elbows on his knees, his vivid blue eyes darting from cousin to cousin. "Do you get it?"

"Well—sort of," Renie allowed, picking up her can of beer.

Judith gave a little shake of her head. "I know what you're saying, Riley. I've never understood abstract art, or whatever you call it. You'll have to forgive my ignorance."

Riley took a big pull from his beer, then shot out of his chair again, apparently struck by inspiration. "I can do better than that!" He lunged across the room once more, this time wrestling with a very large painting that was at the back of the covered collection. At last he managed to pull it away from the others and set it on end in front of Judith and Renie.

"My last landscape," he announced with flair. "It's yours."

Judith remembered Riley's earlier landscapes as falling into two categories—sure, strong strokes of bold color, or muted pastels that evoked a tranquil feeling. His last—or at least his latest—was a hodgepodge of blue, green, brown, pink, purple, and yellow. The colors weren't unpleasing, but the execution was jarring. Riley might have been trying to capture a river scene—or more cole slaw. Judith tried to focus on the subject matter and took a wild guess:

"Oh, Riley," she said with a crack in her voice, "you painted it *here?*" She saw him nod with self-satisfaction. "It's . . . striking! But I couldn't possibly take it. This painting must be worth a fortune."

Tobias, holding the painting with one big hand, gave a shrug. "I knew you'd say that. Then borrow it instead.

Hang it in the cabin. Or would you like it for that B&B you've set up?"

Judith tried to imagine the Riley Tobias original among the English hunting prints, the Dutch florals, and the Hudson River school landscapes that dominated the walls of Hillside Manor. Tobias's work was four feet high and five feet wide. She had no idea where to put it. Maybe, she thought, blinking at the clashing colors, high on the stairwell, where the sun didn't shine . . .

Tobias gingerly set the painting against a large seaman's chest. "I'll wrap it for you. How long are you staying up here?"

"Just three days," Judith replied, watching Riley Tobias wrestle with a roll of bubble-wrap and some sturdy cardboard. She and Renie exchanged quick glances of dismay. "Really, this is too generous. You must have all sorts of old friends and devoted admirers who'd love to have that . . ."

But Riley was chuckling and shaking his head. "When it comes to friends, I travel light. Always have; you should know that. As for admirers, let them pay." Deftly, he tied heavy twine around the covered painting. "Early on, twenty years or so ago, when I was still splitting my time between this place and the houseboat in town, who kept an eye out for me? You and your relatives, that's who. Remember that winter when your Uncle Corky shot a mountain lion that was trying to break into the studio?"

Judith and Renie did. Uncle Corky had come up to the cabin to replace part of the roof that had blown off in a severe November storm. In the process, he had managed to avoid his waspish wife, Aunt Toadie, for almost three blissful, solitary weeks.

"Well . . ." Judith hedged.

But Riley Tobias's decision was final. The threesome resumed drinking their beer and reminiscing. As usual, the subject of Tobias's mentor, Ward Kimball, came up. Renie's inquiry was met with a sad shake of Riley's head.

"Ward hasn't painted for some time. He's feeling his

age, his eyesight is poor, he's pretty shaky. It's a shame." Tobias sighed, shifting around in his chair as if he were uncomfortable with the idea of age overcoming talent. He opened another can of beer. "He was brilliant, a real genius of the Northwest school, right up there with Tobey, Graves, Callahan."

Renie inclined her head and went straight to the bottom line. "But he never made a lot of money. That is, the others didn't command huge prices in their day, either, but Ward Kimball came along just enough later that he could have rung up some big sales if he'd . . ." She paused, apparently trying to figure out the economics of art. "What, Riley? Promoted himself? Had an aggressive gallery behind him? Curried favor with the critics? How have you done it?" Renie's frequently feigned ingenuousness was now sincere.

Tobias frowned, stood up, paced a bit, and scratched at his beard. "Who knows?" he said at last in a musing voice. "A lot of it's luck. Sure, Clive Silvanus has worked his butt off for me. I got sick of haggling with galleries and having to suck up to people. Now I've got Clive, and I couldn't ask for an agent who would have my interests more at heart. But Ward never wanted to be bothered with any of the business side—he wanted to be left alone to paint in peace. That's why he moved up here to the river in the first place. That was what—forty years ago?"

"More like fifty," Judith replied. "I can't remember a time when Ward Kimball didn't live down by the Big Bend."

Renie was nodding in agreement. "That was one of my father's favorite fishing holes. He used to cut through Ward's property from the road. They were buddies."

Riley nodded, a small smile on his face. The image of Cliff Grover carrying his expertly wrapped trout rod, hefting his wicker creel over his shoulder, and moving easily in his fishing boots over the rock-strewn riverside had been as familiar a sight as Ward Kimball with his basket of paint tubes, his easel, and a glass milk bottle full of brushes.

"It'll be the same old story," Riley said with a deeper, sadder sigh. "When Ward is dead, the prices of his paintings will skyrocket. It always happens."

Judith finished her beer. "At least Lark will benefit," she remarked, referring to Ward Kimball's daughter. "A good thing, too, since she's almost blind. Has she ever worked?"

The mention of Lark Kimball's name seemed to dispel the gloom that had momentarily hung over Riley Tobias. "Oh, sure. She got her degree a long time ago in special ed. She's taught off and on in Glacier Falls."

"Good for her," said Judith. "I've always thought it was the greatest of ironies that Ward Kimball should have a daughter who couldn't see his paintings clearly. You know, like Beethoven going deaf. Sort of." Indeed, Judith remembered young Lark vividly, a beautiful child with wisps of curling ash-blond hair and big, unfocused blue eyes. "She must be thirty by now," Judith mused.

"Thirty-two," said Riley, reaching into a picnic hamper and taking out a bag of pretzels. "Want some?"

Judith declined, but Renie couldn't resist. "What was it?" Judith asked. "As I recall, Lark's mother was in her forties when she had their only child."

Riley had surrendered the pretzels to the always-ravenous Renie. "They married later in life, at least for those days. Lark was premature, which is what caused the vision problems. She never could see well, even with glasses. Light, color, vague shapes—that's about it. To make things worse, Mrs. Kimball died before she was fifty. Cancer." The artist had turned very solemn. "Ward didn't paint for two years. In fact, he almost sold the place at the Big Bend. But Lark felt at home there, she was familiar with everything, inside and outside, and Ward decided not to uproot her. Losing her mother was a big enough blow. More change might have ruined a seven-year-old."

Judith got to her feet, anxious to return to their own cabin. She was always a trifle nervous about leaving a fire in the stove when it hadn't been used for a while. "I haven't seen the Kimballs for some time. Seven, eight years ago, Dan and I ran into them up at the Green Mountain Grocery. Ward was still painting then."

Riley Tobias also had stood up, though Renie continued to devour pretzels. "He probably was. It's only been in the past couple of years that he stopped." Riley picked up the painting he'd given to Judith. "Let me carry that. You two have to tote the bucket and the milk can."

Judith gazed at Renie, who suddenly looked guilty, set the half-empty bag of pretzels on the floor, and tried to smile at their host with her mouth full. "Don't bother, Riley. We can manage. I'll carry the water. One in each hand will give me balance."

Riley Tobias offered only a token argument. Five minutes later, the cousins had drawn their water and were about to head back for the cabin when a whirring noise ruptured the forest calm.

The sound grew louder. Judith and Renie both looked up, since the sky seemed to have come alive with ear-shattering resonance. Hovering over the river was a helicopter, its gleaming cockpit sparkling like silver in the afternoon sun. It veered to the right, over the mountain ash, alder, and cottonwood that bounded the meadow, and descended onto the wildly stirring grasses. Hair blowing in their faces, the cousins were forced to brace themselves.

The roto-blades slowed, flickered, and stopped. Judith rubbed at her ears, relieved at the cessation of sound. She and Renie watched curiously as a man in a shiny black helmet and a gray Armani suit got out of the copter. He was carrying a leather briefcase and a huge bouquet of flowers.

"Hi," Judith said in a small voice as the man strode briskly toward Riley's house.

The man nodded, an absent gesture. He was tall and lean, with prominent cheekbones and a sharp nose. Large brown eyes gazed soulfully from under heavy dark brows. His brown hair was combed straight back and hung just above his collar. Judith guessed him to be in his early forties.

Riley had come out of the studio. He was beaming through his beard and waving a hand in effusive greeting. "Lazlo! You came! I thought you were headed back to Budapest!"

The newcomer stopped and saluted Riley with the bouquet. "How could I stay away? I am drawn, as the Danube is pulled to the sea."

With a hearty laugh, Riley rushed to embrace his guest. The big bouquet of mums, lilies, and baby's breath rocked in the stranger's grasp. In his effusiveness, Riley didn't notice. "You're a crazy man, Lazlo. Come in, have a beer. Oh!" Remembering the cousins, Riley hastened to introduce them. "Lazlo Gamm is my favorite Hungarian émigré. We met years ago in the Haight. He was a starving oboe player when I was a starving artist."

Judith resisted the urge to remark that Lazlo's thin frame looked as if he were still starving. But the helicopter and the Armani suit clearly indicated otherwise. "Do you play the oboe nowadays, Mr. Gamm?" she asked with a smile.

Lazlo Gamm's lean face grew morose. "I only play sad songs of love. Alas, I play them often these days."

Riley Tobias clapped Lazlo on the shoulder. "Don't believe a word he says. If Lazlo ever really fell in love, I'd keel over! Meanwhile, he's bringing decadent American art to his newly enlightened homeland. Lazlo is a top-notch international art dealer."

Lazlo nodded in glum acknowledgment. "It is, as they say, a dirty job, but someone's got to do it." He spoke with only the faintest of accents. "I'm not certain the former comrades are ready for Riley's latest works."

Judith tended to go along with the comrades, but she held her tongue. The cousins exchanged a few more pleasantries with Riley and his new guest, then took their leave. Lazlo Gamm still looked gloomy.

"He flew that sucker himself," Renie noted as they

passed the empty copter. "That's pretty tricky, landing in this meadow."

"I take it that Lazlo is a man of many talents," Judith replied. "Having fun isn't one of them, from the looks of him."

Renie walked slowly along the trail behind Judith, careful not to spill any of the water. "I wonder what Lazlo would think if he knew you were lugging a Riley Tobias around the woods."

"I don't know what he'd think, but I'm flummoxed," Judith announced as they opened the front door. "How in the world did I end up with a pricey painting that looks like Sweetums? I've got enough trouble hiding his ugly little hide now that he's back home from your mother's apartment."

Judith's cat and Judith's mother had both ended their exile at Aunt Deb's apartment the previous autumn. The plan to have the cousins' mothers live together had proved disastrous. Although the two sisters-in-law possessed a grudging affection for each other, they had waged an ongoing war that would have taxed the ingenuity of a United Nations peace-keeping force. Judith had said as much to both her mother and her aunt. Deborah Grover had assumed her most martyred air; Gertrude had snapped, Why not?—they'd both been around a lot longer than the UN. Judith had shut up.

"Maybe you could sell it," Renie suggested, carefully putting down the full water containers next to the faucetless sink.

But Judith was shaking her head as she placed the painting against the far wall. "Riley would hear of it. I wouldn't dream of hurting his feelings." She reached behind the drape that matched the curtains and pulled down the Murphy bed. "I think we ought to ditch this for now. It's too unwieldy to haul up to the loft, so behind the bed will have to do. Even if we think the picture's gruesome, somebody else might not. And it's sure worth a lot with Riley's signature."

"Good thinking, coz," replied Renie, pouring herself a glass of well water. "You want some help with that bed?"

Judith, however, had the situation under control. She wedged the big painting between the mattress and the pad that covered it. "It'll just barely fit. Up we go." The bed swung back into place and Judith rearranged the blue-and-white-plaid drape. "I suppose I could forget to take it home with us."

Renie gave Judith a wry grin. "Like fun you will. Once you get used to it, you'll be glad to have a Riley Tobias original. It'll impress the hell out of your B&B guests."

"You're right." Judith sighed, then went to the stove to check on the fire. It was out. She swore softly, crumpled more newspaper, threw in more kindling. "For all I know, Joe might actually like it. After all," she added as she struck a match, "it's a work of art that serious connoisseurs would kill for."

"Right," agreed Renie.

The newspaper caught; the kindling snapped. Judith replaced the cast-iron stove lid once more. And, standing next to the fire on a mild May afternoon, wondered why she suddenly felt cold.

TWO

One load of garbage, a sackful of mildewed linen, and two dead mice later, Judith and Renie had the cabin clean as well as aired out. They had used a machete to hack down the tall grasses that grew in front of the porch, they had done their best to sanitize the outhouse, and a pile of fallen limbs that could be used as firewood was stored under the porch. Lazlo Gamm's helicopter had taken off halfway through their chores, causing Judith to look up from pulling out a large thistle by the porch, and Renie to glance through the window where she was scouring the sink. The emaciated art dealer had departed as noisily—and perhaps as glumly—as he had arrived. Now only the rolling river and the soft rustle of the trees could be heard outside the cabin. Meanwhile, the fire was crackling merrily in the stove, the Coleman lanterns were readied for the evening, and the twin beds were made up in the little back bedroom. The cousins had just poured themselves a drink and were sitting out on the front porch in matching metal deck chairs when they saw a doe across the river.

"Sweet," murmured Renie, sipping at her bourbon.

"Mmm," agreed Judith, admiring the animal's nonchalant grace. "Remember the time Uncle Vince got chased by a porcupine?"

Renie laughed. "He swore it was six feet tall. After they went to bed that night, Auntie Vance stuck him with a hat-pin just to scare him." Renie stopped laughing and looked at her watch. "It's almost five. I'm starved. We missed lunch."

Judith gave Renie a look of mock exasperation. "That's because we ate a late breakfast in Glacier Falls around eleven. Besides, you gobbled up about two pounds of pretzels over at . . ." She paused, turning toward the sound of snapping twigs along the bank above the river. The doe apparently heard it, too, and ambled back into the cottonwoods.

Among the ferns and vine maples, the cousins could see the slim figure of a woman carrying a large paper bag. She moved as gracefully as the doe, and with equal confidence. Judith frowned in the effort of recollection: The newcomer was no stranger. Judith got to her feet, almost spilling her scotch. "Iris! Hi! Remember us? The cousins?"

Iris Takisaki ascended the little knoll and glided across the grassy area that made up the cabin's front yard. "Of course!" She gave the women a dazzling smile. "I hope you don't mind my trespassing. I couldn't get my car started up at Green Mountain. It's been acting peculiar ever since I left the freeway." She hugged the grocery bag. "I just got up here from town and figured that Riley was probably out of some basics. He usually is." Her words were ironic, but the tone was fond.

Judith offered a chair, but Iris declined. "Riley doesn't know I'm here. He probably expected me sooner, but I got tied up with a client who insisted on furnishing his new offices with the very worst examples of cubism. I'm still not sure I convinced him otherwise. I don't understand why corporate executives hire art consultants if they've got preconceived notions."

Renie nodded in vigorous agreement. "You must deal with the same morons I get. Bankers who want Grecian columns on the covers of their annual reports or public utilities that just have to show their workers struggling in an ice storm. I practically have to beat them over the head to get rid of all those clichés."

Shifting the grocery bag from one arm to the other, Iris gave a merry little laugh. "How true! And colors! How these people get locked into combinations! Five years ago it was all teal and gray, then came the Santa Fe pastels . . ."

Judith only half-heard the professional exchange between art consultant and graphic designer. The other half of her mind focused on Iris Takisaki, a handsome woman of Nisei heritage in her forties, with jet-black hair securely held in place with a pewter clip. Her oval face was carefully, if lightly, made up, accentuating her wide-set, almond-shaped eyes and her meticulously plucked, slanting brows. She was tall for a Japanese woman, almost at eye level with Judith. She wore a tan trench coat over coffee-colored slacks and a black turtleneck sweater. Heavy silver bracelets decorated one wrist and a beaten-silver pendant in the form of a swan hung from a chain around her neck. The strap on a large brown hand-tooled leather bag was slung over her left shoulder. She had aged remarkably little since Judith had last seen her seven years earlier. Indeed, Iris's looks had improved with time, from a youthful graduate student's unsure prettiness to the mature woman of sophistication and self-confidence. It occurred to Judith that life as an art consultant had treated Iris kindly. Apparently, being Riley Tobias's mistress for two decades had also been good for her.

Iris and Renie were winding up their mutual horror stories of clients gone wrong. "I'd better get these things to Riley before he sends out the sheriff to look for me," said Iris, giving the grocery bag a hoist. "Come for a drink this evening, all right?"

The cousins accepted the invitation, then waved Iris off. For a few moments they watched her in silence as she made her way over the uneven ground and then disappeared among the tall stand of cedars and Douglas fir that separated the Grover and Tobias properties.

"Preserved or pickled?" said Renie at last.

Judith shot Renie a reproachful look. "Neither, coz. She's one of the lucky ones. Great bones. Model quality."

Renie was unconvinced. "Face-lift. Cosmetic surgery. Went to Bags R Us to erase everything but her nose. Too thin."

"Hey, quit griping," countered Judith. "You aren't exactly fat, coz. You can eat about four million calories a day and not look like Dan."

Mildly placated, Renie leaned back against the top step. "Iris probably doesn't eat much. Gee, I wish she'd asked us to dinner. Japanese food is about my favorite."

Judith looked askance at Renie. "How can you possibly decide? I thought your favorite food was Aisle A to Z at Falstaff's Market. Besides, I'll bet she cooks from one end of the ethnic rainbow to the other."

"Yum." Renie licked her lips. "Still, there's nothing quite like real yaki soba. Or tempura prawns. Then again, I'm extremely fond of beef teriyaki, medium rare . . ." Her voice faded away as she contemplated yet more Asian delicacies. Across the river, the cottonwoods and alders swayed in the late afternoon breeze. Crows cawed overhead, then soared from the evergreens, circling high above the rippling waters. Judith closed her eyes, soothed as always by the sound of the river and the scent of the forest. Fresh. Damp. Primeval. If only Joe would develop a yen for the cabin . . . The two of them could get away for overnights during the slack season. They could hike, make love, fish, make love, rusticate, make love . . .

Judith's mouth had curved into a smile at the thought, when she heard an unexpected sound. Startled, she almost slipped off the middle step. "What's that?"

Renie, holding her tumbler of bourbon in both hands, stepped down to the ground. "I don't know—is someone calling us?"

Setting her drink on the porch, Judith also got up. Iris

Takisaki plunged through the woods, waving her arms and calling to the cousins. Her grace and composure were shaken.

"There's a prowler next door," she announced, her almond-shaped eyes wide. "Do you think I should call the sheriff?"

Judith glanced at Renie. "Well—maybe. What does Riley think?"

Iris gave an impatient shake of her head. "He's working. I didn't want to disturb him. And I could be wrong. Maybe it's just a hiker." She hesitated, rubbing her hands up and down her upper arms. "Would you mind coming over and taking a look with me? If we see anybody suspicious, we can call from the Woodchuck Auto Court."

Although Riley Tobias used electricity, he had never installed a phone. Like Gertrude Grover, Riley considered the telephone an intrusion. On the rare occasions when he needed to make a call, the artist would go next door to the home of Nella Lablatt, who had been the local postmistress until President Dwight D. Eisenhower had closed many of the rural offices in the 1950s. Nella was reportedly still pouting about Ike's decision.

"Nella's out of town," Iris explained as the cousins joined her in heading for the trail. "Riley's been watching the house for her, but he's never mentioned seeing anybody suspicious around. I was about to put a note under the studio door and let him know I was going back to check on my car when I heard a noise over at Nella's icehouse. I went to the fence and thought I saw somebody slip between the bushes and the house."

"It's broad daylight," Renie pointed out. "Who'd be dumb enough to break in now?"

In the lead, Iris had entered Riley's property. "I agree, except with all these crazy people on drugs, there's no accounting for what criminals do. Nella's been gone for over two weeks, so word may have gotten out that the house is empty."

They were passing the studio. Judith glanced through

the big window and saw Riley Tobias poised in front of his canvas. The garish colors of "The Nerd" looked even more jarring in the waning sunlight.

Iris stopped at the corner of the house. "Maybe I should tell Riley," she said in an uncertain voice. "He might get angry when he finds out we tackled this character alone."

"Don't bother," Renie said, moving right along. "We're not exactly The Wimp Triplets. Besides, we outnumber the bozo."

With a little shrug, Iris continued across the grass to Nella's property. The flagpole where Nella still dutifully ran up the Stars and Stripes every morning was bare. Her bungalow with its stained cedar shakes and dark green trim was locked up tight. Above the door, Judith could just make out the faded letters that said, "U.S. Post Office—Mount Woodchuck Station."

The cousins took a quick look around the garden. Nella had a knack for raising herbs and domesticating wildflowers. Despite her great age, she still managed to tend her flowers and shrubs. The small rockery that stood between the road and the front porch sported a profusion of spring color: pink gloxinias, purple anemones, scarlet freesias, golden tigridias, sprung among the boulders Nella had personally carried up from the riverbank. All around the house, new growth was ready to burst into bud. Out back, Nella's gnarled old fruit trees were heavy with white-and-pink blossoms. The little stone path that led to the icehouse was bordered with sweet alyssum and primroses. Judith had a sudden urge to head back for Hillside Manor and start working on her yard. So far this season, she hadn't done much more than prune the rose bushes and put in some new dahlia tubers.

Iris was cautiously circling the icehouse. Judith checked out the shrubbery. Renie tried both front and back doors, then looked in the windows. There was no sign of disturbance.

"Curious," murmured Iris, standing with her fists on her

hips. "Maybe it was one of the kids from across the road. But I could have sworn it was an adult."

"Male or female?" Judith asked, her gaze lingering on the stone walkway where blooms from a bronze cushion chrysanthemum had fallen. Scanning the border next to the walk, she saw bleeding heart, creeping phlox, and crown vetch. Judith frowned.

Iris was taking one last look around the icehouse. "I couldn't say for certain," she answered. "It was just a figure. These days, people dress so strangely that it's sometimes hard to tell a man from a woman."

"That's for sure," Renie replied on a disparaging note, despite her own shapeless Zion National Park T-shirt, baggy cotton pants, and nondescript shoes that could have been worn by anybody but a penguin. As ever, Renie's casual wardrobe looked more like a casualty, and was a far cry from the expensive designer pieces she trotted out for professional duties.

The three women headed away from Nella Lablatt's cozy cottage. Iris thanked the cousins for accompanying her. "Why not have that drink now?" she offered.

But Judith replied that they still had to finish their own, left back on the cabin porch. "Later," Judith said. "After dinner, okay?"

"That sounds fine." Iris smiled. "Riley will be finished up by then and he'll have time to unwind." She walked between the house and the studio with the cousins. "Now I feel silly," she murmured. "I brought you all the way over here for nothing."

"Oh, no," Renie countered. "There've been a lot of prowlers and robbers around. We've had stuff taken over the years, too."

Judith nodded in acknowledgment of the rural crime wave. The Grover cabin had indeed suffered, having been broken into at least four times in the past decade. Except for an antique Victrola record player, little of value had been taken, mainly because the family had furnished the place with so many castoffs.

"Riley's been lucky," Iris replied, gazing over Judith's shoulder toward the studio. "Oh—he's quit for the day. Which reminds me," she added, setting her jaw. "I'd better see if he locked up. He's pretty careless about security." She went to the studio door and flung it open. "You see? He just—" Iris stiffened, then threw up her hands and screamed.

Judith started for Iris, then froze, as if by reflex. Renie didn't move at all, but clamped a hand over her mouth. Iris screamed again, then rushed inside the studio. Unable to contain herself, Judith followed her.

Riley Tobias lay facedown on the floor, one hand flung out, the other at an awkward angle by his side. A bright orange stain spread out on the floor under his body. Judith's first reaction was that it was blood, but of course she was mistaken: It was merely oil paint, used to add brighter nuances to "The Nerd."

Nonetheless, Riley Tobias was dead.

Iris Takisaki crouched on the studio floor, rocking back and forth, her hands covering her face. A very pale Renie had now joined the other two women.

"What happened?" she asked in a hoarse voice. "His heart?"

Judith was trying to examine Riley without touching him. He was facedown, but she could tell his color was an ugly bluish gray. With unsteady fingers, she flicked at the thick hair that grew down over his collar. A little groan surged up from her throat. Iris didn't seem to notice, but Renie caught her cousin's reaction.

"*What is it?*" Renie demanded.

Judith swallowed hard. "It's picture-hanging wire, I'd guess." Her voice dropped to a whisper. "He's been strangled."

Iris's head jerked up. She stared at Judith. "What are you talking about?" Her words were thick, almost incoherent.

Judith closed her eyes for just an instant. "There's some kind of wire around Riley's neck, Iris. He's been strangled."

Iris shook her head, slowly at first, then faster and faster, until Judith thought her neck would snap. A high-pitched cry tore from her throat and seemed to ricochet off the big panes of glass that illuminated the studio with the light of the dying day.

"Crazy!" Iris shrieked. "That's crazy! You're crazy!"

Renie had a hand on Judith's arm, as if to assure her not only that she wasn't crazy, but that, as always, she—Renie—was there to support her cousin in an hour of need. Judith silently acknowledged Renie, but her first concern was for Iris, who was bordering on hysterics.

Then Iris stopped shrieking and grew very still. She turned a drawn, horrified face to the cousins. "But that *is* crazy," she said in a not-quite-normal tone. "It has to be. You mean we're talking about murder?"

It was always murder. Or so it seemed to Judith. It was a violent world, it always had been, yet unnatural death seemed to dog Judith's footsteps. The B&B brought her into close contact with hundreds of strangers every year, most of them decent, kind, gentle people. But occasionally there was the volatile guest capable of smashing up the furniture, jumping out of a window, or committing murder. To make matters worse, some of Judith's travels had brought her face-to-face with malicious mayhem. Now the rustic tranquility of her longtime sanctuary at the cabin had also been invaded. It was no wonder that her husband rarely confided in her about his routine homicide investigations. He knew she was already too well acquainted with violence.

Judith's feet felt like lead as she held a hand under Iris Takisaki's elbow to guide her along the gravel drive that led to the highway. They could see for a half mile in each direction, from the easterly curve in the road where the Green Mountain Inn and Grocery was located, to the west where the highway followed the Big Bend in the river.

The Woodchuck Auto Court was situated across the road from Nella Lablatt's little house. Indeed, Nella and her fifth—and final—husband had once owned the auto court, back in the thirties. Then Franklin Delano Roosevelt had nominated Nella for government service, and the Lablatts had forsaken their commercial enterprise for the federal pork barrel.

It seemed to Judith that subsequent owners hadn't done much to bring the original complex out of the Depression era. The half-dozen cabins that formed a U-shape around the small parking lot were all one-room affairs with small, square windows and weathered shake roofs. They were clean, they were neat, they were *old.* The office was housed in the filling station; the front desk also served customers who wanted gas, oil, soda pop, cigarettes, and bait. Just outside the door stood an old-fashioned wooden phone booth, blistered by sun, wind, and rain.

A pickup truck with a golden retriever in the back was just pulling out from the gas station as the three women set foot on the tarmac. A tall, thin man of about forty was leaning against the ancient glass-topped pump, counting money. Judith tried to remember who owned the Woodchuck now. There had been several changes over the years, and she didn't recognize the man in the dirty denim coveralls.

"There's been an accident," she said, gesturing over her shoulder in the direction of Riley Tobias's cabin and studio. Only the rooftops could be seen beyond the thick stand of trees. "We need to call the sheriff."

The tall, thin man's gray eyes snapped to attention. He pocketed the money and regarded all three women with suspicion. "What kind of accident?" His voice had a nasal quality.

Renie, who wasn't encumbered by Iris's flagging figure, marched briskly to the phone booth. "A bad one," she replied. "As in dead."

The man in the coveralls swore under his breath and spat on the tarmac. "That does it! I'm sellin' this place! I told Carrie Mae we'd have to put up with a lot of guff, like customers and such." He stomped off into the tiny office and banged the door behind him.

Judith rolled her eyes, while Iris chewed on her lower

lip. "That's Kennedy Morton. He and his wife have been here only a few months. Oh, my! I didn't mean to upset him! And I don't even have money for the pay phone! I left my purse at the house! Oh!" She began to weep anew.

"Don't worry about it," soothed Judith, watching Renie cope with the antiquated telephone. "We'll handle the phone. As for Mr. Morton, I gather he isn't the sensitive type."

Renie was giving the interior of the phone booth a swift kick. Obviously, things weren't going well. Judith's gaze roamed around the little parking lot. There were three vehicles pulled up in front of the cabins, which wasn't as amazing as it might seem: The Woodchuck Auto Court and the Green Mountain Inn were the only hostelries on the ten-mile stretch of highway between Glacier Falls and the entrance to the national forest. What did amaze Judith was that one of the three vehicles was a handsome new white Mercedes-Benz sedan. It looked as out of place as a Ming vase at a Tupperware party.

The phone booth was shaking. Renie appeared to be hopping up and down inside, screaming into the receiver. Judith grimaced, then glanced at Iris. She was regaining her composure, smoothing her black hair, wiping her eyes, pressing the swan pendant against her breast.

At last Renie emerged from the phone booth. "What century is this?" she shrieked. "That damned phone must have been the first model after the crank!"

Judith bit back the urge to tell Renie *she* was the crank. Instead, she inquired as to what would happen next, as far as the county law-enforcement officials were concerned.

"They're sending somebody," Renie replied, simmering down and brushing bugs off her T-shirt. "It'll take a while, though. After all, the county seat is thirty miles away, and they don't have anybody in the Glacier Falls area at the moment."

Judith was about to suggest that they go back to wait at Riley's cabin when a chubby redheaded woman bounded out of the house behind the gas station. "Yoo-hoo! Wait! Stop! Hoo!" She bounced down the gravel path, waving a dish towel. "Mort says somebody died. Who? Nella? She must be a hundred and ten!"

Before the cousins could respond, Iris finally relinquished Judith's arm. "It's not Nella, Mrs. Morton. She's still away. It's Riley Tobias. The sheriff is coming." Iris's voice was very thin.

Mrs. Morton moved closer, bosom straining at her coral polyester blouse. "Riley? Riley!" She put her hands to her head and let out a little squeal. As if responding to the sound, three small children came tumbling around the corner of the filling station. Judith thought they were all boys, but couldn't be sure: Their curly red hair, smudged round faces, and rumpled playclothes could have belonged to either sex.

"Now why," demanded Mrs. Morton, batting ineffectually at the children, who were hanging onto her tight green polyester pants, "would the Lord take somebody so young? Riley Tobias couldn'ta been more than fifty."

"Fifty next month," murmured Iris, apparently equally dazed at the thought.

The youngsters were neither dazed nor distressed. "Sweet-Stix! Sweet-Stix! We want Sweet-Stix now!" They spoke in unison, hopping up and down on the tarmac, tugging at their mother, and waving their arms.

She ignored them and reached out to Iris, enveloping the taller but much slimmer woman in her arms. "There there, you poor thing! Why, you must feel just like a widow!" Mrs. Morton crushed Iris to her coral bosom. The children kept on hopping and shouting.

Judith and Renie eyed each other with pained expressions. Iris allowed herself to be comforted for a minimal moment, then drew somewhat awkwardly away from her benefactress.

"I feel numb just now," Iris said in a hollow tone. "Maybe I should sit down."

"Sweet-Stix! Sweet-Stix!" The children were still jumping, though the oldest, who appeared to be about five, turned to glare at Iris. Obviously, Judith thought, he—or she—recognized Iris and her sad news only as a deterrent to childish pleasures.

At last Mrs. Morton made a serious attempt to shush her offspring: She planted both feet firmly on the ground, gave a tremendous heave of her chubby body, and shook off all but the oldest child. "That's it! You behave now! You, too, Velvet," she said to the five-year-old.

Velvet let go, though her face had turned sulky. She immediately led her two younger siblings out toward the edge of the road, as if organizing a mutiny. Mrs. Morton watched the trio with narrowed eyes. "Not another step, Velvet. You hear? Rafe! Giles! Don't you dare cross that road again! You'll get killed." Her gaze was now ferocious, and her voice could have been heard not only on the other side of the highway, but across the river as well. The children seemed unaffected, but they stayed put. Their mother turned back to Iris and the cousins. "Now, as I was saying—or about to, before those little imps tried to get the better of me—why don't you come inside and take it easy on our couch? I'll clear off the laundry and the diaper pail and the dog and the baby and we'll . . ."

But Iris had raised a slim hand in protest. "You're so kind, Mrs. Morton, but no, thank you. We should go back over to Riley's."

Mrs. Morton looked disappointed but undaunted. "Well—if you say so. But come along later, and I'll fix you a nice wine cooler. Bring your friends, too." She nodded at Judith and Renie. "Peach, mango, grape—what's your favorite wine, Iris?"

Iris almost succeeded in hiding her look of dismay. "Uh—I—er, a cup of tea would be fine." She forced a smile. "Thank you." Practically backpedaling straight into Renie, Iris fled in the direction of the road.

Half a dozen cars, a flatbed truck, an RV, and three motorcycles passed before the women could get to the other side of the road. A few yards away, they could hear the chant resumed:

"Sweet-Stix, Sweet-Stix, Sweet-Stix . . . *please!*"

* * *

Iris Takisaki had steered the cousins into Riley Tobias's living room. Judith was seated in an uncomfortable teak chair from Denmark; Renie had commandeered a soft leather armchair that practically swallowed her up. Iris, who had insisted on pouring the brandy despite her trembling hands, was perched at the far end of a colorful futon sofa.

"If only I'd gotten a better look at whoever was at Nella's." Still berating herself for not being more observant, Iris paused to take a sip of brandy.

Judith tried to console her. "You can't be certain that whoever you saw was the killer. And you certainly can't beat yourself over the head, because you had no way of knowing that it was important at the time."

Iris was nervously plucking at the fine fabric of her coffee-colored slacks. "It must have happened very quickly," she said, almost in awe. "How long were we at Nella's? Five minutes? Ten?"

"No more than ten," replied Renie, who had an astute knack for judging time. "Maybe what happened was that the killer sneaked in back of the studio while you were getting us. Then, as soon as we came along and continued to Nella's, whoever it was dashed into the studio and . . . uh . . . ah . . ." Succumbing to an unusual fit of tact, Renie faltered and fumbled with her brandy snifter.

Attempting to steel herself, Iris took a deep breath. "It doesn't seem real, does it? It's as if we're talking about a movie or a play. You can read about murder every day in the newspaper or see it on TV, but when it actually happens—" Iris stopped, a hand to her mouth. Tears welled up in her eyes. Setting the brandy snifter down on a side table, she frantically scanned the small, untidy living room. "My purse . . ." she murmured. "A handkerchief . . ."

Judith spotted the leather shoulder bag at the other end of the futon sofa. She crossed the room to fetch it for Iris, who failed in her effort at a grateful smile.

"Damn," Iris said in a shaky voice. "I don't seem to have any self-control! This is so awful!"

Judith and Renie both offered sympathetic expressions. Patiently, they waited in silence for Iris to marshal her composure.

"We couldn't see him at first because those big windows don't come all the way down," Iris went on in a rush. "If only we *had* stopped to ask him to come with us! I'd have rather put up with a tantrum twenty times over than sacrifice Riley to our silly feminine pride!"

"Regrets are useless," Judith asserted flatly. "You—and Renie and I—would do the same thing again. It's very rare that, when we talk about might-have-beens, any of us would actually change what we did in the first place. We act instinctively and in the context of the moment. You've nothing to regret, Iris." Seeing a resigned expression creep over Iris's face, Judith continued. "What's important now is to move on and try to help the sheriff find Riley's killer. Where did that wire come from, by the way?"

Iris nodded jerkily. "Riley kept some picture-hanging wire in the studio. I don't know why—he never actually hung any pictures there, he just propped them up or put them on easels." The brief resignation was erased by another look of dismay. "Did you see how tight that wire had been pulled? It had cut into his skin and—"

Iris's vivid description was mercifully interrupted by a pounding at the door. Relieved at being spared a recollection of the gruesome details, Judith leaped to her feet. "I'll get it. It must be the sheriff."

It wasn't. A distinguished middle-aged man wearing a khaki safari suit stood on the small, square back porch that faced the highway. Before Judith could say a word, he pushed past her and entered the house.

"Where is Riley?" he demanded in a deep, resonant voice. "If he isn't really dead, I'm going to kill him anyway."

Staring from over the top of the sofa, Iris took one look at the newcomer and let out a piercing scream.

THREE

In a flurry of sound and motion, Iris Takisaki flew off the sofa, dashed through the narrow corridor that separated the kitchen from the living room, and attacked the newcomer. Judith grabbed at Iris, vainly trying to pull her away. Renie struggled with the soft leather armchair, attempting to get up. In the end, it was the distinguished-looking man in the safari suit who was able to stop Iris from doing serious damage. He grasped her around the waist and lifted her bodily into his arms, then marched into the living room and threw her back onto the sofa. Iris gasped for breath; the visitor dusted off his safari suit.

"Really, Iris," he remarked in that deep, cultured voice, "you've no cause to do me harm. All I want is my painting. I'm paying seventy thousand dollars for it, you know. Riley has stalled me long enough. If he had one of his fits of whimsy and sold it to that hangdog Hungarian, I'll sue."

Somehow, Iris managed to look graceful in the aftermath of her tumble onto the sofa. She lifted her head and glared at the visitor who had now moved into the center of the room and was smoothing his silver hair.

"You killed him!" The words shot out of her mouth.

Judith involuntarily retreated a few steps from the man Iris had just accused of murder. It was possible, of course. Obviously, somebody had killed Riley Tobias. "Excuse me," Judith ventured. "Who are you?"

The man gazed at Judith in a bemused manner. She had the feeling that he thought she ought to know—or wasn't worthy of enlightenment. "I'm Dewitt Dixon. And you?" He didn't offer his hand.

The name rang no bells. "Judith Flynn," she responded, then gestured at Renie, who had finally managed to extricate herself from the leather chair. "My cousin, Serena Jones."

To Judith's astonishment, Renie went over to Dewitt Dixon and planted a big kiss on his cheek. "Hi, Dewitt. I haven't seen you since the gallery opening at the university last spring."

Judith couldn't believe her eyes or her ears. Dewitt Dixon was giving Renie a bear hug. "How's Bill?" he inquired. "Your husband had teeth problems that night, as I recall."

"Right." Renie stood back as Dewitt released her. "Ulcerated, root canal, gold crown, the works. We sold two out of our three kids to pay for it. How's your spouse?"

Strolling to the stone fireplace that Riley Tobias had built with his own hands, Dewitt Dixon leaned against the natural pine mantelpiece. "She's fine, the last I heard, which was Florence. She found the Uffizi redundant." It suddenly seemed to strike Dewitt that his conversation with Renie was inappropriate under the circumstances. His cool blue gaze shifted to Iris, who was half-sitting, half-lying on the sofa. It would have been a seductive pose had her black eyes not been rimmed in red and filled with malice. "Tell me, Iris," Dewitt queried, "is Riley playing some practical joke?"

Iris glared some more at Dewitt Dixon. "It's not a joke, you fool. Riley's dead. Someone killed him. Was it you?"

Dewitt shed a fraction of his seemingly imperturbable air. "*Killed* him? Good Lord! When?"

Sitting up straight, Iris reached for her purse and pulled out a gold-leaf cigarette case. Still silent, she extracted a black cigarette tipped in gold and lighted it with what Judith had thought was an eagle sculpture. The sharp beak spewed flame. Exhaling, Iris stood up and walked out, presumably headed for the house's only bedroom off the narrow hall.

"Well." Dewitt Dixon chuckled softly and shook his head.

"She's very upset," Judith explained, sniffing at the lingering cigarette smoke and almost wishing she hadn't kept her vow to quit. "She found him. We were with her."

"Where?" Dewitt had taken out his own case, sleek silver with his initials tastefully engraved.

Renie motioned through the nearby window. "Out there, in the studio. It happened between five-fifteen and five-thirty." Catching a warning glance from Judith, Renie shut up. If Dixon had anything to do with the murder, it would be better if he didn't find out how much they knew.

A spiral of smoke drifted from Dewitt's cigarette to disperse among the pine rafters. "This is most extraordinary! Why aren't the police here?"

Judith sniffed again. "They will be. Not police, but sheriff. It's a big county, you know. They could be fifty miles away."

The room turned quiet. Outside, dusk was descending, the soft spring light softening behind the mountains and over the river. Judith's gaze took in her immediate surroundings. Riley Tobias had lived among clutter, with piles of books, magazines, tapes, clippings, and file folders. The furniture was ordinary, neither cheap nor dramatic. Comfort appeared to have been Riley's goal. But the art that hung from the walls, reposed on tables, and stood in corners was a wildly eclectic representation of contemporary Pacific Northwest painters, sculptors, glassblowers, and printmakers. Some, like the lotus-shaped white bowl, were stunning. Others, such as a suit of armor covered with purple eggshells, were ghastly. As far as Judith could tell, only two of Riley's own works hung on the living room walls—an early cloudscape and a pen-and-ink drawing of Mount Woodchuck. It occurred to her that she would much rather have either one than the ugly—if expensive—painting Riley had given her. It also occurred to her that she was being crass.

It was Dewitt Dixon who broke the silence. "Tobias had an agent. He used to deal strictly with galleries, but he was too much of a maverick to work in the normal way. And he was big enough to get his way. I dealt with his agent initially. What is his name? Silvanus? Shouldn't he be told what's happened?"

"That's up to Iris," Judith replied.

Dewitt nodded once. "And family? I think there was a brother, back in New England."

There was. Judith remembered that, along with the fact that Riley's parents had been dead for years. She also recalled that he had been born in Indiana, on a bulb farm, and had gone west as a very young man in the fifties. He had heard the call of the Beat Generation and had hit the road. Making the North Beach scene had strengthened his resolve to become an artist, but the Bay Area hadn't suited him. San Francisco had physically and spiritually hemmed him in, he'd once said. A brief, disastrous marriage had rounded out his disillusion.

"He couldn't go any farther west, he couldn't go back home, and L.A. appalled him," Judith said, more to herself than to Dewitt and Renie. "So he had to head north. That's how he ended up here, where he found his artistic soul." She gave a little jump, a bit startled by her own musings. "Excuse me, I seem to be eulogizing out loud. Family?" She gazed at Dewitt Dixon. "Yes, of course, the brother . . . Iris would know how to get hold of him. That's up to her, too."

Indeed, it was all up to Iris, Judith realized. Iris had been Riley Tobias's mistress for twenty years; Iris had found his body. She had divided her time between a waterfront condo in town and the cabin on the river. Iris must know everything there was to know about Riley Tobias. Judith was strictly an outsider. She locked gazes with Renie; the cousins communicated wordlessly. It was habit as well as kinship, a communion forged in childhood.

"Look," said Renie, taking her cue, "we should go. If the sheriff wants to talk to us, we're next door." She gestured in an easterly direction.

Dewitt Dixon looked surprised, even a trifle alarmed. "You're leaving?" He inclined his head toward the bedroom, where Iris presumably had fled. "What about *her?*"

Judith was not without sympathy. "It's terrible, I know. But she's got to cope. We all do. I gather she wants to be alone right now. Iris strikes me as a very strong, capable woman. If she needs us, we're only a shout away."

The dew was already beginning to settle on the grass in the meadow. Renie started off at an angle, clearly intent on circumventing the studio. In a low voice, Judith hailed her cousin.

"Hold it—we ought to take another look at the body, coz." She stopped, standing next to a ramshackle fence decorated with all manner of objects from old horse collars to new ceramics.

Over her shoulder, Renie looked askance. "Why? Seen one body, seen 'em all. I don't feel like a ghoul this evening. Besides, I'm starving. It's almost seven o'clock."

Hesitating, Judith finally gave in and followed Renie through the woods. Her cousin was right: It would be ghoulish to study Riley Tobias's corpse. It would also be difficult, since there were no lights on inside the studio. Judith knew better than to touch anything until the law enforcement personnel arrived. Which, she realized, was taking a very long time. Carefully stepping over the uneven ground, she tramped along the primitive trail that zigzagged among the vine maples, cottonwoods, hemlock, cedars, and fir.

The old cabin seemed to welcome them back. Even its flaws were a sign of comfort in a world turned suddenly violent.

"Don't tell me," said Renie, going straight to the stove to make sure the fire hadn't gone out, "you're sleuthing. Dammit," she went on with considerable fervor, "you're going to get us involved. I should have known your sudden departure had nothing to do with my attitude to cease and desist. You just didn't want me to bitch about being hungry." She yanked open the icebox and began hauling out steaks, lettuce, and tomatoes.

Judith was holding up her hands in protest. "Wrong, coz, wrong. We were with Iris when she found the body. We were also the last people to see Riley alive—except for the murderer. We're witnesses. We have a very real obligation. Surely you can see that."

Renie gave a little snort. "Let's try seeing where you put the potatoes. It's going to take forever to bake them in that old oven. I suggest we have hash browns."

"Fine." Judith rummaged under the little counter that divided the kitchen from the living room. A moment later, she was at the sink, peeler in hand. She was also humming.

Renie gave her cousin a suspicious, sidelong look. "You're putting Riley Tobias out of your mind?"

Judith kept peeling potatoes. "Of course I am. I'm thinking about calling home after dinner. I'm thinking about Joe. And Mother. Oh, and whether or not Mike will really graduate from college this year."

Renie paused in the act of putting a thick New York steak in the heavy cast-iron skillet. "Then how come you're humming Strauss's *Artist's Life* waltz?"

Her big dark eyes looking startled, Judith dropped a potato. "I am? Oh, dear!"

Placing the two steaks in a puddle of hot butter, Renie sighed. "You're hopeless. Get another frying pan for the spuds. I'll light the lanterns." She stomped out into the living room.

Judith watched Renie fill and pump the lanterns. "I was sort of surprised when you greeted Dewitt Dixon like an old college chum. You've never mentioned him to me."

"Probably not," murmured Renie, waiting for the first lantern to catch. "He's one of those people I run into at art and design shows. Most of them are a pain in the butt, but I have to be nice just in case they turn into potential clients. It drives me crazy. Being nice, I mean." The lantern flared and she nodded approval at her handiwork. "Dewitt's a real stuffed shirt. Big bucks, good taste, dedicated art buff. But he's still a pain."

"An urbane pain," Judith noted. Renie didn't reply; she was concentrating on not setting fire to her fingers.

Five minutes later, the potatoes were frying, the steaks were sizzling, the salad reposed in the icebox, and Judith and Renie had poured fresh drinks. Two Coleman lanterns hung from sturdy hooks in the rafters. In the kitchen, a bracketed brass lamp fixture glowed on the wall. Darkness was settling in over the cabin, and the only sounds were the rippling river, the crackling fire, and the tremor of the leaves in the gentle spring breeze. It would have been a perfect setting for repose—had a dead body not been lying two hundred feet away.

As if to remind the cousins that the world was seriously flawed, sirens wailed out on the highway. Judith and Renie looked at each other.

"The sheriff?" Judith turned but didn't get up from her place on the sagging sofa.

"It's about time," Renie replied. "Maybe he won't bother us until we're done with dinner."

Judith didn't respond. The sirens drew closer. But before they stopped, she heard the sound of footsteps on the porch. Startled, she almost spilled her drink.

Renie got up out of the mohair armchair that had once sat in their grandparents' front parlor. "Maybe it's Iris," she said, crossing the room. Cautiously, she opened the top half of the Dutch door.

Judith was right behind her. The balding middle-aged man with the mustache appeared much more frightened than the cousins. He all but cringed when Renie asked him to identify himself.

"Clive Silvanus, at your service," he said with more than a hint of a Southern accent. "Good Lordy-Lord, isn't this a d-d-dreadful day?"

Renie opened the other half of the door. "You got that right. Come on in, or are you armed and dangerous?"

"Ah'm t-t-terrified," Clive Silvanus replied, scooting across the threshold. Indeed, Judith noted that his teeth seemed to be chattering. He was neatly, if blandly, dressed in a tan sport coat, beige slacks, and a brown tie. The white dress shirt seemed at odds with his saddle shoes. Upon closer inspection under the lantern light, Judith saw that Clive Silvanus had soft brown eyes, a small, soft mouth, and a very soft chin. His pale skin looked soft, too, despite the soft brown mustache. Judith wasn't surprised to see him collapse onto the sofa.

"It's th-th-the end of the world. As Ah know it," he added, eyes rolled back into his head. "Who could have foreseen this d-d-dire d-d-day?"

Nearby, the sirens stopped. Presumably, the sheriff had arrived at Riley Tobias's house and studio. Judith pretended she didn't notice the police activity, lest her acknowledgment cause Clive Silvanus to get the vapors.

"Yes," she agreed, holding her scotch against her breast. "It's pretty terrible. Would you like a drink?"

With his head lolling against the floral pattern of Auntie Vance's old sofa, Silvanus let out a little gasp. "Strong drink! Oh, my, yes, bourbon and branch water, if you p-p-please. It will do me good."

Renie also rolled her eyes, but for a different reason. "It's my bourbon and I only brought a pint. As for the branch water, you're lucky to get any at all. We had to haul these containers from Riley's well and my arms still hurt. You can forget about ice, because I'd have to chip it off the old block. Thank your lucky stars we've got glasses. When I was a kid, we used to drink out of old jelly jars." Renie swished off into the kitchen.

Judith was torn between amusement and dismay by her cousin's minor diatribe. Clive Silvanus, however, appeared unmoved. In fact, he looked traumatized, and Judith really couldn't blame him. Silvanus was Riley Tobias's agent, and no doubt his client's sudden death had come as a terrible shock. While Renie made Silvanus's drink and checked on dinner, Judith said as much to their visitor. But Clive Silvanus surprised her.

"A shock? Not entirely." His teeth had stopped chattering as he sat up and began digging into the pocket of his sport coat. "Riley enjoyed livin' on the edge. He delighted in antagonizin' people. Rilin' Riley, that's what Ah called him. To mahself, of course." At last, Silvanus pulled out a pack of cigarettes and a book of matches. "Do you mind? Ah may not be surprised, but Ah *am* shocked."

Obligingly, if enviously, Judith handed Silvanus an ashtray that Aunt Ellen had made from her firstborn's baby bottle. Silvanus lighted up and puffed with relief. Renie handed him his drink, and after the first sip, he seemed to implode.

"Now that's what Ah call a *help!*" Arms and legs splayed all over the sofa, his head shot back, his chest sunk in, and his stomach suddenly bulged at his belt. Ashes flew from his cigarette; a small leather-bound notebook fell out of the pocket inside his sport coat. Clive seemed not to notice. "Yessir, Ah'm gonna live after all! Is what Ah smell taters fryin'?"

The cousins traded perturbed looks. "No," said Renie emphatically. "That's wax facial-hair remover. We're going to depilate each other after dinner. I mean, after you leave."

Although an expression of either disbelief or disappointment crossed Clive Silvanus's soft face, he seemed content to console himself with his bourbon. Renie retrieved the notebook and placed it at Clive's elbow. Judith sat down next to him on the sofa, intent on getting an explanation.

"You said you were shocked but not surprised, Mr. Silvanus. What did you mean by that?"

Swirling the pale mixture of bourbon and water, Clive Silvanus turned ruminative. "Like Ah said, ol' Riley had a way about him. He put people off-balance. He made 'em sit up and take notice. He despised complacency, Riley did. Friends, foes—it didn't matter. It was one and the same to him. Way back, he went the usual route, sellin' his paintings on consignment through a gallery. But he'd always get mad—riled up, you might say—and move on. Finally, he hired me." Silvanus shrugged, drained his drink, and handed the empty glass to Renie for a refill. Renie grimaced, but went into the little kitchen to comply. "Ah was always warnin' him. 'Riley,' Ah'd say, 'you behave now. Don't go shootin' your mouth off and antagonizin' folks.' But he wouldn't listen. It was just his way." Silvanus paused to accept another drink from Renie. She also pointed to the notebook. Clive gazed at it blankly, then put it back in his inside pocket. "Thank you, ma'am. Yessir, it was just Riley's way. And it got him killed."

As Clive Silvanus took a deep swallow, Judith saw her chance to interrupt the monologue: "Do you know who did it?"

The soft brown eyes widened as Silvanus gazed at Judith. He brushed at his mustache and wrinkled his nose. "Sure Ah do. Fine bourbon, by the way." He made a little bow to Renie. "Ah ought to know—Ah am aware of who called on Riley this afternoon. Ah heard the quarrel. Ah heard the threats. Ah must say Ah'm sorry."

Judith raised her dark eyebrows. "You knew Lazlo Gamm?"

Clive's face sagged. "Lazlo? Ah've met the man. But what has he got to do with the price of pigs?" He shook his head sadly. "Alas, Ah'm not referrin' to that foreigner. Oh, no. It grieves me to say as much, but who else could have killed Riley but Ward Kimball?"

FOUR

A HUNDRED YARDS upriver, on the former site of a gold prospector's shack, stood the A-frame owned by Trent and Glenna Berkman. The Berkmans were skiers who used their river retreat mostly as a base for going up to the lifts on Mount Woodchuck. They were rarely seen in the summer, never in the autumn and spring. Through the trees, Judith could just make out the very tip of the Berkman cabin. A full moon was rising behind it, casting a silver sheen over the forest.

At Clive Silvanus's startling statement, Judith tore her gaze from the perfect picture framed by the homely window with its four square panes. "Ward Kimball?" she echoed. "No! You can't mean that, Mr. Silvanus."

Mr. Silvanus looked as if he didn't mean much of anything. He was pulling on his bourbon, rocking to and fro, and making a noise that sounded like, "Ummm-mm, ummm-uh-mm, ummm-mm." Judith wondered if he was singing himself to sleep.

"Mr. Silvanus!" Judith spoke sharply. The agent jumped, then shook himself and almost dropped his drink. He gave the cousins a shamefaced look.

"Sorry. Ah tell you, Ah'm very upset." With exaggerated effort, Clive began to rearrange himself on the sofa. "Ah'm not prevaricatin'. Riley and ol' Ward were havin' a real ruckus this afternoon."

"Where were *you?*" Judith queried, perching on the arm of the sofa.

Clive reflected, drank, and reflected some more. His soft brown eyes were growing downright fuzzy. He started to put his cigarette out, missed the ashtray, and was about to singe the couch when Renie yanked the butt out of his hand. "Oh! Sorry." Clive gave Renie a penitent, sickly smile. "Where was Ah? Literally and figuratively? Ah'm all at sea . . . Oh—outside the studio, that is. Ah had just arrived and heard them goin' at it tooth and toenail. Then Ah skedaddled away."

Judith frowned at Renie, who was looking quizzical. "What were they fighting about?" asked Judith.

Draining his glass, Clive started to slump again. "A row . . . a real donny . . . brook . . ." His head lolled. Judith leaned over and propped him up. She gave him a little shake. He flipped and flopped, like a soft rag doll. "Ummm-mm, ummm-uh-mm . . ." The odd noise faded; Clive Silvanus was also fading.

Crouched in front of the sofa, Renie caught the empty glass as it fell from Clive's limp hands. "We've got to get him out of here," she whispered. "He's going to pass out and we'll be stuck with him. Besides, we only have two steaks."

"Rats!" muttered Judith, giving Clive another, harder shake. "Wake up! Mr. Silvanus! Hey!"

But it was too late. Clive fell away from Judith, his head nestled on a pillow Grandma Grover had covered in crimson corduroy. He began to snore. Softly.

"Great," said Renie, getting up. "Now what?"

Judith was still perched on the arm of the sofa, chin on her fist. "What do you think he weighs? One-fifty?"

Renie considered. "He's not much taller than you. Five-ten, maybe one-sixty, I'd guess. Which end do I take?"

It wasn't easy to cart Clive Silvanus from the sofa to the little bedroom off the kitchen. The cousins had only about fifteen feet to cover, but Clive was a dead weight. They ended up hauling the unconscious man across the floor and dumping him on the bed. Judith threw a striped Hudson Bay blanket over him; Renie tugged off his saddle shoes. Closing the blue plaid curtain, they left him in peace.

"He's not only drunk," Judith declared as she went to the stove to rescue their dinner, "he's crazy. Ward Kimball wouldn't—probably couldn't—kill Riley Tobias."

Renie nodded. "Silvanus is crocked. If Ward's as feeble as Riley said he is, he could hardly have overpowered his victim and garroted him with picture-hanging wire." She stared at the steaks. "They're too well done. Damn."

"We'll manage." Judith quickly sautéed a half-dozen mushrooms while Renie tossed the green salad. The drop-leaf table, which could be expanded to seat twelve, stood in front of the Murphy bed. Sitting down to eat, Judith queried Renie about Clive Silvanus and Lazlo Gamm.

But Renie had never heard of either man before today. "I'm on the fringes of the art world," she pointed out. "My only connection is when I attend a gallery showing to get ideas for new designs, use of colors, general trends. Lazlo may not live in this area. As for Clive, I figure that under that boozy Southern exterior, he must be pretty sharp. And shrewd. He's helped parlay Riley Tobias into the Big Time. I suspect his image is carefully cultivated to sucker potential buyers."

Dishing up the hash browns, Judith considered Renie's assessment. From the bedroom, Clive's snores erupted like a combustion engine run amok. Indeed, the sound struck Judith as almost inhuman. She cocked her head to one side and listened. The noise abated to a dull rumble. Judith turned her attention back to Renie. "Could be," she said. "I wonder where Clive went after he left the studio. Do you think it was his Mercedes parked at the Woodchuck Auto Court?"

Renie shook her head. "I think Dewitt Dixon drives a Mercedes. Wherever Clive was, I'll bet a buck he had a bottle with him. Nobody, not even in shock, could get that blitzed on two bourbons. I wasn't exactly generous."

"Right." Judith cut into her steak, which happily remained pink in the middle. "Once Clive sobers up, maybe he can deliver Dewitt's painting. He should get a nice commission off that sale."

Renie was stuffing herself with steak, salad, and hash browns, all at once. "He will. I don't know the percentage, but with a gallery it's anywhere from ten to sixty percent. All Clive has to do is hand that baby over and . . ." She paused, which was just as well, since Judith was having trouble understanding her cousin talk with her mouth full.

"And what?" prompted Judith.

Renie's brown eyes strayed to the curtain that covered the Murphy bed. She swallowed. "He can hand it over if he can find it," she amended. "What do you think, coz?"

Judith also stared at the blue plaid curtain. Then she dismissed Renie's insinuation with a wave of her fork. "Riley Tobias wouldn't give me a seventy-thousand-dollar painting he'd already sold. That doesn't make sense." Judith's logical mind was offended by the mere idea.

From the bedroom, Clive Silvanus's snores had become muffled. The cousins gathered up their dishes, put a tea kettle on to heat water for washing up, and opened a tin of sugar cookies Judith had baked the previous day. The cabin smelled of woodsmoke and no-nonsense food. Judith marveled anew at the contentment within her grasp. If only Riley Tobias hadn't gotten himself killed . . .

It was going on nine when they finished the dishes. The cousins were wondering if they should leave Clive Silvanus alone while they called home from the auto court when a harsh knock rattled the Dutch door. The plaid drapes had been drawn; Judith peeked through the window over the sink to see if she could identify their latest visitors.

"Swell," she muttered, heading for the door. "It's the sheriff and company."

Two uniformed men wearing trooper hats marched into

the cabin. Both were average height; one was in his early forties, the other no more than twenty. The older of the two surveyed the living room before looking directly at Judith and Renie.

"Abbott N. Costello," he announced in a voice devoid of inflection.

Judith looked puzzled. "You're Abbott? And he's . . . ?"

The fortyish lawman shot Judith a look of reproach. "I'm Abbott *N.* Costello. The 'N' is for Norman." He gave a nod at the younger man. "Deputy Dabney Plummer."

"Oh." Judith worked hard at not smiling. She didn't dare glance at Renie, who seemed engrossed with her shoes. "You're investigating the Tobias murder, I take it?"

Abbott N. Costello didn't reply. He moved ponderously in a small circle, absorbing every detail of the cabin's interior. His uniform was steel gray; so were his eyes. The sideburns under the hat were dark, with a touch of gray. He was solidly built, but without an ounce of fat. His features were even and ordinary, except for the stern set of his mouth. By contrast, Dabney Plummer was lean, blue-eyed, pink-cheeked, and boyish. The shock of fair hair that jutted over his forehead was almost white. He struck Judith as both anxious and eager.

Costello concluded his survey. He pointed a sturdy finger at Dabney "Go."

Judith expected the younger man to leave, but instead, he took out a ballpoint pen and hoisted a clipboard he'd been holding at his side. It was obvious that he understood Costello's method of communication. Judith and Renie were both wearing an air of bewilderment.

"Name?" The word shot out of Costello's mouth, aimed at Judith.

"Uh . . ." Judith reeled a bit, taken aback by the lawman's abruptness. "Judith Flynn. I actually live in—"

"Name?" Costello had swung around, now fixing Renie with his frozen stare.

Renie couldn't resist. "Smith N. Wesson. The 'N' is for

Nincompoop." Unable to control herself for another second, she burst out laughing.

If Judith was dismayed by Renie's verbal high jinks, Abbott N. Costello was infuriated. He puffed out his chest, lowered his head, and looked as if he intended to charge at the still-giggling Renie.

"You think homicide is *funny?* What's *funny* about death? What's *funny* about Murder One? What's *funny* about *me?*" His ferocious glare would have terrified any woman who hadn't been married to the same man for almost thirty years.

If not intimidated, Renie was at least seemingly chastened. "Yeah, right, murder's not a lot of laughs, Sheriff. Sorry. We've been under a strain." She attempted her middle-aged ingenue expression.

It got nowhere with Abbott N. Costello. "That's better," he muttered. "And don't call me 'Sheriff.' I'm the undersheriff. The Boss is over on the other side of the county, chasing a serial killer."

Having elicited the pertinent information about the cousins' names, addresses, phone numbers, occupations, and why they were not back in the big city where they belonged, Costello shifted into the investigation at hand.

"You knew this Tobias?" he demanded, his steel-gray eyes darting back and forth between the cousins.

Judith briefly thought about asking the lawmen to sit, mainly so she and Renie could, too, but if they remained standing, they might not stay as long. "We've known him for over twenty years," she answered, trying to be accommodating. "He bought that property next to ours from the Kirbys. They were here when my grandparents started building back in the thirties."

If Judith thought that the Grover family's presence for half a century would make a favorable impression, she was dead wrong. Costello scowled under the brim of his hat. "Summer people. A home in the city, a place in the mountains, a beach house, a ski lodge, an island getaway. Yachts, helicopters, limos, private jets—there's no end to it." He pulled out a rumpled handkerchief and wiped his nose.

"Uh . . . actually, in 1938, these lots went for less than four hundred dollars . . ."

"The Leisure Class. The Rich are different." Costello trampled Judith's explanation, then turned to Dabney Plummer. "Take that down, it's a good quote. We can use it somewhere."

Judith decided it would be best not to tell the undersheriff that his quote had already been used. Often. She waited for him to continue with his questions.

"So you went over to party with Tobias this afternoon?" The scowl had been replaced by a mere frown.

Renie chose to field that one. "We went to get water. From Riley's well. We always do that. He asked us to have a beer. We did. We left. With our water."

Costello was looking skeptical. "How long were you there drinking?"

Judith and Renie exchanged questioning glances. "Half an hour?" ventured Judith. "We went over around one o'clock. We didn't want to stay too long because we'd just built a fire in the stove. I know we were back here shortly after one-thirty, because I looked at my watch when I started cleaning out the cupboards."

Dabney Plummer was writing assiduously. Costello fingered his blunt chin. "What was his mood?"

Judith considered. Riley Tobias had seemed much the same as always: gregarious, open, a bit mercurial. Or was there something else? She couldn't put a finger on it. Maybe she was mistaken. She and Renie hadn't seen Riley for a long time.

"Was he drunk when you left?" queried Costello.

The question made Judith think of Clive Silvanus. She refrained from glancing in the direction of the bedroom. Fortunately, she could no longer hear him snoring. "Drunk?" Judith repeated. "Heavens, no. He had one beer. No, he took a second. We didn't."

The undersheriff waited for his deputy to finish writing. "You went back, though. How come?"

Judith gave a nod. "Iris—Ms. Takisaki—asked us to help her look for a prowler over at the neighbor's on the other side of Riley's property. Mrs. Lablatt?" Judith raised her even, dark eyebrows in a question.

"Old lady Lablatt?" Costello spoke in a disrespectful tone. "Probably a new boyfriend. She's a corker."

Judith ignored the comment. "Mrs. Lablatt's out of town. Iris thought someone was lurking around the icehouse. But when we got there, whoever it was had disappeared."

Costello snorted. "Handy. So the three of you trooped back to the studio and found Tobias zapped, huh?" He didn't wait for Judith or Renie to respond, but instead smirked at Dabney Plummer and went right on talking. "How about this? You three broads crash into the studio, wrestle this poor guy to the floor, and strangle him." He glowered at Renie. "I figure you for the one who sat on him while the two bigger dames did him in. Whose idea was it? The Dragon Lady's?"

Judith gnashed her teeth. Abbott N. Costello struck her as a character out of an old B-movie. "That's idiotic," she declared. "Why on earth would we kill Riley? We hadn't even seen him—or Iris—in ages!"

"A likely story," Costello muttered, unembarrassed by the cliché. "How come you didn't stick around over there with your Japanese ally?"

Renie passed a hand over her forehead. "Oh, for heaven's sake! Iris was born right here in the Pacific Northwest! So were her parents, as I recall. In fact, they got stuck in one of those awful internment camps during World War Two. Where were you, Costello? Leading your Boy Scout troop on a raid of the sauerkraut section at the local Safeway?"

Costello had stiffened. "I was a babe in arms," he retorted.

"An armed babe is more like it," Renie snapped back.

"I can see you in the hospital nursery, demanding that the black babies be put in isolettes. Wake up, this is almost the twenty-first century!"

Instead of roaring at Renie, Costello looked mystified. "What's an isolette?" he asked of Dabney Plummer. The deputy merely shrugged. Renie retreated to the sofa, shaking her head.

"Okay, okay," huffed Costello, momentarily distracted. "Now about this lurker—you never saw him?"

"Or her," Judith said mildly. "It's almost the twenty-first century, remember?"

Costello made an impatient gesture. "Whatever. Well? A no-show, you say?"

"That's right," Judith replied calmly. "He—or she—apparently left or hid. Naturally, we can't be certain that the person who killed Riley is the same one Iris spotted over at Nella's."

"Naturally." Costello's voice was coated in sarcasm. "You see anybody else lurking around this afternoon?"

Judith said they hadn't. The ear-shattering arrival of Lazlo Gamm's helicopter hardly qualified for Costello's description. "Hovering, not lurking. An art dealer from Hungary landed his helicopter in the meadow just as we were leaving earlier."

Costello was wreathed in skepticism. "Boy, you people up here on the South Fork sure put on airs. What's wrong with a good old Chevy?"

"Funny you should ask," Renie snapped, looking up from her place on the sofa. "First it was a leak in the brake fluid, then it was the power steering, and finally the whole damned transmission went out. Seventeen hundred bucks later, and it still doesn't reverse like it should. That's why we brought my cousin's compact. Any more dumb car questions?"

It seemed to Judith that Renie and the undersheriff weren't hitting it off. "Rhetorical," she murmured, moving toward the sofa and attempting to jab at Renie's upper arm. "Shut up." Judith turned back to the glowering

Costello. "Lazlo Gamm—he's the art dealer—landed just as we were leaving with our water buckets. Riley Tobias greeted him like a long-lost pal."

Costello finally stopped giving Renie the Evil Eye. "Hungarian, huh? They're pretty sinister, aren't they? What did he have against Tobias?"

"Nothing," Judith answered hastily. "As I said, they seemed to be friends from way back. The helicopter took off about an hour later, maybe less."

Costello fixed his steely-eyed gaze on Dabney Plummer. "You know how to spell 'Lazlo'?" Plummer nodded. "Who else?" demanded the undersheriff.

Judith considered; Ward Kimball's visit was hearsay. She decided not to mention it. "Iris Takisaki came down from the Green Mountain Inn along the river, but that was later—just before she came back to tell us about the prowler. You certainly don't have a problem with time of death—it had to be in that five- or ten-minute interval while Iris and my cousin and I were over at Mrs. Lablatt's."

Costello gave Judith a disparaging look. "Hey, this isn't television. All we can say right now is that Riley Tobias died somewhere between four-fifteen and five-forty-five this afternoon. Maybe we'll never come any closer. It's a shame we couldn't get here sooner, but whoever reported this homicide was either on drugs or slow in the upper story." He tapped his graying temple.

"Hey," Renie exclaimed, "what are you talking about? I was the one who called! I may have been ticked off by that stupid phone, but I don't do drugs and I'm not slow. Who've you got manning the phones? Dumbo?"

Costello sneered at Renie. "Right, sure. I guess when you're filthy rich, you can afford to be dumb as dirt. Not to mention take as many drugs as you please. Well, in the end, it's all the same—an OD in a body bag." For the first time, he gave the merest hint of a smile.

Renie leaped up from the sofa and spun around the room. "Oh, good grief!"

Judith intervened. "Is that all? I can't think of anything else we can tell you that would be helpful."

The threatened smile actually materialized, though Costello bestowed it on Dabney Plummer. Plummer grinned in response, looking a lot like a rabbit. "You hear that, Dabney? The suspect says she can't think of anything that would help us." The undersheriff chortled nastily, then swung back to face the cousins. "How about the deceased's plans for the afternoon? How about all those empty beer cans? How about *grand theft?* What does the suspect have to say about *that?*" The last words came out on a roar.

"Theft? Suspect?" It was Judith's turn to be annoyed. "Now just a minute, Mr. Costello—my cousin and I aren't suspects. In fact, my husband is a policeman. He probably knows more about homicide than you and all your deputies put together."

Abbott N. Costello again refused to be impressed. But he did lower his voice. "You think that people related to law enforcement officers never commit crimes? Don't make me laugh."

"Okeydokey," murmured Renie, who had slipped over to the bedroom door. Surreptitiously, she glanced around the curtain to make sure that all the commotion hadn't awakened Clive Silvanus. It hadn't.

"Then drop the 'suspect' stuff," Judith demanded, her black eyes snapping. "And what's this about grand theft?" Involuntarily, her gaze darted to the Murphy bed.

"Never mind," huffed Costello. "Just answer the question about Tobias's plans for the afternoon."

Judith gave an impatient shrug. "If he had any, he didn't tell us. I think he was surprised by Lazlo Gamm's arrival. But I suppose he was expecting Iris. She said so, anyway. Did he have an appointment book or a calendar?"

Again Costello gave his deputy that snide smile. "Listen to that, Dabney! The policeman's wife wants to know if the victim had an appointment book! Or a calendar! Now isn't that clever detective work? Her husband must have taught her everything he knows!" He chortled and Dabney grinned.

The cousins exchanged more glances, both of them angry, yet trying to warn each other to keep calm. They waited in silence for the next outrage from the undersheriff. He was now scowling, his gray eyes raking over the cabin one more time. Judith thought he lingered a bit too long on the curtain that covered the Murphy bed.

But a moment later, he was pointing that beefy finger at Dabney Plummer and saying, "Out."' The lawmen left without another word. In fact, Judith realized, Dabney Plummer had never spoken at all. She said as much to Renie.

"I wouldn't talk to Costello, either," Renie replied. "What a creep."

Judith went over to the window next to the stove. She could see the undersheriff's and his deputy's flashlights bobbing through the woods. When they disappeared among the trees, she turned back to Renie.

"Let's go. Clive Silvanus won't wake up until next week." Judith grabbed her jacket from the hook next to the bedroom door.

Renie was puzzled. "Go? Go where?"

Judith rummaged in her purse for her car keys. "First, to see Ward Kimball. And Lark. Second, to use the phone at the gas station to call home. Third, to Xanadu, or any place where I wouldn't expect to ever see Abbott N. Costello." In her agitation, she dropped her keys, stooped to retrieve them, and looked up to see the perplexed expression on Renie's face. "Oh, right—and fourth, to keep out of this murder case. I wouldn't get involved with that bozo for a million bucks!"

"So," Renie inquired as they headed down the road in Judith's Japanese compact, "why are we going to see Ward Kimball and his daughter if you don't intend to play sleuth?"

Judith turned just enough to give Renie a baleful look.

"To offer our condolences. I don't care what that drunken case of Southern Discomfort said about Ward and Riley quarreling—they've been close for years. Ward wasn't just a mentor to Riley; he was a father, too. Riley's death must have devastated Ward, especially if he's in poor health."

Judith slowed to take the curve in the road that followed the bend in the river. Putting on her turn signal, she slowed a bit more to make a left off the highway and onto Ward Kimball's private road.

There was no gate. Ward Kimball was of a generation and a disposition that trusted other people. His home, as well as his studio, was farther off the highway than the Grover cabin. Judith drove slowly along the winding road until she came to a clearing. She pulled up to a big log, next to an aging but well-cared-for Volkswagen bus. Ward had owned the bus for almost as long as Judith could remember. He had never become wealthy, but he had made money from his art. Yet it hadn't gone for material possessions. Briefly, Judith speculated on what Ward Kimball had done with his earnings. Travel, perhaps. He had certainly roamed the globe. Art, certainly. His private collection was small but magnificent. And Lark, of course. Ward Kimball had spared no expense where his daughter was concerned.

The house was modest yet handsome. It had been built just after World War II, when Ward had gotten out of the Army. Then he and his wife had remodeled it in the early sixties, after Lark had been born. Her handicap had dictated certain changes, but Ward had wanted to emulate the architectural style of Native Americans in the western part of the county. Interestingly, many of the coastal tribes' traditional houses had an uncanny resemblance to beach homes in southern California: High ceilings, big windows, shake exteriors, shingled roofs, and huge stone fireplaces were prominently featured. Judith had always wondered if the white man's builders hadn't stolen more than just the land from the Indians.

In a typical Pacific Northwest display of skittish weather,

the moon was now obscured by clouds. The outlines of the studio and the other outbuildings could be seen across the open area in front of the house. Oddly enough, Ward Kimball had not built right on the river. Perhaps he was afraid of floods; the Grovers had suffered for their temerity, having had to move the cabin twice in the past forty years. Of course, Kimball owned a great deal more property. Judith figured he had at least a full acre.

It appeared that only one room was lighted inside. Kimball had electricity, running water, and a telephone. Real plumbing, too, Judith reflected, vaguely recalling that she'd heard he'd had a hot tub installed a few years back.

The single swing of the brass knocker with Kimball's name engraved on it brought no immediate response. The cousins waited at least two minutes before Renie reached out to rap again. Before she could, the door swung away from her hand. Ward Kimball's shadowy figure stood before them.

"Ward?" Judith peered into the semidarkness. "It's us, Judith and Serena Grover. From up the road . . ."

"Come in." Kimball gestured urgently, as if he thought the cousins might have a posse at their heels. "Here, we're in the study. The Higbys up the road stopped to tell us about Riley. Isn't this a terrible day? I've lived too long."

The study was illuminated by a desk lamp with a green shade and a pair of wall sconces shaped like tulips. It was a small room, made even smaller by the crammed bookshelves, folios, cassettes, and heavy oak furniture. In a dark green leather chair next to the rolltop desk, a slim figure seemed folded up, like one of life's discards.

"Lark," said Ward Kimball in an uncertain voice, "we have guests. The Grover girls, from next door to Riley."

Judith couldn't help but smile faintly at Ward's description. But of course, in Ward Kimball's mind, she and Renie would always be the Grover girls.

"Hi," Judith said, going straight to Lark and reaching for her hand. "We had to come and say how terrible we felt about what happened today."

Lark Kimball lifted her head. Her blighted, beautiful blue eyes were red, and the perfect complexion that Judith remembered was blotchy. She didn't wear glasses, which Judith assumed would do no good. There were tiny lines on Lark's brow and around her eyes, no doubt caused by making an onerous effort to see. But the golden hair shimmered in the lamplight, the fine features had been honed by time, and the slender figure had blossomed in a delicate yet provocative manner. Judith felt an awful pang: How sad to be so lovely—and not be able to fully appreciate it.

Lark's smile was tremulous, touching. Except for those fine lines, she looked much younger than thirty-two. Perhaps her limited ability to see the ugliness of the world had helped preserve her innocence—and her youth. "I remember you!" Lark cried. "Your husband has a wonderful voice. He's a jolly man, isn't he?"

Judith saw Renie smirk. "Dan *had* a wonderful voice—and he could be sort of jolly." Judith gulped. *Jolly,* as in tight as a tic, or on a sugar high. The last jolly memory Judith had of Dan was when his fifty-four-inch belt had broken and his pants had fallen down. "I'm afraid Dan passed away a few years ago. I've remarried." Gently, she squeezed Lark's slim hand.

Lark lowered her head. "Oh! I'm so sorry! He must have been young, too." She paused to gather her composure. "Is that your sister with you? The designer?"

"My cousin. Serena. Yes. She's still married to Bill Jones, the psychologist at the university." Judith let go of Lark's hand and stepped aside for Renie.

Lark took Renie's hand in both of hers. "I went to the university. I took a class from a Dr. Jones. Was that your husband?"

"Could be," said Renie. "Did he rant like Hitler?"

Lark laughed, a small, painful sound. "Only if you had a late paper. He was very good. I found his lectures enlightening as well as refreshing. He had more to offer than most professors. And he didn't toe the academic party line."

"That's my Bill," said Renie.

Judith had accepted a straight-backed oak chair from Ward Kimball. Discreetly, she studied the renowned painter as he sat down in front of the rolltop desk. Riley Tobias was right: Ward Kimball had aged, and not particularly well. His white hair was still thick, as was his beard, but his hazel eyes were tired and the skin sagged on his cheeks. He was not a big man, and his spare frame had a fragile air. The Roman nose that had dominated and lent strength to his face now had a predatory look, as if the goodwill he had shown to men had been replaced by a need to be wary, even aggressive.

Yet his eyes were still kind, if guarded. "Lark could make tea or coffee." He spoke with pride. "We have seltzer, wine, and mineral water, too."

Judith declined, saying they'd just eaten. "We just finished when the undersheriff and his deputy showed up. Did you talk to them?" she asked artlessly.

"Not yet, but I know him." Ward Kimball's expression was wry. "Dreadful man. The undersheriff, I mean. I met him when someone broke into my studio a year or so ago."

Judith leaned forward. "Oh, no! Did they take anything valuable?"

Kimball shook his head. "There was nothing to take. I haven't painted for some time. My personal treasures are all here in the house. We've got an alarm system for it." He waved a hand at a Kenneth Callahan watercolor, a Dale Chiluly vase, a Mark Tobey sketch, a Ward Kimball mixed media of Glacier Falls. "Lark paints," he added with another proud smile, and pointed to a small oil on tempera depicting wildflowers. "Isn't that enchanting?"

Judith marveled at the exactness of the work. Slim silver stems boasted graceful white flowers. A cluster of purple blooms drew the eye to the background. The grass seemed to move on a summer breeze.

"It's wonderful. Amazing," she added as Renie got up

from the dark green leather footstool to admire Lark's work.

"Can you tell how good this is?" Renie asked, as usual abandoning tact for the sake of truth. "Lark, you're very talented."

Lark turned in the direction of Renie's voice. "Oh, I can sense that it's right. I'm able to discern colors and shapes. I spent as much time as Nature would allow studying those flowers—mostly with my fingers, of course. But I have a photographic memory. Or is it photographic fingers?" Her smile was faintly impish.

Judith turned to Ward Kimball. "Did you teach her?"

"In the beginning." He looked away. "Then Riley helped a bit with her technique." His tone was flat.

In the leather chair, Lark coiled as if she were going to spring across the room. "Riley was marvelous! He was patient, understanding, kind! And *he* never patronized me!" The last was hurled as an accusation that made Ward Kimball flinch.

"Lark," he said wearily, "you know it's not easy for a parent to teach a child. A father is always a father. It can't be helped."

With surprising agility, Lark jumped up from the chair and left the room. A sob tore from her throat as she slammed the study door.

Ward emitted an embarrassed little laugh. "Lark's upset. She was fond of Riley. So was I," he added a bit hastily.

"Of course you were," Judith said smoothly. "Everyone knows that."

"Of course." Ward's shoulders sagged; he looked not only old but defeated. "It's a terrible tragedy, not just for those who knew him, but for the entire art community."

To Judith, it seemed like an exit line. Yet she was loath to leave Ward Kimball alone with his grief-stricken daughter. "Had you seen Riley lately?" Judith kept her voice natural. It was a polite stall, she told herself—not an attempt at sleuthing. She ignored Renie's bemused expression.

The guarded look intensified in Ward's eyes, but his response came easily enough. "I stopped by this afternoon, as a matter of fact. He was working, so I didn't stay long."

Riley Tobias had not been at work when the cousins had seen him, and Judith doubted he was when Ward came calling. But she only had Clive Silvanus's word for the quarrel. "Was he upset or anxious?" she asked.

Ward adjusted the shawl collar of his loosely woven navy blue sweater. "No, he was his usual self. Caught up in his painting, of course. I understand that very well."

Renie leaned forward on the footstool. "What was he working on?"

Ward's forehead wrinkled. "One of those so-called portraits. I'm not keen on them, but Riley would call my opinions archaic."

Judith saw Ward's gaze stray to the door. No doubt he wanted to check on Lark. But Judith had one more question: "Did Riley have any enemies who'd want to see him dead?"

Sitting up straight in the oak swivel chair, Ward seemed to consider the query very briefly. "Oh—not really. Rivals, possibly. Any successful artist invites a certain amount of envy and spite. Riley could annoy, he could shock, he could be perverse. But enemies? There was always a lovable quality about him. Allowances have to be made for creative people. I suspect he was forgiven as much as any man ever was." A wistful note had crept into Ward Kimball's voice. He stared up at the ceiling where the tulip lamps cast scallop-shaped shadows. "Yes, he had a knack for repentance. In the end, everyone always forgave Riley Tobias."

Judith shook her head. "No. Not everyone. His killer didn't forgive him."

Ward seemed unshaken by Judith's pronouncement. "Oh? I wonder. It wouldn't surprise me if whoever murdered Riley has forgiven him." The old artist's voice took on a harsher edge. "Now that he's dead, of course."

FIVE

JOE FLYNN URGED his wife to flaunt her talents. She had a gift for piecing odd lots of information together. She could get anybody, even killers, to open up. She was a born observer, a student of human nature, a font of logic. So what if the investigating officer was a crude, unprofessional boor? All the better. Such a backwoods boob couldn't catch an anteater in an elevator. Judith had aptitude, perception, and experience. Coupled with Renie's knack of going for the jugular, they made a terrific team. Joe would cheer them on from the sidelines, at least when he wasn't being distracted by such mundane matters as chasing down murderous gang leaders, doped-up convenience-store killers, and a wacko who had carved up three people with a grapefruit knife.

Judith still couldn't believe what she'd heard as she dialed her mother's separate line in the converted toolshed that stood behind Hillside Manor. Joe couldn't be serious about telling her to get involved in the Tobias investigation. That wasn't like him. On previous occasions he had warned her off, even forbidden her to join the hunt. It was too risky, too dangerous, too out of her league. Judith waited through seven rings before Gertrude Grover answered.

"What's the matter with you?" Gertrude barked. "It's after eleven. I was asleep."

"Fraud," countered Judith. "You and Sweetums always watch the news. Besides, I had trouble making the call. This pay phone at the auto court is really outmoded. Is everything okay?"

Gertrude snorted. "Okay? Is it okay to live in a paper box? That's about how big this stupid toolshed is. No room to swing a cat. And believe me, I tried. That mound of mange is still dizzy."

Judith leaned against the glass door of the booth, waiting for an eighteen-wheeler to pass. After six months, she was used to her mother's complaints about the apartment in the former toolshed. But she knew Gertrude wouldn't want to be anywhere else—unless it was back in the third-floor family quarters of Hillside Manor. That, of course, was impossible, since she refused to live under the same roof as Joe Flynn.

"You probably called that shanty Irishman first," Gertrude accused. "Or did Serena tie up the line with that addled sister-in-law of mine? Deb rang up *twice* today, just because she fell out of her wheelchair."

Alarmed, Judith glanced through the glass at Renie, who had not yet called her own mother. Renie looked back with a question on her face.

"What happened?" Judith demanded. "Is Aunt Deb all right?"

"Black and blue always were her colors," Gertrude replied blithely. "Oh, Deb's fine. She just bounced around a little. Mrs. Parker and her ugly mutt, Ignatz, were there, so she stuffed Deb back in the wheelchair and screwed in all her missing parts. Deb was reaching for a doughnut. Serves her right. I'm sure glad I'm not stuck living with her anymore." Gertrude let out a little hiss as she caught herself making an admission that might be construed as positive. "I mean, at least I don't have to listen to her whine and jabber here while I'm trying to sit down with my entire body *in the same room.*"

Aware that Renie was growing anxious as well as impatient, Judith told her mother to take care and prepared to hang up.

"Take care? Of what?" Gertrude huffed. "My health, which stinks? My belongings, which have shrunk to about fourteen items? Your wretched cat? He hauled in an almost-dead pigeon today. I baked it and sent it over to Deb." Gertrude chortled in Judith's ear.

"You didn't—Aunt Deb wouldn't eat pigeon," Judith protested.

"I wasn't talking about the pigeon." Gertrude chortled some more.

Judith sighed. "Now, Mother, stop trying to horrify me. Renie and I got a real start on cleaning and fixing up the cabin today. If you need anything, you can call Joe."

"I know what to call him," growled Gertrude. "Lunkhead, for starters. He had the nerve to come by this evening and tell me I should open a window to get some fresh air. Since when do I need advice from that twerp? You don't need it, either, Judith Anne. Any wife who listens to her husband is a certified sap." She banged the receiver in Judith's ear.

"What's wrong?" Renie demanded as Judith emerged from the booth.

Judith explained. Renie attacked the phone, knowing that her mother was a night owl, too. Indeed, the sisters-in-law had more in common than they'd admit. The experiment of having them live together had failed, but deep down, they both loved—and needed—each other. At least at a distance.

Judith knew Renie's call to her husband would be brief. Indeed, Bill Jones was an early riser who had probably already gone to bed. Renie's three grown children—Tony, Tom and Anne—never lingered on the line with their mother. But Aunt Deb would chat forever. Judith contemplated waiting in the car, but was afraid she might fall asleep if she got comfortable. To stay alert, she began to amble aimlessly up and down the drive.

Traffic on the highway was very light. The filling station and the office were both closed. Five vehicles, including the white Mercedes, were now parked in front of the little cabins. Lights glowed behind the curtained windows of two of the units. Wandering around in front of the auto court, Judith noted that somebody was still up at the Mortons'. She was only half-surprised to see Carrie Mae Morton come outside in a gaudy floral print bathrobe.

"I know you," said Carrie Mae, keeping her voice down. "You were here today with Riley's girlfriend." She glanced at the phone booth, where Renie was propped up against the wall. "Her, too. Were we introduced?"

"Not really. It was pretty hectic." Judith extended her hand, introducing herself—and Renie by default. Carrie Mae remarked that the Grover cabin didn't get used much, at least not during the year that the Mortons had lived across the road. Judith admitted that was so, but explained how she and Renie were spending a few days doing some maintenance work.

"You sure picked a bad time," Carrie Mae said cheerfully. "Did you see those TV cameras and reporters? Newspaper people, too. They were here for almost an hour. Me and Mort got ourselves on the ten o'clock news."

Judith let out a little gasp that Carrie Mae took for excitement. But it wasn't. Judith had purposely avoided telling her mother about Riley Tobias's murder. The ten o'clock news was aired over a local station; Gertrude always watched the network affiliate at eleven. Riley Tobias was sufficiently famous to make both broadcasts. Judith hoped that she had been talking to her mother when the story hit the airwaves. As much as her mother criticized Aunt Deb for being a worrywart, as often as she raked Judith over the coals, Gertrude couldn't stand it if she thought her only child was in the slightest danger. If Judith was protective of her mother, Gertrude, in her own way, was equally protective of her daughter.

Carrie Mae was rambling on about the interview, which, according to her, could have filled up an hour time-slot.

Judith tried to refocus, but she was getting very tired. She had risen at six, prepared breakfast for Joe and her four guests, packed, checked on Gertrude, picked up Renie, and driven more than sixty miles to the cabin. The cousins had put in a busy afternoon, working around the cabin. Then all hell had broken loose. Now it was eleven-thirty, a stranger was sleeping in the spare bedroom, and Carrie Mae Morton was talking Judith's ear off.

". . . a hippie type, that's what I told them," Carrie Mae was saying as Judith finally tuned back in. "There's still a few of 'em, living by the old sawmill up the Jimmy-Jump-Off Creek Road. They come in for gas now and then. It figures, don't it?"

"It . . . could," Judith allowed, not quite following Carrie Mae's brand of logic. "Do they do drugs?"

Carrie Mae gave Judith a condescending look. "Does a dog have fleas? 'Course they do—they even grow the stuff. You'd think that dopey undersheriff would have busted 'em a long time ago. On the take, that's what. Those hippies have money to spare, believe me." She sniffed with disdain, red curls and big bosom shaking.

Carrie Mae's hippie theory wasn't implausible. Abbott N. Costello *had* mentioned grand theft. Maybe it was a relatively simple murder, with robbery as the motive.

Judith pointed to the white Mercedes. "Is that Mr. Dixon's car?"

"Dixon?" Carrie Mae's mouth twisted in the effort of remembering. "Oh, right. Sort of a spiffy guy. I guess he knew Riley, huh?"

Judith nodded. Inside the phone booth, Renie looked paralyzed. "When did he check in?" Judith tried to keep the question casual.

Again Carrie Mae screwed up her face. "This time? Let me think . . . it was soon after that whirlybird took off from Riley's and just before Rafe put peanut butter on the pig. We keep a few animals out back, you know. Well—I guess it was around four, maybe sooner. It's hard to keep track of time."

Briefly, Judith commiserated. "I take it Mr. Dixon was here to see Riley?"

"Must have been. Lousy timing for him, too, huh?" Carrie Mae smiled broadly.

It was, of course. Unless . . . Judith put another question to Carrie Mae: "Did you or your husband happen to see anybody over by Nella's house around five o'clock?"

Carrie Mae tugged at the ties of her floral bathrobe. "You mean around the time Riley was killed? Nope. I was thrashing the kids. They were trying to put a dress on the dog. My best dress, too." Carrie Mae's full lips puckered in disapproval. "As for Mort, he was out feeding the chickens and slopping the pigs. He always does that about then. When he's done, I fix dinner and we all sit down to the family trough." She squealed with laughter at her own humor, sounding not unlike one of the Morton pigs.

Renie finally staggered from the phone booth. After a few more desultory exchanges with Carrie Mae Morton, the cousins got into the blue compact and drove the short distance to the family cabin.

Both the fire and the lanterns had gone out. Although the night air had grown cool, the cousins decided against coping with the stove. Renie lighted a single lantern while Judith peeked in on Clive Silvanus. She stood in the doorway for several seconds, waiting for Renie to illuminate the room. When the light finally flared up, Judith let out a resigned sigh.

"I knew it," she said, turning away and letting the plaid curtain fall into place. "He's gone."

"Good riddance," said Renie, yawning.

"Probably," responded Judith, kicking off her shoes. If she hadn't been relieved, and tired, she would have felt uneasy.

Instead, she went to bed. Renie carried the kerosene lantern into the back bedroom. Yet more blue-and-white plaid covered the twin beds. It occurred to Judith that Grandma Grover must have bought the stuff in bulk, rather than by the yard.

The cousins settled down; the lantern light faded into darkness. Less than two feet separated the beds. On many a long-ago summer night Judith and Renie had gotten into trouble for talking too much, getting up repeatedly, insisting on using the chamber pot, or beating each other over the head with their pillows. They would complain of grizzly bears at the window, garter snakes on the floor, and ghosts hiding outside in the woods. On this night in early May there were potheads up the road, burglars on the loose, and a murderer lurking in the shadows. Times had changed, and so had Judith and Renie.

Forty years after making mischief and giving their imaginations free rein, the cousins simply went to sleep.

The morning mist was on the river; the dew was still on the grass. Mount Woodchuck was partially obscured, but the cousins knew that by noon it would reappear. Unless it rained. Judith and Renie breakfasted on buttermilk pancakes, link sausage, fried eggs, orange juice, and hot coffee. They talked of mothers, matrimony, and murder, but not necessarily in that order.

"Joe must be using reverse psychology," Judith asserted. "You know how he is about me playing sleuth. So why has he changed his tune? Because we're leaving tomorrow afternoon?"

"Maybe. But I think you were right the first time," Renie said, buttering four dollar-sized pancakes in turn. Not a morning person, she seemed more alert than usual. Judith figured that her cousin was also responding well to the rustic comforts of the cabin. It was much more agreeable to wake up to the sound of a rippling river than to the buzz of an alarm clock.

"Bill's the one who knows psychology," Judith mused. "Then my mother tells me I'd be a sap to ever listen to anything Joe said. If I keep out of this case, I'd be playing right into his hands. But if he's serious, then I'm defying him. What would you do, coz?"

"Be confused," Renie replied, drizzling syrup over her

pancakes. "Which I am. I don't know what the hell you're talking about."

For a few moments the cousins ate in silence. At last Judith spoke again. "If Carrie Mae Morton is right, it shouldn't take too long for even a dim-bulb like Costello to track down those aging hippies."

Renie nodded. "They'd know Riley had valuable artwork. I've no idea how you fence a curlew sculpture, but I suppose it can be done. Face it, coz, there may not be much of a mystery about this case. The way things stand, I don't even know where you'd begin."

Judith was cutting up her sausage and didn't see Renie's eyes dance. "Oh, there could be other motives besides robbery. Why hadn't Riley handed over the painting to Dewitt Dixon? What's their mutual history? How much is Clive Silvanus really hiding behind that overdone Good Ol' Boy exterior? Where *is* Clive, if it comes to that? *Did* Ward Kimball have a serious quarrel with Riley, and if so, what was it about? Was Lark in love with Riley? How did that sit with Iris Takisaki? Why did Lazlo Gamm suddenly show up, literally out of the blue? Where were all of the above between five and five-thirty yesterday afternoon? We know where Iris was. Dewitt had checked into the motel by four, Ward and Lark were in the vicinity, so was Clive, and we know approximately when Lazlo Gamm left because we heard his copter. But how do we know he didn't come back?"

Renie tried not to smile. "Yes, I can see there are a few other possibilities. But if we're going to tackle those downspouts, we won't have time to follow any of them up."

"That's true." Judith gazed beyond Renie to the windows at the far end of the cabin. "Do you think the old ones are usable?"

"They looked pretty beat-up to me. We could drive into Glacier Falls and get some new ones." Renie complacently devoured egg white.

Judith finished her juice. "Where's Grandpa's ladder?"

"It broke. Mike and Tony used it to play pirates about ten years ago. My dad had one up here, but Bill took it home so it wouldn't rust. It was aluminum or something."

"The toolbox is under the house." Judith got up to get the coffeepot.

Renie reached for another sausage. "There aren't any tools in it. Cousin Marty borrowed them to fix his doghouse and never brought them back."

Judith's oval face sagged a bit. "Cousin Marty has never had a dog."

Renie gave Judith a bland look. "I know. Did I ever say Cousin Marty was *bright?"*

Pouring out coffee, Judith shook her head. "Our maintenance plan doesn't sound so good. Let's scratch the downspouts. We'll clean out the gutters instead."

Renie raised both eyebrows. "Without a ladder?"

"We'll borrow one." Judith sat back down in the cherrywood dining room chair that had belonged to Uncle Vince's mother.

"Oh." Renie was now looking ingenuous. "Where, coz? The Berkmans aren't around, neither is Nella Lablatt at the old post office, and we really don't know the Mortons that well."

Judith leaned forward, glaring at Renie. "Okay, okay, so we'll go ask Iris. It'll keep her mind off her loss."

"Good idea." Renie brushed her hands together. "I was wondering when we'd come to that."

Judith snorted and speared another pancake. "We never left it."

Renie grinned. "I know, coz. I know."

SIX

"BY THE WAY," said Judith as the cousins prepared to head over to Riley Tobias's property, "did your mother say anything about seeing the murder on TV last night?"

"Are you kidding?" Renie pulled on a pair of black sweatpants. "My mother never watches the news. She's afraid she'll see something unpleasant. Like the anchorman's bad toupee on Channel Six."

"Lucky you," Judith replied, brushing her short, silver-streaked black curls into fashionable disarray. "I have a feeling that my mother missed it last night because she was talking to me. But both of them could see it in the paper today."

"Maybe not," Renie said. "They're playing bridge all day."

Judith hoped Renie was right. Five minutes later, they were going through the meadow approaching Riley Tobias's house and studio. If they needed a further excuse, they'd brought along another bucket for more water.

But the place appeared to be deserted. The studio exhibited the telltale black-and-yellow tape of a crime scene. The house showed no sign of life. The doors to both buildings were padlocked. Out back, by the highway, there were no vehicles in the drive. Just to be sure, the cousins went around to the front and knocked. They knocked again. There was no response.

Judith wore a disappointed look. Renie tried to cheer her. "Maybe it's just as well, coz. Now you don't have to turn yourself inside out worrying about whether you're pleasing Joe or toadying to your mother. Think about it—why shouldn't they all be gone? Dewitt came to get his painting. Iris probably went back to her condo to mourn. Clive Silvanus must have to wind up Riley's business affairs in town. Lazlo Gamm flew away. And the Kimballs don't live here."

Taking in a deep breath, Judith squared her wide shoulders. "Okay, you're right. Let's get our water and go home."

She lowered the beige enamel bucket with its dark green trim into the well while Renie noted that the clouds were already beginning to lift off Mount Woodchuck. It appeared as if they were going to have a warm, clear day ahead of them.

Judith scanned the horizon, from the emerging crest of the mountain to the cottonwoods behind Riley's studio. "Hey—there's a ladder!" She pointed to the north side of the studio. "We might as well help ourselves. Who else is going to use it?"

The ladder was ten feet long and made of very heavy wood. Judith struggled, trying to swing it away from the wall.

"Need any help?" Renie was holding the bucket.

"No, I can get it." But the ladder slipped from Judith's grasp, fell back against the studio, and crashed through one of the big windows. Judith jumped out of the way, shielding her face from shards of sailing glass. Renie ducked and let out a squeal.

The cousins finally dared to look at the damage. The ladder had struck the plate glass in such a way that its downward descent had virtually taken out the entire window. Crime-scene tape was tangled in the rungs; the studio lay open like a big wound.

"We'll have to call somebody," Judith said, picking glass out of her Rugby shirt.

"Not the sheriff," Renie exclaimed in horror.

Judith bit her lip. "Yes, the sheriff. Or in this case, the undersheriff. And Iris. She'll know about the insurance."

Renie emptied the bucket. "I'm not taking any chances. Glass might have landed in the water. Let's draw some more, take it home, and then go make our calls."

This time, Renie lowered the bucket into the well. Judith leaned against the small woodshed by the decorated fence. She was eyeing the studio speculatively.

"As long as we're here . . ." She paused, nodding at the broken window. "What do you say, coz?"

Renie rolled her eyes. "Would it matter?"

With great care and diligent effort, the cousins managed to remove the ladder. With it, they also removed much of the crime-scene tape. A chopping block provided the needed height for them to reach the window opening. Tiptoeing around broken glass, Judith and Renie studied the interior.

Except for the damage caused by the ladder, the studio looked much the same as it had less than twenty-four hours earlier. The Nerd's portrait still reposed on the easel, looking, if possible, even uglier than it had the previous day. If anything was missing, Judith assumed it had been taken away as evidence by the undersheriff and his deputy. The only addition was the crude outline of Riley Tobias's body on the orange-paint-spattered floor.

"*His* portrait," murmured Judith, and winced.

"Ugh." Renie gave herself a shake. "The spilled paint has dried. I wonder how it got all over the floor."

Judith spotted a cardboard box just behind the easel. "There are a bunch of tubes and jars. Maybe Riley was using one of them when he was attacked."

Renie glanced into the box. "Could be. What about all

those beer cans Costello mentioned? Gone for finger-printing?"

"Probably." Judith prodded at the floorboards with her canvas shoe. At least two of them appeared to have been loosened by the impact of the ladder. She bent down, careful not to touch any glass. A slight pressure sprang one of the boards like a seesaw. Judith gaped. Empty liquor bottles lay in a jumble, at least a foot deep. Bourbon. Gin. Vodka. Scotch. Rum. A single beer can.

"I don't get it," said Renie, joining Judith by the opening in the floor. "Why didn't Riley put these in the trash?"

Judith replaced the board. "I don't know. Lazy? I always thought of Riley as a beer drinker, but there's only one can in here."

"I never thought about him as any kind of a serious drinker," Renie said. "Still, I haven't seen much of him in recent years."

Judith steeled herself to take another look at Riley's outline. "He fell face-forward. See, there are skid marks in the paint. He must have been working at the easel when he was strangled. Interesting."

"Yes, interesting, gruesome, ghastly. I may soon puke. Let's go, coz." Renie was heading for the open window.

But Judith was still browsing. Kneeling on the hearth of the big stone fireplace, she reached into the grate and pulled out a crumpled ball of paper.

"I'll bet this is what Riley was throwing away when we arrived yesterday. I'm surprised the undersheriff didn't check it out."

"I'm not," Renie replied with a touch of impatience. "What are you expecting? A death threat?"

Judith had smoothed the wrinkled paper, which consisted of a single, typed sheet of plain white stationery and an envelope addressed to Riley Tobias. The return bore the surname of Tobias as well, and the address was a rural route number in Old Bennington, Vermont.

"It's a letter from somebody named Yancey," Judith said, ignoring Renie's remark. "His brother, I bet." She scanned the first two paragraphs, which included an excuse for not writing sooner, news about a minor car accident presumably involving a teenaged son, and mention of a family outing to St. Catherine Lake. Judith read the third and final paragraph aloud:

" 'Honest to God, Riley, I don't know what to say about that painting you sent me for my birthday. What are you trying to do these days? You always say you want me to be candid, and usually that's not hard. Your work—in general—has been brilliant. But this thing looks like you tap-danced on it. With clogs. Go back to your old stuff, kid. I'm putting this one in the garage. Peace—Yancey.' "

Renie's impatience had flown. "Wow! He took the words right out of my mouth. You think that's Riley's brother?"

Judith nodded, stood up, and put the letter in her pocket. "It must be. The name on the envelope is Tobias, and who else but a brother would be so blunt?"

Renie grinned. "A cousin?"

Judith grinned back. "Good point. However, we'll assume that brotherly love didn't extend to Riley's new style."

"Riley's a generous guy," Renie mused. "He sends Yancey a painting for his birthday; he gives one away to you." Her brown eyes swept around the studio. "What's here? A dozen canvases? Not a huge inventory. There might be more in the house, though."

Judith agreed. The cousins also agreed to abandon the ladder, as well as their plans for the gutters. After taking the water back to the cabin, they struck out for the Woodchuck Auto Court. Crossing the highway, Judith and Renie simultaneously saw that the white Mercedes was still parked at the auto court.

"So Dewitt Dixon didn't leave after all," Judith remarked as they reached the tarmac.

Kennedy Morton came out of the office, followed by two redheaded children somewhat older than the trio the cousins had seen the previous day. This time, Judith could distinguish between the sexes, mainly because the girl had a huge yellow satin ribbon in her hair and the boy was naked.

"Thor!" Kennedy Morton made a pass at swatting his son's bare behind. "You get in there and put some clothes on! Just because you got a day off from school don't mean you can lollygag around here in your birthday suit!"

Thor galloped off toward the house. His sister seemed unmoved by the incident, standing pigeon-toed and staring at the cousins. The children's father wiped his dirty hands off on a greasy rag.

"Dang these kids—if they ain't squabblin', they're pesterin' the livestock. Want to buy a chicken? The Little Woman can wring a neck for you in less time than it takes to say cock-a-doodle-doo."

"No, thanks," Judith replied, feeling a little dazed. "We came over to use your pay phone. And to call on Mr. Dixon." Seeing Morton's blank expression, she gestured at the white Mercedes. "That's his car. He spent the night here."

"Oh, him." Kennedy Morton grimaced. "Fancy fella, puttin' on airs. Why can't people be real?" He started for the second cabin, while his daughter scuffed at the gravel and wandered off. "You go use the phone. I'll fetch Mr. Dixon," Morton called to the cousins over his shoulder.

After the initial wrestling with the antiquated telephone, Judith finally reached the sheriff's office. Her explanation about the ladder and the broken window was taken by a woman with a monotone voice who sounded bored to tears. The second call, to Directory Assistance, yielded Iris Takisaki's number in the city. Judith dialed, but got no answer.

"Maybe she's making funeral arrangements," Renie suggested after Judith had gotten out of the booth.

Kennedy Morton returned alone. He waved the greasy rag at Judith and chuckled in an apologetic manner. "Sorry, I forgot Mr. Dixon was going up the road to have breakfast at the Green Mountain Inn. He walked."

So did the cousins, covering the distance in just over five minutes. The Green Mountain Inn was of the same vintage as the Woodchuck Auto Court, but it had been built with more imagination and a bigger budget. The faux thatched roof was an Irish green. The second story, which housed the guest rooms, was gabled with dormer windows and shutters that matched the roof. The stucco exterior was whitewashed at least every other year. A quaint sign printed in Olde English style stood at the edge of the road. Half of the first floor was a grocery; the other half, a restaurant.

Judith and Renie had known the original owners quite well. But the business had changed hands twice since the early sixties. The cousins were only nodding acquaintances with Dee and Gary Johanson, who had owned the property since 1989.

Dee was working in the restaurant as both hostess and waitress. A rangy woman in her late thirties, she wore her blond hair in a Dutch bob and disdained cosmetics.

"Two for breakfast? Or lunch?"

It was not quite ten-thirty; the cousins had eaten only a little more than an hour ago. "Coffee," said Judith.

"With pie," put in Renie.

Dee led them to a place by the window. Flowered oilskin covered the tables, providing a cheery note. Otherwise, the decor was kept to a minimum—a copper warming pan on one wall, a mounted rainbow trout on another, and a montage of old photographs depicting loggers, miners, and railroad men from the early part of the century. An impressive rack of antlers loomed over the entrance to the bar.

It being midmorning in the off-season, the restaurant was virtually deserted. Except, Judith noted with satisfaction, for the two men who sat at a table across the room: Dewitt Dixon and Clive Silvanus were deep in conversation.

Dee Johanson proffered menus, but Judith held up a hand. "Just coffee for me. Really."

Renie ordered coffee and blackberry pie with whipped cream. Dee started to move away, then turned back. "You look familiar. Are you up from Glacier Falls?"

Judith and Renie identified themselves. Dee visibly relaxed. She had the common Pacific Northwestern rural suspicion of people who didn't belong. Judith and Renie did—however tenuously.

Dee's eyes widened and she lowered her voice. "You knew Riley? Are you the ones who were with Iris when she found the body? Isn't it awful? Did you want to pass out?" Without waiting for affirmation, she leaned closer, gesturing with the menu pinned under her arm. "See those two men over there? They knew Riley, too. They've been sitting at that table for over an hour, talking like a couple of spies."

Judith also spoke softly. "The one with the mustache is Riley's agent. The other one bought a painting from Riley." A sudden thought struck Judith. "Is the Southerner staying here?"

Dee Johanson nodded. "He checked in yesterday around two. He went out, came back, went out again—and didn't get in until going on midnight. I suppose he was busy with the murder. You know—answering questions and helping the sheriff."

Neither Judith nor Renie said anything to correct Dee's assumption. It appeared to Judith that Clive Silvanus hadn't yet talked to Costello. If the lawman had called on Clive at the Green Mountain Inn, Dee would have mentioned it. But Dewitt Dixon might have stayed on at Riley's house and been interrogated on the spot. Judith wondered if the two men would notice her and Renie.

"They look like they're plotting the overthrow of a Third World government," Renie noted after Dee had gone off to hand in their orders. "Does Clive seem hung over to you?"

It wasn't easy to be discreet when the objects of Judith's attention were the only other two people in the dining room. "I can't tell. At least he doesn't have an ice bag on his head."

At that moment the two men sat back in their chairs and began the ritual of Picking Up the Check. Clive seemed to be short of cash; Dewitt claimed the bill. Clive used the stairway near his table, apparently to return to his room. It appeared he hadn't noticed the cousins.

Dewitt, however, headed straight toward Judith and Renie on his way to the cash register. He seemed mildly surprised, but gave them a debonair smile.

"Good morning, Serena. And . . . Judith, is it?" He stopped next to Renie, the smile disappearing. "I'm still in shock. Indeed, I feel like a fool for being so callous with Iris. Have you heard anything new about Riley's murder?"

Renie shook her head. "Nothing of interest. Did you talk to the undersheriff?"

Dewitt Dixon pulled a face. "Yes, much to my sorrow. The man is an incompetent clod. I was still at Riley's house last night when that Costello and his stooge showed up. I'm quite certain they don't have a clue—literally."

Renie suggested that Dewitt pull up a chair and join them. He hesitated, then gave in. Dee appeared with a pot of coffee and a piece of pie topped with a mound of real whipped cream. She asked if Dewitt wanted anything, but he demurred. She coaxed in vain. Judith had the feeling Dee wanted to linger, but the woman was forced to retreat with curiosity stamped all over her plain face.

"Did you get your painting?" Renie asked, doing her best not to decorate her upper lip with whipped cream.

Dewitt's tanned forehead furrowed. "Not yet. Clive Silvanus—the chap I was just speaking with—says it has to be properly wrapped for transport. That may take a few days. I'd rather carry it back to town myself."

Judith tipped her head to one side, regarding Dewitt with sympathy. "I can certainly understand that. It must be a stunning work. Had you seen the finished product before yesterday, or was it a commission?"

"I'd seen it, about three weeks ago." Dewitt's gaze

roamed around the ceiling beams. "My wife is the one who wanted to buy it. She's starting up her own gallery. That's why she went to Europe, to scour the Continent for new talent."

Under the table, Judith gave Renie a nudge. Renie responded to her cue. "Was the one you bought a new work? One of those portraits he'd started lately?"

Dewitt drummed his fingers on the oilskin and gazed up at the beamed ceiling. "A portrait? No, it's a landscape. It has charm, I suppose. Erica was determined to have it. I'm afraid our tastes sometimes differ. For example, I don't find the Uffizi at all redundant."

"On our first two tries, we couldn't find it at all," Renie asserted with a gleam in her eye. "Of course, that was over twenty-five years ago and we were young and naive and Judith spent all her time in Florence leering at Michelangelo's 'David.' She said it reminded her of Joe. I can't think why." She paused just long enough to acknowledge Judith's incensed glare. "What did Riley call the painting you bought? It sounded to me as if he'd given his new series some really stupid names. He didn't do that with his earlier works."

Dewitt didn't know, and apparently didn't care. "It's a large sum of money, But Erica refuses to change her mind. She wants it for the centerpiece of the gallery. Given the rumors about Riley, perhaps it's not an entirely frivolous decision."

"Rumors?" Judith turned in her chair. "About what?"

Dewitt shrugged, then pulled out a package of foreign cigarettes. "Do you mind?" The cousins didn't. Nor did the Green Mountain Inn have a no-smoking policy. And with the number of carousing loggers who frequented the bar on a Saturday night, the owners would have been lucky to enforce a no-combat zone.

"There's been talk in recent months that Riley's talent has diminished," Dewitt explained, lowering his cultivated voice. "His output has slowed, too. Erica points out that's because he drastically altered his approach. But Riley Tobias was well known as prolific, without sacrificing genius. For years he's pleased critics as well as admirers. Then, about a year ago, everything changed, including his style. Erica and I were fortunate to discover that he'd painted one last landscape. There have been only three of his new, so-called portraits completed, and the two that have been placed on exhibit were scorned by everyone. Except," he added with a pained expression, "my wife. It wouldn't surprise me if she made an offer on one of those blasted nerds now that Riley's dead."

"Your wife sounds like a devoted fan," Judith remarked.

Dewitt scoffed. "Not a fan. A fanatic." He exhaled a cloud of blue smoke. "But what could you expect? I don't believe Erica has ever gotten over Riley." He saw the puzzlement on the cousins' faces and gave them an ironic look. "Ah—I gather you didn't know. Years ago, Erica was Riley's wife."

"I *told* you I didn't know much about the artsy set," Renie declared as the cousins took the river route from the Green Mountain Inn. "As for Riley, you knew him as well as I did. Better, maybe."

Judith wore a chagrined expression. "I knew he'd been married briefly. But that was over twenty years ago, before he moved up here from San Francisco. I don't think I ever heard him mention his ex-wife by name. Oh, well, it's not as if we've acquired another suspect. Erica Tobias Dixon is in Europe."

Traversing the riverbank, the cousins alternated between sizable boulders and patches of sand. In some places where the river cut close to the shoreline, they had to step warily and cling to vine maples to keep from getting their feet wet. When they reached the Berkman property, the bank began to rise. The cousins disdained the trail that led up to the A-frame and kept walking next to the river.

Just beyond the Berkmans' A-frame, a movement caught Judith's eye. She stopped, with Renie following suit just behind her.

"Deer?" Renie whispered, taking Judith's silent, motionless stance for animal-gazing.

Judith shook her head. The figure had disappeared behind the Berkman cabin. The cousins waited, with Renie's expression growing curious. At last Judith sighed and turned to her cousin.

"I saw a man at the back of the A-frame," Judith said, keeping her voice low. "He may have headed for the road."

"Trent Berkman? A hippie?" Renie sounded dubious.

"Neither. It wouldn't have been Trent—the place is all closed up. And," Judith added with a knowing look, "even well-heeled hippies don't wear Armani suits."

"Lazlo Gamm?" Renie sounded incredulous as the cousins again took up the trail. "But he flew off yesterday."

"His *helicopter* flew off," Judith replied, but she, too, spoke in a disbelieving voice. "And even if he was in the copter, what's he doing now, lurking around the Berkman place?"

Naturally, Renie had no explanation. The cousins trudged on in puzzled silence. They were just below their own cabin when they noticed a figure perched on a big rock downstream. "Iris," murmured Judith, nodding at the seated woman who seemed totally self-absorbed.

Here, in front of the Grover and Tobias properties, the bank rose at least twenty feet. Much of it was undermined by floodwaters. The stretch of river that flowed between the Green Mountain Inn and the Big Bend was relatively smooth, yet swift. In early May, the river ran about waist-high. In summer, the channel remained quite wide, but the water barely reached an adult's knees. The cousins had plenty of room to roam between the river and the bank. They got within fifteen feet of Iris before Judith called out a greeting:

"Hi, Iris! How are you doing?"

Iris seemed to move in slow motion. A ghost of a smile played at her lips. She raised an uncertain hand. "What can you expect?" she responded in a feeble voice as the cousins drew closer. "I'm not sure I really believe Riley's dead."

Judith and Renie each chose a big rock and sat down. The river rumbled by, reassuringly constant. "Have you heard from the undersheriff?" Judith asked.

Iris had her arms wrapped around her knees. She barely breathed as she spoke. "He's coming by in about an hour. I've already answered every conceivable question. What can he want now? Maybe he thinks he should look at that broken window."

Judith winced; Renie squirmed. "Did he tell you how that happened?"

Iris's nod was indifferent. "Thieves, coming back to loot the place. Why didn't they take what they wanted when they killed Riley? It must have happened this morning, after I went into Glacier Falls to see the undertaker." She didn't notice that both Judith and Renie had started to speak at once. "Riley had insurance. It'll cover the theft. What's important is to find his killer."

"Ah . . ." Judith glanced at Renie. The cousins were equally ambivalent. "The theft? Of what, exactly?"

With a heavy sigh, Iris sat up straight. "I'm not sure. The main thing that's gone is the painting Dewitt Dixon bought. He doesn't know it's disappeared. I should have given it to him last night, but I was too upset. Besides, that's Clive Silvanus's business. And I can't reach him. I called twice from Glacier Falls, but he wasn't in his office or at home."

Judith decided it was time to level with Iris. There was no reason not to, except some little corner of her soul hated to part with Riley Tobias's gift, especially now that the artist was dead. It was very unlikely that she'd ever own any of his work, no matter how ugly. For the first time, she understood why Erica and Dewitt Dixon would spend seventy thousand dollars on an eyesore: Love it or hate it, any painting by Riley Tobias carried the hallmark of genius.

At first, Iris reacted listlessly to Judith's account of

Riley's generosity. Then, when Judith got to the part about the ladder falling through the studio window, Iris showed a hint of excitement.

"You mean it was you two and not a thief?" She rose quickly from the rock, brushing off her tailored navy slacks. "Let's go see it. I'll know if it's Dewitt's purchase. I saw the work in progress. This is all very strange."

Iris and the cousins climbed the zigzagging trail that led up to the meadow. Heading through the woods, Judith offered to pay for the damage she had caused. Iris brushed the notion aside.

"As I said, Riley had a lot of insurance. He had to, with all his own works and those he'd collected from other artists. If we can find Dewitt's painting, the insurance company ought to be grateful that we put in for only a broken window."

The fire in the stove had gone out, which was just as well, since the day was growing warm. The aroma of breakfast still lingered on the air. Judith went to the Murphy bed and lifted the plaid curtain.

"We had to ditch it someplace," she explained, tugging at the bed. "We've tried all sorts of locks, but the jerks who have broken in always figure out a way. And frankly, we'd rather have them come in, see that there isn't much worth stealing, and leave that wonderful old Dutch door in one piece." The bed came down, curiously light. Judith snatched at the covering. The painting was gone.

"Damn!" She stared at Renie, then gave Iris a helpless look. "It must have been Clive," Judith murmured, shaking both fists.

"Clive Silvanus?" Iris gaped at Judith. "What are you talking about?"

It seemed to Judith that there was a lot of explaining to do where Iris was concerned. "Clive was here last night. Drunk. He passed out, we left for a while, and when we came back, he was gone. He must have taken Riley's painting with him. We found out this morning he'd checked in at the Green Mountain Inn. Dewitt Dixon had breakfast with him. Or something like that," Judith finished lamely.

Iris sat down on the Murphy bed. "Good heavens," she murmured. "So much has happened that I don't know about. I saw the undersheriff last night, sent Dewitt off with a flea in his ear, and collapsed. The last thing I remember was a bunch of snoopy TV reporters banging on the door. I took a tranquilizer and ignored them."

A sudden thought struck Judith. "Iris, what happened to your car? You said it broke down when you stopped at the Green Mountain Inn." Judith wondered why Iris hadn't seen Clive if she'd gone back to check on her car.

Iris gave Judith a vague look. "Oh—Gary Johanson got it started for me this morning. He drove it down here and walked back. It was some silly thing that only men understand. Who else would want to worry about their ignition?"

Since Judith and Renie were both married to men who didn't know a combustion engine from a compost heap, they kept quiet.

"Maybe we'd better drive up to the inn and talk to Clive," Judith suggested. "You need to see him anyway, don't you, Iris?"

But Iris seemed to have lost her spine. "I'm not up to it just now. If Dewitt wants that picture badly enough, he'll get it out of Clive. Maybe Clive thought you two had stolen it." She saw the shocked expression on Judith's face and waved her hands. "I don't mean that *literally*—I meant that *Clive* thought . . . oh, never mind." She yanked off the white bandeau which held her hair in place and let the long black waves fall over her face.

Judith was willing to let Iris's remarks slide. Renie, however, was not. "I'd like to know why Clive was tearing our furniture apart. How did he know we had that canvas?"

It was, Judith thought, a good question. But maybe Renie had posed it at a bad time. Iris didn't seem ready to cope with much more than getting through the day. Perhaps once the funeral was over, she'd rebound as her normal, capable self.

Iris apparently felt the same way. "Look," she said, getting to her feet and replacing the bandeau, "I'm utterly worthless right now. If Clive has the painting, he'll see that Dewitt gets it. It's too bad you met Clive when he was . . . under the weather. He's actually a very astute businessman. Or so Riley always said."

Judith couldn't resist at least one query. "Then Riley has been doing well lately?"

Iris lifted her chin. Her gaze was level with Judith's. "Clive has handled Riley very successfully. Have you heard otherwise?"

"He changed horses," Renie replied, putting on what Judith called her boardroom face. "In the art world, that can make a difference in perception by the public. And in sales."

Iris shrugged her cashmere-clad shoulders. "The artistic community is rife with gossip. There's so much envy of anyone who is commercially successful. Riley dared to go beyond what had already proved profitable. Naturally, he stirred up a few malicious people." With a trace of her customary tensile inner strength, Iris moved toward the Dutch door.

As Judith went to see Iris out, she felt the crumpled letter in her pocket. "What did Yancey Tobias think of his brother's new style?" Judith met Iris's curious gaze unflinchingly and lied like a rug. "Riley told us about sending Yancey a recent painting for his birthday."

Small creases appeared on Iris's brow. "That's odd. I don't recall Riley sending his brother one of his works. Yancey's a botanist. He doesn't know the first thing about art. Though," she added as an afterthought, "Riley somehow prized his opinion. I suppose that's because Yancey is the older of the two."

Judith was prompted to ask one last question. "Iris, do you know why Lazlo Gamm came to see Riley yesterday? He arrived by helicopter, around one-thirty."

Gamm's visit obviously wasn't news to Iris. She made an indifferent gesture with her left hand, causing a dozen slim silver bangles to jingle at her wrist. "Mrs. Morton told me about the helicopter. I figured it must be Lazlo. If Riley lived at the beach, Laz would have come by submarine."

"You know Laz?" Renie asked.

Iris examined the bangles, frowning as if in disapproval of their inappropriately merry sound. "Oh, yes. He's been in and out of Riley's life for years. He's always talking about buying a painting, but he never does. If you want to know the truth, I always thought he liked Riley but didn't like his work."

Judith hesitated, then put another query to Iris. "You haven't seen him this time, though?"

"No. I gather he left before I arrived." Iris shoved the bangles higher up on her arm to keep them from jangling. With a thin little smile, she bade the cousins good-bye.

"Well?" inquired Renie after their visitor was out of hearing range. "Do we call Yancey in Old Bennington, hunt down Lazlo, or go see Clive up at the Green Mountain Inn?"

"I wouldn't know what to ask Yancey," Judith pointed out. "We don't bother the grieving kin, in any event. Lazlo could be anywhere. As for Green Mountain, we were just there."

"But we didn't see Clive," Renie countered. "Not to talk to, that is. Besides, it's lunchtime. I'm so hungry I could eat a mole."

"You can't be hungry," Judith protested. "You just ate a pound of pie and a pint of whipped cream. I thought we'd make some sandwiches here. There's ham and hot dogs and—" She broke off, struck by a sudden thought. "On the other hand, if we're somewhere else, we can't be here, right?"

"Huh?" Renie looked mystified.

Judith was heading for the door. "Remember what Iris said was going to happen pretty quick? The undersheriff is coming, coz. He is to be avoided at all costs. Let's be gone."

The cousins didn't get very far. Instead of walking this time, they decided to take Judith's car. But driving out to the road, they saw Ward Kimball's Volkswagen bus turning into the drive. Judith reversed and pulled the compact to one side. Renie got out and wrestled with the sagging wooden gate that deterred casual intruders from the Grover property. Cautiously, Ward drove onto the rutted dirt drive. Lark was next to him in the van.

"Hello there," Ward greeted the cousins, going around to assist his daughter. "Are we keeping you from something?"

"Nothing vital," Judith replied, wondering if she spoke the truth. For all she knew, Clive Silvanus could be headed back into the city with a seventy-thousand-dollar painting stashed in his trunk. If, of course, it would fit.

Lark smiled faintly as she held onto her father's arm. They walked slowly over the unfamiliar, uneven ground. "I have to apologize for last night," she said, turning in the direction of the cousins. "I was very distraught. Riley's death has been a terrible blow."

Ward patted his daughter's hand. "I agree, Lark, absolutely. Shared grief isn't much comfort, though." He smiled fondly at her, and though she could not have seen his face clearly, Judith sensed that she heard the warmth in his voice. "Be honest," Ward urged as they reached the cabin. "You two were on your way out. We mustn't impose."

Judith and Renie insisted that the Kimballs' arrival was perfectly convenient. Inside the cabin, Ward explained that he and Lark had intended to call on Iris Takisaki, but a sheriff's car had been pulled up by the house.

"Now, that was definitely bad timing," he said, sitting next to Lark on the old sofa. "Iris must be taking this very hard. That bumbler of a Costello came by to see us first thing this morning. We can't expect much from him, you know. I imagine Iris feels the same way, poor woman."

Lark might not have been able to convey much with her eyes, but her face was extremely mobile. At present it registered derision. "Iris! As if she really cared about Riley! The only thing she wanted from him was having fame and success rub off on her. His reputation gave her a certain cachet as an art consultant. I doubt that she'd know Monet from Manet."

"Now, Lark, that's very unkind. Iris has been devoted to Riley for twenty years. You shouldn't say such things, especially under the circumstances." Her father's tone was disapproving.

"Devoted to Riley's *work,*" Lark corrected with a smug expression. "That is not the same as being devoted to Riley."

Judith feared that she and Renie were about to be privy to another father-daughter squabble. "Murder is always devastating," Judith declared, hoping to strike an ameliorating note. "I'm sure Iris will be glad to see you—once the undersheriff is gone."

Lark was turned toward Judith. "She might like to see Dad. She won't be so pleased to see me. She never was." The smug look intensified.

"Stop it, Lark!" Ward Kimball spoke sharply, flushed, and apologized to his hostesses. "You must think we wrangle all the time. That's not so. Riley's death has unsettled us."

"It's unsettled us, too," Renie remarked. "After all, there's a killer somewhere around here."

Judith gave Renie a curious look. It was true, of course, yet it dawned on her that neither she nor Renie had lost a wink of sleep over the possibility of being murdered in their beds. Had they grown accustomed to violent death? Or did they know, deep down where it counted, that whoever killed Riley Tobias had no reason to kill them? The insight made things more clear to Judith. The pot-growing hippies evaporated in her mind's eye.

"Let me make some coffee," she suggested, then remembered that the fire had gone out. "Or some pop? A drink? Ice water?" She grimaced slightly at the thought of chipping chunks off the ice block.

But both Kimballs declined the offer of beverages. Indeed, Ward was on his feet, fingering his beard and gazing out the window. Mount Woodchuck stood watch over the forest, the clouds dispersed along the river valley.

"I think I'll head over to see Iris," Ward said, touching Lark's shoulder. "The law should be gone by now, and if not, I'd like to hear what they've found out. If anything. Lark?"

His daughter shook her head. "I told you, I'd rather not play out a farce with Iris. She doesn't like me any more than I like her."

Ward Kimball sighed with resignation. "As you will, dear heart. I'll amble over there. I shouldn't be long." He sketched a courtly little bow and was gone.

"Come on, Lark," Renie urged, "have a beer. A sandwich? A couple of hot dogs?"

Judith heard the hunger pangs and made a face at Renie. "Don't force food and drink on people, coz. Not everyone is a Big Pig."

But Lark said she would like a glass of wine after all, if the cousins had any. They didn't. She settled for a beer. Judith and Renie joined her, trying to be companionable.

"I suppose," Judith mused as she sat down next to Lark on the sofa, "that Riley never married Iris because his first bout with matrimony was so unhappy."

To the cousins' surprise, Lark laughed. "No, it wasn't. Riley just didn't like the idea of the institution. Not when he was young, anyway. It wasn't part of his philosophy then. He was into Kerouac, and all those British Angry Young Men. But he changed. Riley matured late, but fully." She held her bottle of beer as if it were a case of jewels.

Renie cut to the heart of the matter. "Then why didn't he marry Iris?"

Lark's laughter took on a jagged edge. "He didn't love her." The beautiful, unworldly face turned from cousin to cousin. For one brief moment, Judith could have sworn that Lark Kimball was not only seeing but studying her hostesses.

"Did he tell you that?" Renie, as usual, had sacrificed tact.

"Of course he did. Why should he love her?" Lark sounded defensive. "She's well connected in the art community; she's supposedly glib, handsome, and articulate. Useful, in other words. But she's also a rapacious conniver. It didn't take him twenty years to figure that out."

"Yes, it did," retorted Renie. "They were still together when he died."

"That's only because he couldn't figure out how to get rid of her." Lark's voice had risen and her face no longer looked so unwordly. Indeed, she was blushing, and her jaw was set in a hard line. "Riley needed some time to tell her how he felt. How *we* felt." She flounced a bit on the sofa. "He wasn't merely my teacher, he was my lover. And we intended to be married. As soon as he told Iris to go to hell." Lark Kimball sat back on the sofa, now smiling serenely.

SEVEN

"SHUT UP AND pass the salt," Renie said as the cousins assessed their order of hamburgers, French fries, green salad, and Pepsi. "I'm sick of all these people. Everybody seems to have a hidden agenda. And nobody seems to be telling the whole truth."

Judith shot Renie a rueful look. "So when did anybody ever do that except us? In fact, even we don't, all the time. I lied to Iris about Yancey Tobias, and I don't even know why I did it. Stop being crabby. It's just because we're an hour late for lunch and you're out of sorts."

"Bag the ham and the hot dogs for tonight," grumbled Renie. "Let's go into Glacier Falls and eat at the Virgin Forest Cafe. They've got a London broil that makes me weep."

"That was in 1968, and the place has changed hands four times. It's Thai food now, you dope." Judith bit into her burger.

Renie swore under her breath, ate three fries, two bites of hamburger, and a forkful of salad, then relaxed in the same chair she'd sat in that morning at the Green Mountain Inn. "Face it, coz, Riley was trying to play two fiddles at once. Which one stopped the music?"

Judith tipped her head to one side, chewing thoughtfully. "Neither, maybe. Besides, we only have Lark's word for it that Riley wanted to marry her. It's possible that she's playing out a fantasy."

Renie stabbed at her lettuce. "So what were Riley and Ward fighting about?"

"*If* they were fighting." Judith's gaze wandered around the dining room. It was after one-thirty, and the lunch rush was over. But the Green Mountain Inn was still busier than it had been in midmorning. Nine of the twenty tables were full, mostly, Judith judged, with locals. "I'm inclined to believe there was a row, if only because, when we showed up at the Kimballs' last night, Ward seemed surprised to see us."

Renie swigged down about half of her Pepsi at once. "So? I haven't seen Ward in years."

"That's not what I meant," Judith explained as an elderly couple tottered past. She smiled, recognizing them as longtime occupants of a mobile home in the stretch of road between Nella Lablatt's and Ward Kimball's. "If Ward had merely dropped by to visit, Riley probably would have mentioned that we'd been there, too. But Ward didn't know we were at the cabin, so I have to conclude that he and Riley weren't engaged in chitchat."

"Ward didn't know we'd been with Iris when she found the body," Renie pointed out.

"True," Judith agreed. "He hadn't yet talked to Iris last night. He and Lark were probably given only the bare bones by the neighbors who called on them. I suppose the news of Riley's murder spread like wildfire. The bottom line is that Clive may be right about Ward and Riley having a quarrel."

"Speak of the devil," murmured Renie, looking beyond Judith to the dining room entrance. "Here comes Clive now."

Clive Silvanus could not avoid the cousins, nor did he try. "Mah soul and body," he exclaimed, coming directly to their window table, "Ah'm surprised to see you two charmin' ladies here. Ah thought Ah'd have a bit of luncheon."

"Pull up a chair," Judith offered. "Have you heard anything new about Riley's death?"

Seating himself in the same place where Dewitt Dixon had joined the cousins earlier in the day, Clive expelled a heartfelt sigh. "Ah spoke with the sheriff's people within the hour. They stopped by before goin' to call on poor Iris. Naturally, there was very little Ah could tell them." Graciously, he beckoned to Dee Johanson to bring him a menu.

"Did you tell them about the argument between Riley and Ward?" Renie asked.

Clive looked affronted. "Ah did not. Why make trouble?" He gave Dee a grateful smile as she handed him the plastic-covered menu.

"This afternoon," Dee said, mainly for Renie's benefit, "we have boysenberry pie, fresh-baked."

But this time Renie demurred. Dee took Clive's order of chicken fried steak and again retreated reluctantly.

"You never did say what they were quarreling about," Judith remarked, willing to leap into the fray now that Renie had broached the subject.

Clive brushed at his mustache and looked pensive. "Ah didn't mean to eavesdrop. Still, Ah couldn't help but overhear a snatch or two. It seemed to be about that lovely child, Lark. Ah gathered her daddy thought Riley was takin' advantage of her. You know how daddies can be."

Judith tried to picture her own father in a similar situation. The rational, even-tempered, intellectual Donald Grover would no doubt have turned the discussion into a debate on morality and ethics. On the other hand, his brother, Cliff, who appeared to be such a quiet sort, would have quelled any man who forced his attentions on Renie by breaking his skull with a coal shovel. Perhaps Ward Kimball fell somewhere in between.

"It wasn't a violent quarrel, was it?" Judith asked as Clive lighted a cigarette.

"Not while Ah was in the vicinity," he replied. His expression was conspiratorial. "Ah know what you're thinkin'. But Ah've known Mr. Kimball for a very long time, and upon sober reflection, Ah know he wouldn't hurt a bug."

Judith agreed with Clive's reassessment—as far as it went. But she knew all too well that under certain circumstances, almost anyone could be driven to violence. Ward Kimball, who had been both father and mother to his handicapped daughter for twenty-five years, might react more strongly than most men. He had a right—and a reason—to be protective of Lark.

Judith let the point ride. "What time were you at Riley's?"

Clive cocked his head. "Oh—about three. Or was it four? Ah forget. The day's a blur."

Judith grimaced. "Did you tell the undersheriff when you *thought* you were there?"

Clive gave Judith a coy little smile. "Ah did mah best. Oh, Ah know—if Ah could be more precise, it would give me an alibi. Knowin' Ah'm innocent isn't enough for the law. But there's no point in makin' things up just to please, is there?"

Judith allowed that there probably wasn't. Maybe Ward had fixed the time of his own visit more accurately. But Clive wasn't finished yet.

"That Hungarian fellow and Dewitt were there before me. Maybe before Ward, too. Ah'm sure that Costello lawman must have asked."

"Dewitt was at the studio, too? Before he came to the house after Riley was killed?" Judith stared at Clive.

"He said he was," Clive asserted as Dee arrived with his chicken fried steak. "Why, thank you, darlin'. That looks just delicious. Like my momma used to fix." He gave Dee a big smile. "Ah had breakfast here this mornin' with Mr. Dewitt Dixon, didn't Ah, sugah?" His admiring gaze was lifted up to Dee's plain face.

Dee laughed, a bit uncomfortably. "You had breakfast

with *someone,* Mr. Silvanus. I thought the two of you were going to stay on and have lunch, too."

"Well, Ah am doin' that now. Mr. Dixon has gone into Glacier Falls to the bank. He won't find better home cookin' in that town, Ah assure you." Clive turned his attention to his plate.

Judith and Renie finished their meal in silence. Judith's brain was spinning. The window of opportunity was slowly closing. Lazlo Gamm seemed out of the running; his copter had lifted off before three o'clock. Clive Silvanus must have shown up at the studio after Gamm's departure and Ward's arrival. The art agent hadn't stayed long, but Ward Kimball was still there when he left. Had Ward gone off to brood and returned later? Judith couldn't picture the elderly, infirm Ward Kimball overcoming the strapping, middle-aged Riley Tobias. Which, she realized, also ruled out the women involved in the case. Even if the cousins hadn't been with Iris at the time, she would have been ill-matched against Riley. And Lark was not only small, but her vision was exceedingly poor. Judith realized that left only two known suspects—Dewitt Dixon, and the man who was sitting between the cousins, complacently eating chicken fried steak.

Pushing herself back from the table, Renie broke the silence. "Say, Clive, what's this we hear about Riley losing his audience with his new style?"

Clive used his paper napkin to wipe a dab of gravy from his upper lip. "That's poppycock. Oh, it takes folks a while to get used to something new, no matter who does it. But Ah'm willin' to wager that those portraits would soon become all the rage."

"Is that what Dewitt bought?" Renie asked, trying to look guileless.

Clive soaked a biscuit in honey. "No, he got himself a landscape. Or got it for his wife, Ah ought to say."

Renie darted a quizzical look at Judith. "So it was an earlier work that Riley's ex-wife wanted."

Briefly, Clive Silvanus seemed genuinely puzzled. "His

ex . . . oh, Erica. Ah never knew her when she was married to Riley. Ah don't think of her as anything but Missus Dixon. That is, *Miz* Dixon, which she prefers."

Clive hadn't precisely answered the question. Judith pressed on. "Let me get this straight. Riley showed us one of his portraits, 'The Nerd,' I think he called it. Is that still in the studio?"

"It is, though, alas, it will now be called 'The Unfinished Nerd.' Still, it ought to fetch a fine price." Clive sighed heavily. "Riley's last work. Such a sad thought."

"Not so sad for Riley's estate," Renie remarked. "Who gets it?"

Clive was still looking morose. He brushed at the strands of hair that lay limply over his bald spot. "Riley wasn't much of a businessman, but Iris saw to it that he made provisions. He set up The Riley Tobias Foundation for Disadvantaged Minority Youth. The money is to be used for study and just plain ol' appreciation."

"That sounds very worthy," Judith said, wondering why she should be surprised at the artist's humanitarian spirit. Indeed, it occurred to her that it wasn't Riley's humanitarianism that she was questioning, but the fact that he'd done something practical about it. Of course, he had acquiesced to Iris's urging. Still, Judith thought the foundation was an admirable concept. "I don't suppose you know why Lazlo Gamm came to see Riley yesterday?" Judith asked, changing the subject.

Clive rubbed his mustache. "Well, now, Ah couldn't rightly say, since Ah didn't talk to poor Riley after Mr. Gamm had called on him. Mah guess is that he was canoodlin'."

Renie grimaced. "Canoodling? As in *to canoodle?"*

Clive nodded solemnly. "That's right. Lazlo Gamm is a great canoodler."

Gazing at the beamed ceiling, Judith found not only inspiration but memory. "Grandma Grover used that word, coz. It means to romance someone. Right?" She lowered her eyes to seek Clive's confirmation.

"It means to snuggle," Clive agreed with a sage nod. "Or cuddle or what you will. Perhaps there are regional differences in the doin' of it, but you get the idea, Ah'm sure." He wiggled his eyebrows in a lascivious manner.

Just then a pair of forest rangers walked past the table, carrying their hats in their hands. Fleetingly, Judith thought of Mike, and wondered if he would someday join their ranks. But her attention quickly went back to the matter at hand.

"With whom is Lazlo canoodling?" Judith inquired.

But Clive couldn't enlighten the cousins. "His fancy moves quickly. Indiscriminately, too. Ah will say that he is very discreet. Those European counts are like that, Ah'm told."

Renie evinced surprise. "He's a count?"

Clive shrugged. "Or a no-account, some might say. He claims to be of noble birth, goin' way back. No doubt it helps his cause with the ladies."

Having run out of food as well as questions, the cousins took their leave of Clive Silvanus. During the brief drive back to the cabin, Judith reviewed her chronology of the previous afternoon.

"We show up about one," she said to Renie. "We stay half an hour or so. Lazlo Gamm flies in circa one-thirty, leaving about an hour later. Dewitt Dixon comes along next, let's say around two-thirty. Then Ward Kimball, with Clive Silvanus lurking in the background. Clive comes and goes around three, Ward leaves later. How much later, we don't know. Iris shows up before five, comes to our place, gets us, and we go over to Nella's. Then we find the body. It could be any of the above, on a return visit." She signaled for a left-hand turn, noting that the sheriff's car was still parked by the road in front of Riley's house.

Judith pulled the car into the little clearing next to the cabin. When they got out, Renie headed for the riverbank. The afternoon was warm. The sunlight sparkled on the rolling water. Up on Mount Woodchuck, the outline of the fire-watcher's hut could be seen against the blue sky. A few feet away, two young cedar trees gave shelter to a bluejay, a pair of cedar waxwings, and several robins. Judith took a deep breath of the unspoiled country air and smiled.

"You saw that, too?" Renie said with a nudge.

"Huh?" Judith was jarred out of her reverie.

Renie gestured at the river. "That trout. He must have been ten inches. Remember how we used to catch that size all the time when we were kids? When was the last time you had a ten-inch trout for breakfast that didn't come from Falstaff's Market?"

Judith drifted back in time to summer mornings when she'd awaken to the caw of the crows, the rumble of the river, and the aroma of fresh fish in butter, of buttermilk pancakes on the old cast-iron griddle, of sizzling eggs, purchased just out of the nest at a farm on the other side of Glacier Falls.

"If you saw a fish, it's probably an orphan," Judith declared. "Your father gave up on this river twenty years ago."

"Not exactly," Renie replied. "He literally died with his boots on. Fishing boots, that is."

And so he had. Judith had not been at the cabin that Memorial Day weekend when Uncle Cliff had succumbed to a heart attack at a favorite fishing hole down by the Green Mountain Inn.

Judith's mood had darkened. Not all the memories of the cabin were happy ones. Her own father's renovation plans had died with him. Meddling in-laws from Aunt Toadie's side of the family had ruined the camaraderie of at least one season. There had been the floods, sweeping away the entire riverfront, surging right up to the front porch. And now, Judith thought with a pang as she glanced over her shoulder, there was Dan—resting among the vine maples.

". . . in that cupboard above the sofa." Renie had been chattering away, and Judith realized she didn't know the topic.

"Whoa!" She grabbed Renie by the arm. "Sorry, coz, I was ruminating. You know—Life. Death. The meaning of existence. What mundane prattle have you been spewing while I waxed sentimental and philosophical?"

Renie rolled her eyes. "Deep thinking—and you? Jeez." She put her fists on her hips. "I was talking about breaking the law—namely, going fishing, even though the season doesn't open for another week. There's still a bunch of gear stowed in that cupboard over the sofa. I'll bet there's even a jar of salmon eggs."

Judith didn't think it was a very good idea. Game wardens were known to prowl the river. The sheriff's men were all over the place. This wasn't like the old days, when there were fewer people around and everybody knew each other.

Renie seemed to consider Judith's rational arguments. She stood motionless for a few moments, staring out over the river. "Do you remember those Dolly Vardens my dad used to get once in a while? And sometimes even a cutthroat. Mmm-MMM!"

Judith slumped, then turned and stalked toward the cabin. "Okay, okay, but we wait until dusk so we can't be spotted so easily."

"Of course. It's dumb to fish with the sun right on the water." Renie trotted along, grinning at the prospect, however remote, of fried rainbow trout for breakfast.

The cousins had just reached the door when they were hailed from the distance. Undersheriff Abbott N. Costello and Deputy Dabney Plummer were coming through the woods from the direction of Riley Tobias's property.

"Let's keep them outside," Judith murmured. "Costello's easier to take in the open."

"We should take a powder." Renie sighed. "What do you suppose he wants now?"

Costello approached with his hands swinging at his sides, striding across the rough ground like General Patton trooping through North Africa. Or so Judith imagined.

"I see you didn't run off to the city," he said, stopping

at the edge of the porch. "A good thing. It would have looked bad for you."

"Worse, if you knew my mother," Judith said under her breath.

"What was that?" Costello cocked an eye at Judith from under the brim of his hat. Deputy Plummer already had his notebook out, pen in hand.

Judith ignored Costello's question. "How's the investigation going? Did you do an autopsy?"

Costello snickered. "Now why do you ask that? The man was garroted, plain and simple."

Judith leaned on the stair railing and shrugged. "Even so, I know it's often procedural. Under suspicious circumstances, death isn't always caused by the obvious."

Slapping Plummer on the back so hard that the pen flew out of the deputy's hand, Costello roared with laughter. "The obvious! Suspicious circumstances! Hee-hee! You got the lingo, lady. What do you and the old man do at night, sit around and read forensics reports?"

Dabney Plummer was scrambling around on the ground, trying to retrieve his pen. Costello sobered and squinted at Judith. "As a matter of fact, Mrs. Smarty-Pants, we did do an autopsy. You bet your booties Riley Tobias died from being choked with that picture-hanging wire. The only thing we learned from taking blood samples was that he was drunk as a skunk. No wonder, with all those beer cans around. I'm surprised the guy's liver didn't look like it had been soaked in lye."

"Gack," Judith exclaimed, then stared at the undersheriff. "Riley wasn't drunk when we left him between one-thirty and two o'clock. In fact, he was working when we saw him a little after five."

Costello rested one hand on his holster and gazed up through the trees. "So you say. Time of death is never exact unless somebody sees the evil deed being done. We only got your word for it—and that live-in babe's—that he was killed sometime after five. But let's say you're all full of bunk. Or lying. The western sun hits those studio windows in the late afternoon and it gets pretty warm inside. Changes in the corpse would be slowed down, see? He could have been knocked off as early as four-thirty. I suppose you know all about taking the deceased's temperature and such?"

Judith didn't, except in the vaguest of laymen's terms. She said nothing, and somewhat to her surprise, Renie also kept quiet. Indeed, Renie had sat down on the bottom step, her chin resting on her folded arms, and her attitude was one of detachment. Judith didn't trust her cousin when she grew aloof. It was a sign that she was either cooking up something outrageous or wrestling with the demons of her explosive temper.

"Now let's get this straight," Costello was saying as he jabbed a finger at Judith. "You two didn't hear anything unusual? You didn't see anything strange?"

Judith shook her head. "Nothing, not even when we went over to Mrs. Lablatt's with Iris. We were busy cleaning all afternoon. Mostly we were inside. We cut down the grass out here"—she made a sweeping gesture that took in the open area in front of the cabin—"but that was more like around three. Then we hauled everything out to the garbage hole in back of the house and went inside to fix drinks. We were here on the porch when Iris came by both times."

Costello turned to look back toward Riley's place. Not only did the forest hide the house and the studio, but it muffled sound. Judith guessed that was what the undersheriff was probably trying to gauge.

"There was quite a parade over there yesterday afternoon," Costello noted. "The only ones you saw were the Hungarian and the girlfriend?"

Judith nodded. "We saw Lazlo Gamm arrive in his copter. Riley introduced us and we left. Then we happened to meet Iris, but that's only because she came through here on her way from the Green Mountain Inn. We wouldn't have seen her at all if she'd gone by the road instead of the river."

But Costello was waving a hand and frowning. "No, no, I don't mean that Takisaki dame. I'm talking about the other one. You know—the girl who can't see so good. Lark Kimball."

Renie came to. But she still didn't speak. Neither did Judith at first. "Now just a minute," she finally said, floundering in confusion. "Lark was never here. Who said she was?"

Costello looked smug. "She did. About three o'clock. Of course, she can't tell time so easy. She came down to Riley's with her father, but she didn't go in. I guess they were having an artistic discussion, or whatever people like that do when they get together."

"Oh, good grief!" Renie jumped up from the porch step and stomped off toward the row of ferns that lined the path to the outhouse. It dawned on Judith that her cousin hadn't dared to talk for fear of saying something acerbic that would enrage Costello. Renie had no patience with incompetents.

"Let me get this straight," Judith said, trying to ignore Renie's pique and hoping that the undersheriff would do the same. "Lark Kimball came with her father to Riley's studio. She didn't go in. She claims to have come over here. But she didn't. So where does a girl with impaired vision go on her own?"

Costello uttered a knowing little chuckle. "You'd like to know the answer to that, wouldn't you?" He stabbed a finger at Dabney Plummer. "Hut!" The lawmen tromped off on the path that led to Riley's property.

Renie was still standing with her back turned, feet planted firmly in the damp, dark earth. "Are they gone? Will they come again? Can they be recalled through a popular vote of the electorate?"

"Okay, so Costello's a moron and Plummer's a mime." Judith drew up alongside Renie. "That doesn't explain Lark Kimball. But Riley's drunken state might explain something else."

"Such as?" Renie moved her head just enough to look at Judith. "How the lame, the halt, and the blind could strangle Riley Tobias with picture-hanging wire?"

Judith clapped Renie on the shoulder. "Right, coz."

Renie shrugged. "So what? We might know it, but Costello and Company won't figure it out. They not only don't have the right answers, they're not even asking the right questions. We'll be damned lucky if they don't arrest *us.*"

It was Judith's turn to gaze off into space. "Lucky?" She tipped her head to one side, vaguely taking in the blossoms on the salmonberry bushes. "We can't count on luck, coz. We've got to start doing some serious sleuthing."

"I thought we already were," Renie countered.

Judith headed back to the cabin. "We have been, but it hasn't gotten us anywhere. Let's put our bodies to work, along with our brains. We've got slightly more than twenty-four hours to figure out whodunit—and to finish cleaning this place up. Let's hit the loft and then we'll fill the woodbox. Maybe tomorrow we can tackle those downspouts. The Mortons might lend us a ladder that doesn't weigh two tons."

The loft had a ladder of its own, but it was fixed in place, flush with the wall. The cousins ascended cautiously, abandoning the one-handed, one-footed antics of their youth. They found the double bed neatly made, covered with yet more blue plaid. The single window had matching curtains, and the small bureau, which was the only other piece of furniture, sported a runner of the same material. Except for sweeping, there wasn't much cleaning to do.

"Should I check for mice under the bed?" Renie asked.

"Go ahead," Judith replied, whisking up dust bunnies. "See if the chamber pot is there. I didn't find it anywhere else."

"It probably got stolen," Renie said, getting down on her hands and knees. "We might consider it a pain in the butt—literally—but there are some who would call it an antique." She used a yardstick to delve under the bed. "No pot, no mice. But there's a box or something. It's just out of reach."

"Maybe it's the badminton set," Judith said, batting away cobwebs with her broom. "Or the croquet stuff. Didn't Cousin Sue take up archery for a while?"

"Yeah, until she got Uncle Corky in the rear end while he was panning for gold in the river. She also shot my mother's angel food cake." Renie stretched, groaned, and gave a big heave. The object of her efforts skidded out on the other side of the bed, to land at Judith's feet.

Judith glanced down. "That's not a box," she began, then bent over for a closer look. "Hey, coz, it's Clive's notebook!"

Renie struggled to stand up. "What? Let me see." She scooted around the end of the bed to join Judith. Together, the cousins flipped through the loose-leafed pages. "I'll be damned," said Renie. "It's a list of Riley's paintings. I can't make out the rest without my glasses."

Judith sat down on the bed, hearing the frame creak beneath her. Renie knelt on the floor while Judith perused the pages. "It seems to go back only to the first of the year. Here's a sale to P. A. Kwan in Hong Kong last January—something called 'Autumn Images,' sold for forty thousand dollars, dimensions, mixed media, blah-blah. In March, A.—no other name given—bought 'Spring Meadow,' sixty grand, more details. Check this—'Pending—D. and E. Dixon, "Spring River." ' What do you think, coz?"

Renie gave a little shake of her head. "Not much. We know Riley was selling a landscape to the Dixons. But who's A.? And why do we care?"

Paging through the rest of the notebook, Judith found nothing of interest. Gallery listings, art critics, and museum contacts seemed to make up the rest of Clive's notes. "I guess we don't care about this," she admitted, closing the notebook. "At least not about the contents. But we do care about how it got here."

Climbing up onto the bed, Renie rubbed at her little

chin. "Why was Clive in the loft? Why was he looking for Riley's picture here before he found where we hid it? Is the answer obvious, or have I got cobwebs on my brain as well as on my pants?"

Feeling the mattress sag under their weight, Judith frowned. "There's only one way Clive could have known that we had that painting." She gave Renie a perplexed look. "Somebody told him. The question, coz, is, who?"

EIGHT

THE COUSINS COULDN'T see any reason not to return Clive's notebook. But they weren't about to return to the Green Mountain Inn. They decided to wait until Clive showed up. They were convinced that he would, eventually.

"Was Clive looking for another painting in the loft?" Judith wondered aloud as she emptied the dustpan into the garbage. "Having found one Riley Tobias in the Murphy bed, did he think we had a second one up in the loft?"

"Oh, great." Renie groaned. "Is there more than one canvas missing from Riley's inventory? Iris should know. She mentioned only the work the Dixons bought. But Riley wouldn't have given us that painting. Do you think the cabin has been used as a regular stash of some kind?"

Judith considered. "No. It wouldn't be safe. We've been broken into. Riley hasn't. Whatever this was, I think it must have been a temporary situation."

Renie twirled the broom and shook her head. "This is the damnedest mare's nest. Absolutely nothing makes sense."

"Yes, it does." Judith picked the axe up from the

woodbox. "We have three separate things going here which may or may not be connected. Come on, let's go chop wood while I explain. The saw's under the house."

The previous day, Judith and Renie had collected a pile of blowdown from windstorms. Judith grabbed the axe and Renie took the saw. The vine maple would make decent kindling; the alder would provide excellent fires.

"First," Judith said, making sure Grandpa Grover's venerable chopping block was secure, "there's Riley's murder. What's the motive? Gain? Not directly, if his entire estate goes into that foundation he set up. But there must be insurance, which I would guess has Iris as the beneficiary. Maybe she gets the house and the studio, too. There's another type of gain, though. Riley told us about it—he was referring to Ward Kimball, but he might as well have included himself."

"Ah." Renie glanced up from the sawhorse. "You mean with regard to how an artist's work goes up in value after he dies?"

"Right." Judith took a swing at a chunk of cedar that probably had been lying on the ground for at least four years. "Clive gets his percentage, which will now grow larger. Who knows how much inventory Riley—or Clive—has stashed away. Even if it's just his private collection in the house and those dozen or so canvases in the studio, we're looking at close to a million bucks."

"And if Clive gets a fifty–fifty split, that's nice," Renie noted, stopping to mop her brow. "It's nice for Dewitt and Erica Dixon, too, since they paid seventy grand for a painting that now may skyrocket to twice its original price. It's not a fortune, of course, but as a motive, profiteering is acceptable."

"Which brings us to Number Two," Judith continued, wincing a bit at discovering muscles she hadn't used for a while. "The Perambulating Painting. Riley gives us a picture that sounds as if it could be the one Dewitt Dixon bought for his wife. Now why does Riley do such a thing?

The only answer I can come up with is because he doesn't want his ex-wife to have it. Spite, maybe."

"So why not just refuse to sell it?" countered Renie.

"You got me," Judith admitted. "All this stuff about the painting is really baffling. Where does Lazlo Gamm fit in? Is it possible that he, too, wanted that painting? Why did he come back—or maybe stick around? Who is the lady in his life? Could he have been pursuing Iris? If so, why not put the make on her in town rather than under Riley's nose up here?"

"Maybe," Renie suggested, "Lazlo is still here so he can comfort Iris in her time of need. But it doesn't sound as if she's seen him. Or cares."

"All of the above could be side issues," Judith said. "Reason Number Three is much more up-front. There were two women in Riley's life—three, if you count the ex-Mrs. Tobias. Lark could be fantasizing about Riley's intentions, but she was definitely in love with him. As for Iris, she and Riley may never have married, but they've been together so long that the emotional tie is the same. Maybe Riley was bored. He could scarcely *not* find Lark enchanting. Like any man, he'd be flattered by her feelings whether he reciprocated or not. Iris might have been jealous."

Renie began piling the logs she had cut to fit into the stove. "And, conversely, Lark might have been jealous of Iris. Are you suggesting Riley was murdered as the third part of a triangle or that he was killed by an overly protective father?"

Judith tucked the axe under her arm and gathered up the kindling. "Any of those are possible scenarios. It would depend on who thought Riley was doing what to whom."

"So in point of fact," Renie mused as they carted firewood into the cabin, "we have several motives for murder: monetary gain, jealousy, paternal outrage, and possible theft. I'd cross off gain if I thought Riley was going to keep painting best-selling works for the next thirty years.

But if you can believe Dewitt Dixon, his career was on the wane."

Judith nudged the Dutch door open with her foot. "You might not believe Dewitt, but you can believe all those empty bottles. I'm still curious about finding just one beer can. What happened to the rest? We know Riley had two, and we each had one. That can was the same brand as what we were drinking. Why throw a single can in with a bunch of bottles? And what did he do with the other three?"

"When you're sloshed, you're not exactly rational," Renie replied, stacking wood in the box by the stove.

"True," Judith allowed. "It's probably not important. Still, I don't remember Riley as a big drinker. But what if he had started guzzling in recent months? It happens. And maybe it affected his artistic output."

"I can nose around about that when we get home," Renie said. "My pipeline in the art community is short, but I do have a couple of contacts who might know."

Having finished their chores as well as the airing of their current theories, the cousins decided to get ready to go fishing. It was going on five, and the sun would soon be off the river. Judith grimaced as she checked her watch. Twenty-four hours earlier, Riley Tobias had been alive. A great deal had happened since Iris Takisaki had come hurrying through the woods with her alarm about a prowler. Yet no one knew what had really happened. With a sigh, Judith approached the problem of getting at the family fishing tackle.

The sofa was too soft to stand on, so Judith and Renie pulled it out from the wall. Placing a chair beneath the cupboard, Judith climbed up and opened the latch. Sure enough, there were four rods, a spare reel, several tins of leader, a container of lead, extra hooks, two creels, three cherry bobbers for steelheading—and a jar of unopened salmon eggs. Judith handed down two of the rods, one creel, and the salmon eggs, then leaped off the chair.

"Bless somebody," said Renie, examining the old bamboo rods tied with thread in various bright colors. "These babies are all set up and ready to go. Look out, trout, here we come!"

Judith returned the chair to the table. "Do you want to go down to the Big Bend or try it out in front?"

Renie was going through the creel where she found some extra nylon leader, hooks, a small knife, and an almost-empty jar of spoiled salmon eggs. "This was Uncle Al's, I think. Look—six pre-computer tote tickets from the race track. They must have been losers." She pitched the jar and the tickets in the trash.

"Knowing Uncle Al, he probably had a few winners, too," Judith remarked, shoving the sofa back against the wall. "He's always been lucky. Did you know he got five of the six lottery numbers a couple of weeks—" She stopped, gazing at a gleaming object on the cracked linoleum. "Hey! Look at this! Is it familiar or what?"

Renie scooted over to join Judith. Both cousins bent down, staring at the sleek silver cigarette case with the engraved initials "DDD."

"It's Dewitt's," said Renie in a wondering tone. "I saw him use it yesterday at Riley's house."

"But not at the Green Mountain Inn this morning," Judith stated with certainty. "He had a pack of cigarettes with him there. *Hmm.*"

Going over to the kitchen, Judith fetched the dustpan and scooped up the cigarette case. Carefully, she slid it onto the counter. Fingerprints probably weren't important, but Judith was taking no chances. "We swept under the sofa yesterday afternoon, but, of course, that was before we ran into Dewitt at Riley's." She gave Renie a wry look. "Do we cross Clive off as the thief or do we give him an accomplice?"

"Jeez." Renie seemed bewildered. "How about this? Dewitt came here last night while we were down at Ward Kimball's and making phone calls at the auto court. Clive let Dewitt in, and they found the canvas in the bed. No." She shook her head vigorously. "Dewitt says he doesn't have the painting. Clive has it, preparing the canvas for transport. Check that—the painting was wrapped and ready to go. Dewitt comes in after Clive has left with the canvas. Or maybe Dewitt comes in while Clive's asleep and steals the canvas. How does Dewitt know it's in the cabin? Why does he deny he has it?" Renie shook her head again.

"Because Riley told Dewitt instead of Clive about giving me the painting?" Judith framed the question in a doubtful voice. "Because Dewitt's pulling a scam?"

Renie considered. "Maybe. We can't be sure Riley told anybody he'd given the picture away. Lazlo Gamm might have guessed we were carrying one when he saw you carting off that big package. Did somebody else see us leave the studio with the painting in tow?"

Frowning at the window that looked out toward Riley's property, Judith gave a little shudder. "I feel as if those trees are full of eyes, watching us. Like the jungle." She paused, then became more brisk. "Come on, let's go fishing. I propose we go down to the Big Bend. There aren't any decent riffles in this stretch of river, as you know perfectly well."

Renie was grinning as they left the cabin. Judith asked her what was so funny. "You, coz," Renie replied. "There aren't any riffles in front of the cabin—and there aren't any suspects. Just what are we fishing for?"

Judith ignored Renie.

Not wanting to waste the daylight, Judith and Renie began fishing at what was known as the Little Big Bend. The hole was just beyond the meadow, formed by a slight curve in the river and several large boulders. The best angle for casting was provided by an old cedar tree that had fallen across the hole, with its exposed roots on one side of the bank and its truncated top on the other. The cousins sat on the tree for ten minutes without a nibble. Giving up, they returned to the bank and followed the trail down to the Big Bend, where the river widened as it tumbled over a rocky bed that reached to both banks.

Smoke drifted among the trees. The clawprints of birds and the impressions of deer hooves could be seen in the damp patches of sand. Mount Woodchuck was now slightly upstream, with the sun slipping behind it and the light fading too swiftly.

Renie hooked into something, gave a yip, and then swore. "A snag," she called to Judith, who was downriver. Tugging and muttering, she finally freed her line but discovered she had lost not only her salmon egg, but the hook and part of the leader. Renie sat down on a big rock to make repairs.

Feeling serene, as she always did with a fishing rod in her hand and the river rolling past, Judith cast again at the riffle formed by a triumvirate of smooth brown boulders. She, too, felt something hit her line. There was play, just enough to give her that old thrill that warms every fisherman's heart. One quick jerk on the rod, then Judith began to reel in slowly. A big smile spread across her face when she saw the flash of the trout as it broke water.

"Whitefish!" jeered Renie. "Even Sweetums wouldn't eat it."

"It is not!" Judith grasped the line, then wrapped her fingers around the wet, slippery, wriggling fish. "Clean kill," Uncle Cliff had always insisted. Judith unhooked the trout, picked up a stone, and shut her eyes. One whack on the head later, and the fish was still. She gathered up a handful of salal leaves and put them in the creel, then placed the fish inside, too. Renie saluted her cousin and made another cast.

Half an hour later, darkness had settled in over the river. Judith's eleven-inch rainbow trout had not been alone. The cousins ended up with two fish apiece, and, though small, they would be tasty.

"Best of all, we didn't run into a game warden," Renie chortled as they headed up the path that led to Ward Kimball's house and, eventually, to the road. "Do you think we should walk along the highway with all this gear? I mean, could we be more obvious unless we stuffed and mounted the trout and wore sandwich boards saying 'We're Not Only Out-Of-Season, We Haven't Bought a Fishing License in Ten Years'?"

"I do feel a little guilty," Judith admitted. "But then again, we haven't caught a fish in ten years." She nodded at the lights up ahead in Ward's house. "We'll have to stop. Otherwise, we might get arrested for trespassing."

"Talk about a crime spree," murmured Renie. "Let's see—breaking and entering, violating at least two Fish and Wildlife statutes, illegal trespass, concealing stolen goods, and suppressing evidence in a murder investigation. Oh, I almost left out sassing a law officer. We may show up yet on the post office wall."

Judith gave Renie a droll look, then used the brass knocker on the Kimball front door. Ward Kimball appeared almost at once, as if he'd been waiting for someone. He seemed pleased, but not surprised, by the cousins' visit. This time, he invited them into the living room, a spacious area with soft furniture in brown-and-green tones. Although Ward had an extensive collection of artwork, the sense of clutter apparent in Riley Tobias's house was absent here. A dozen examples of Japanese netsuke reposed on the mantel. Judith was particularly charmed by a turtle, caught forever in ivory with an inquisitive look on its wrinkled face.

"We can't stay," she said, pointing to the fishing creel. "We were out breaking the law and we want our ill-got gain to stay fresh."

"Tsk-tsk." Ward shook his head, but his eyes twinkled. "You were very lucky. Not only to avoid the game wardens, but to get anything worth keeping. Would you like a drink?"

Renie declined for both of them. "We don't want to get picked up for drunken strolling. Besides, we're going into Glacier Falls for dinner."

Ward apologized for Lark's absence. "She's painting.

She's been at it all day. I suppose it helps to keep her mind off . . ." He made a vague gesture with his hand. "For her, the quality—or lack—of light doesn't matter as much."

Backing into her subject for the sake of tact, Judith asked Ward if he knew when Riley's funeral service would take place. Ward thought it would be Saturday in Glacier Falls. Judith lamented the fact that she and Renie would be gone by then. Renie remarked that she thought it might have been more fitting if the service had been set in town, where Riley had so many professional connections.

"Knowing Riley," Ward said, with an ironic expression, "he would feel that they could come to him instead of the other way 'round. That's the way he lived—that's the way he died. He had no time for the city these last few years."

"Nor do you," Judith noted, pleasantly sinking into the plush leather sofa. "You and Riley had a great deal in common. It's no wonder you were his mentor. I imagine you had some arguments over the new direction he was taking with his work, though."

Ward considered Judith's words carefully. "No, not arguments. There was no point in arguing with Riley once he had set his mind on an artistic course. There never is, not with any creative person. Besides, you can never be sure you're right. Art is too subjective. What the public might despise today will be considered visionary a generation hence. You see that time and time again in the history of art."

"True," Judith allowed. "Riley certainly seemed to have great enthusiasm for his new venture."

"Passion," Ward corrected. "Riley was always fueled by passion. And self-confidence. He'd come to believe he could do anything and get away with it." A touch of bitterness tinged Ward's speech.

Renie stopped stroking the Chinese aster bowl on a teak side table next to her. "Self-confidence? Or arrogance? They're not the same."

"Quite right, Serena." Ward nodded his approval. "Had Riley lived, he might very well have done some truly foolish things, like going up on the roof and spilling paint onto a canvas twenty feet below. That's not art, it's flimflam. His mind-set was such that he was heading in that direction."

"That's not Riley," Renie protested. "Passion notwithstanding, he always seemed to have quite a bit of discipline."

Ward shrugged. "He did. But what do you people call it? Mid-life crisis? He reached his late forties and changed rather drastically. He even talked about selling his place and moving further out into the woods. He said this area was getting too populated, too civilized."

Judith made an effort to sit up straighter. "How did Iris feel about that?"

Ward's eyes darted to the door, as if he were making sure Lark wasn't lingering there. "Iris is an amazing woman," he declared, lowering his voice. "She has put up with a lot all these years. I suspect she would have gone along with him. I don't see her often, but it has occurred to me that she's been under a greater strain lately."

"Somehow I thought she might confide in you," Judith said, also speaking more softly. "After all, who knew Riley better than the two of you?"

Ward turned somber. "Who indeed?" he murmured, his gaze now focused on the shadowy far corner of the living room. "Iris kept her own counsel."

"It's too bad she and Lark weren't pals," Renie said brightly. "You know, girl stuff. It seems to me that both of them could have used a confidante."

The comment elicited no response from Ward Kimball. Indeed, Judith thought he looked quite grim. When he finally spoke, it was not of Lark or Iris or even Riley, but of trout. "Tell me," he said, forcing his voice into a normal tone, "have you heard if the Fish and Wildlife Department has plans to plant the rivers again in the near future? It seems a shame to keep the streams on this side of the mountains so depleted."

For the next five minutes, the threesome discussed the problems of the sportsmen versus the Native Americans versus the environmentalists versus public indifference to all of the above. Judith and Renie took their leave, feeling thwarted in their quest for new knowledge about Riley's murder. They had collected their rods and were heading for the road to the highway when they heard a door shut nearby.

"Lark," whispered Judith, touching Renie's arm.

The cousins turned toward the studio, which lay in darkness. A slim figure was moving surely, yet carefully, down the gravel path that led to the house.

"Is someone there?" Lark's voice was low.

Judith acknowledged their presence. "Your father told us you were painting," she said as they met Lark halfway. "How is it going?"

"Fitfully." Lark wrung her hands, a curiously ingratiating gesture. "I can't concentrate today."

"That's understandable," said Judith. "Say, Lark, we're confused. Did you try to call on us yesterday while . . . we were gone someplace?"

Fleetingly, Lark appeared confounded. "Yesterday? Oh! I started out for your cabin, but I couldn't remember exactly where the trail went. Of course," she added quickly, "I didn't know you were there. I mean, I was just sort of ambling around, waiting for my father."

Putting a hand on Lark's arm, Judith began gently steering her back toward the studio and away from the house. She didn't want Ward Kimball to see her and Renie talking to his daughter. "You came with your father to Riley's place? Why didn't you go in, too?" She saw no way to skirt the direct question. Subterfuge had failed with Ward Kimball.

Lark avoided turning in Judith's direction. "I only came along for the exercise. Dad wanted to talk to Riley about something. I wasn't interested."

Feeling frustrated, Judith chewed on her lower lip. "I would think you'd always find conversations between your father and Riley fascinating. It would be like a meeting of the Titans. What did they talk about, besides art?"

"Oh . . . things." Lark sounded vague. "You know, what was happening around here in terms of development and new people and all that." She smiled, as if pleased with her glibness.

Renie let out an odd little sound of dismay. "And here I thought they might be planning your future." The cousins saw Lark stiffen, the smile gone. "Of your paintings, that is. You know, a showing or something."

"You're not very subtle," Lark declared with fervor. "If you're referring to the feelings between Riley and me, say so. They're no secret. I'd like to shout it from the top of Mount Woodchuck."

She was, in fact, shouting, and Judith turned quickly to see if Ward Kimball had heard. But the house remained closed up; the lights in the living room had gone off. Perhaps Ward had retreated to his study.

"Okay," Renie agreed, "so we're dancing around your love life. We gather your father didn't approve."

"Of course he didn't," Lark replied impatiently. She nudged the single step that led into the studio. "Come inside; hear this."

Judith and Renie exchanged puzzled looks, put down their rods, and followed Lark into the studio. A mixture of fragrant flowers and sharp turpentine filled the air. Lark didn't bother to turn on any lights, which left the cousins staggering around and bumping into unfamiliar objects. Lark, however, went straight to a cupboard from which she retrieved a small, rectangular object from a drawer.

"Dad insists that Riley was patronizing me—or worse. He went so far as to warn poor Riley to leave me alone. Silly, misguided Dad! I'd play this for him," she went on, pressing switches on what Judith could now see was a tape recorder, "but it might kill him. His heart is weak, you know. He's been ailing for the past year."

In the darkened studio with its alien accoutrements, Judith heard the voice of Riley Tobias and felt a shiver crawl up her spine. At her side, Renie swallowed hard. The ghostly surroundings and the voice from the dead unnerved both cousins.

"This is my version of a love letter," Riley said in his hearty, yet somehow caressing, voice. "I'm not clever with words, only with brushes and paints and knives and chisels. You are springtime, dear Lark, fresh blossoms and turbulent brooks and sweet grasses in the new-mown meadow. You are everything I've dreamed of, the embodiment of emotion in my lifework. Be my lover, my friend, and my wife. We belong to each other, and will face the wind and rain and sun and snow with our faces turned to heaven—together."

The tape stopped. Lark's alleged fantasy had turned into irrefutable reality. And then it had disappeared forever. Judith knew Lark couldn't see the sympathy on her face, but it would be conveyed in her voice.

"I'm so sorry, Lark. Riley's loss is doubly difficult for you."

Lark shut off the tape recorder and replaced it in the cupboard drawer. "I know what you're thinking. 'Poor Lark, she finally found a man to love her, despite her handicap, and then he died. Now she'll never know love again.' " Her attitude was hostile. "I don't want your pity."

Not for nothing had Judith hustled drinks to self-pitying customers at the Meat & Mingle for almost ten years. "What you need is to get out of here," she replied briskly. "Two eyes, three eyes, no eyes, your chances of meeting a decent, eligible bachelor up here on the river stink. Too many people use a personal flaw as an excuse for failure when they have it within themselves to succeed. It's not pity you hear, Lark, it's compassion. And I know what I'm talking about. You should try being a better judge of character. You thought Dan was wonderful because he had a pleasant voice. You should have heard him calling me a fat, ugly moron twice a day and three times on Sunday when the football team he bet the grocery money on didn't beat the point spread." Judith flushed, surprised and embarrassed by her heated little lecture.

"You met Dan in a downtown bar," Renie murmured dryly.

Judith bridled. "That's beside the point. It was his *character* I couldn't judge. Or wouldn't." She stopped glaring through the gloom at Renie and gave herself a sharp shake. It wasn't like her to be so blunt—or so presumptuous when speaking to others. She sighed and put a hand out to Lark. "I'm really sorry. What I should have said was some sort of placebo about Time Healing All Wounds and You've Got A Lot Going For You, So Chin Up."

Lark Kimball gave Judith a tight little smile. "You were right the first time. Maybe. But there's nobody anywhere like Riley. He was absolutely unique."

The point was not arguable. If nothing else, Riley Tobias had been a rugged—and talented—individualist. He had also been two-timing Iris Takisaki. Judith considered probing about Iris's reaction, then decided against it. Perhaps Iris didn't know what was going on behind her back. But Lark had implied that there was antagonism between her and Iris. Having heard Riley's tape, it was easy to understand why. Judith and Renie chose to leave Lark in peace—assuming she could find any, given the circumstances.

"Holy cats," Renie remarked as they finally got to the highway, "I thought you were going to take Lark's head off back there. And you criticize me for being tactless!"

The cousins were on the other side of the road, walking against the traffic, which was light on this evening in early May. On their left was the Higby farm, owned by an elderly couple who had weathered the Depression by trading eggs, milk, and produce, and had survived the next five decades to now sport a huge RV parked near a TV satellite dish. The field where cows had once grazed was empty; the old red barn stood derelict, with an advertisement for baking powder fading under the sagging eaves.

"You should have kicked me," Judith replied, glimpsing the moon through a few scattered clouds. "I can't think what set me off."

"That's not too hard to figure. Yesterday we planted Dan. He's dead as a dodo, you're alive, and happy as a clam. You feel guilty. It's stupid, but it's natural." Renie made a circular motion with her fishing rod, as if she were casting a spell with a magic wand. Or, it occurred to Judith, exorcising old demons.

"You're right, I suppose. But it's not just putting Dan's remains out there under the vine maples," Judith said as they passed the mobile home that housed the old-timers they'd seen earlier that day at the Green Mountain Inn. "It's all the memories from fifty years of being here. There are a lot of ghosts around the cabin, coz."

"Friendly ghosts," Renie declared. "Those ghosts loved it at the river. I can hear them laughing when I lie in bed. Do you remember when we were kids and the grown-ups would stay outside at the picnic table with a couple of lanterns and play six-handed pinochle until all hours?"

Judith smiled. "They'd get bitten by mosquitoes and deer flies and no-see-ums, and then the bats would come and get in their hair and the chipmunks would swipe the peanuts right out of the bowl, and one time Grandma thought Uncle Al was looking over her shoulder, trying to see her cards, and it turned out to be a bear. Yeah, I remember." She laughed aloud.

The neon Vacancy sign at the Woodchuck Auto Court beckoned up ahead. Renie, who had also been laughing, sobered. "Should we stop and call home? Or wait until after we get back from dinner in Glacier Falls?"

"We're leaving tomorrow," Judith pointed out. "Joe's at a police guild meeting tonight and Mother will only be annoyed. But go ahead, call Bill and your mother if you want."

Renie peered at her watch in the darkness. "It's after seven-thirty. There's a big NBA play-off game on tonight and Bill will probably ignore the phone. Mother has her pedicurist coming this evening. I guess I'll hold off, too."

The cousins were waiting in front of the auto court to cross the highway when they heard someone calling to them. It was Carrie Mae Morton, followed by four children, one of whom Judith and Renie had never seen before.

"Yoo-hoo!" shouted Carrie Mae, bouncing down the driveway. "I thought it was you! There was a phone call here for Mrs. Flynn about half an hour ago." She caught her breath as she pulled up next to Judith. "My goodness, have you been *fishing?*"

"In a way," Judith replied vaguely. "Who called?"

Carrie Mae shushed the children, among whom were numbered Velvet, Giles, Rafe, and a girl of about eight Judith didn't recognize. "I sent Thor and Jade here over to your place with the message. They put it on your door. But I got it written down someplace in the parlor. Come on in, I was changing little Fabio. Shanna is watching him for me."

Shanna turned out to be the girl with the satin bow who had been with her father and brother that morning. Judith mentally toted up eight children—so far. The so-called parlor was jammed with Morton offspring, a-tumble and a-jumble on furniture, appliances, and the floor. In the midst of the cramped confusion, Kennedy Morton sat in a well-worn recliner, watching a *Star Trek* rerun. He lifted a hand in salute, then immersed himself in outer space. Judith didn't much blame him.

"Right here," Carrie Mae said over the din of the TV, the screeching children, a barking dog of mixed ancestry, and the howls of little Fabio. She extracted a slip of notepaper she'd been using as a bookmark in a dog-eared historical romance. It dawned on Judith where all the unlikely names for the children had been found.

"Arlene," said Judith with a little gasp. "Oh, dear—I hope nothing's happened to Mother." Thanking Carrie Mae, and grateful to escape the Morton parlor, Judith hurried out to the phone booth. Renie trailed, carrying both fishing rods and the creel.

After the usual telecommunications difficulties had been surmounted, Judith got through to the Rankerses' house, next door to Hillside Manor. Arlene answered on the second ring.

"Hi," said Judith, a little breathless. "What's happened? Is it Mother?"

"Mother?" Arlene sounded puzzled, then laughed. "Oh, no, your mother is fine. We had her over to dinner. She'd won the quarters at bridge today and we thought she should celebrate. I made chicken breasts in a white wine sauce with fresh asparagus and brown rice. She enjoyed it very much. Carl and I get so tickled with her when she pretends to be so crusty. What a tease she is!"

Judith collapsed against the phone booth. "Yeah, right, a real tease, like Hitler kidding around with the Sudetenland. Well? If it's not Mother, what is it?" A sudden lurch of her heart caused Judith to put a hand to her breast. Joe? Mike? Sweetums?

"Nothing to fret over," Arlene replied in her breezy manner. "Who carries your homeowners' insurance? I would have asked Joe, but he's out tonight at some meeting."

"My—wait a minute, what's going on? Did a guest have an accident?" Judith flung open the phone booth door so that Renie could try to listen in.

"Not a guest," Arlene answered, then apparently turned away from the receiver. "Carl—put down that sledgehammer! I've got a perfectly good nutcracker in the kitchen, third drawer down on the left from the stove." She made an exasperated little noise in Judith's ear. "Honestly, men are so impatient! That's the last time I ask my husband to help me make a dessert for the Altar Society luncheon up at church. Did you hear about Father Hoyle? Somebody hit his car while it was parked in front of Moonbeam's, where he was having coffee with—"

"Arlene," Judith interrupted firmly, "I'm sorry about our pastor's problems, but it sounds as if I've got some of my own. What on earth is happening at the B & B?"

"Oh." Arlene seemed vaguely offended. "Well, it's

nothing to worry about, now that the water in the living room has gone down."

"What?" Judith closed her eyes; Renie practically fell on top of her.

"It was the main-floor bathroom," Arlene explained calmly. "The Rooter man said it was Gabe Porter's weeping willow across the street. Personally, I think it was that couple from Walla Walla who were here night before last. She tried to stuff her wig down the toilet after you left yesterday morning. Anyway . . ."

While the vast majority of visitors to the B&B were considerate, well-behaved people, Judith was accustomed to a few who did peculiar things. Explanations for erratic deportment were unnecessary. Since she was sixty miles from Hillside Manor, they were also futile.

"So what happened?" Judith asked in a limp voice.

"It flooded," Arlene said as if Judith ought to know. "Into the entry hall, the dining and living rooms, and just a little bit in the kitchen. Luckily, these old houses are crooked because of all the earthquakes. Yours must slant to the north. I think ours goes west. Anyway, it's fine now, or will be when everything dries out. But I did want to call your insurance company. The repairmen and the cleaning crew and the people with the big blower will come in the morning. The fellow with the pump turned out to be a classmate of Kevin's from Our Lady, Star of the Sea. He's living out in the North End now and got married last November to a dental hygienist who works for . . ."

Judith held her head and let Arlene rattle on. Not that any of it was her neighbor's fault: There was no accounting for strangers—or sprawling tree roots. Visions of damaged Oriental carpets, matching beige sofas, the grandfather clock, and every other treasure in the old Edwardian saltbox house danced in her head. Arlene couldn't have prevented the disaster any more than Judith could have if she'd been home. Indeed, Arlene Rankers wasn't just a cherished friend, but an extremely capable woman.

"Carl," Arlene barked, "take that baseball bat back downstairs this instant!" Carl Rankers's impatient rejoinder was heard in the background, but Judith couldn't make out what he said. "I told you, the *third* drawer, on the *left.* Honestly," Arlene continued, now speaking into the receiver once again, "men can never find *anything.* And they don't *listen!*"

Dutifully, Judith gave Arlene the information about the homeowners' insurance policy. Thanking her lucky stars that she had increased her coverage in the past few months, Judith hung up. After hearing a detailed explanation, Renie commiserated. Her sympathy was cut short by Iris Takisaki, who was dashing across the road.

"Well, hello," Iris said, surprised to see the cousins at the auto court. "Have you been fishing?" She looked dubious.

"You could say we've been practicing," Judith replied. "How are you getting along, Iris?"

Iris gazed down the road, where a large sedan was cautiously passing two bicyclists with reflectors on their spokes and helmets. "Maybe I'm still numb," she admitted. "I don't feel much of anything right now. The funeral is Saturday morning at the community hall in Glacier Falls. Riley's brother, Yancey, is flying in Friday night. Clive will meet him and his family at the airport and bring them up here."

It occurred to Judith that she and Renie should drive back for the services. But the B&B was full over the weekend. It was also at post-flood stage. To make up for their absence, Judith impulsively asked Iris to join them for dinner in Glacier Falls.

Iris, however, had already eaten. "I had some soup and crackers," she said. "I came over here now to check on my messages in town. It's a nuisance that Riley hated the phone so much. Usually, I use Nella's."

At that moment four of the Mortons burst out onto the tarmac. All were now clad in pajamas of varying hues, their red curls dancing and their voices piping:

"Sweet-Stix! Sweet-Stix! We want Sweet-Stix now!"

The cousins took the cry as their cue to be gone. Iris barricaded herself in the phone booth while the foursome continued chanting outside. Judith and Renie scurried across the highway, relieved to escape the din.

Inside the gate, Judith paused, then ambled over to a grove of cascaras and vine maples that shielded the Grover property from the highway. "Remember how we used to peel off the cascara bark and sell it in town?"

"Right. We got as much as nine bucks for it once," Renie replied impatiently. "Come on, let's get these fish put away before a game warden shows up in a bear suit."

"And the swamp back there," Judith mused, ignoring Renie. "Quicksand, we called it, but it wasn't really. It was just very marshy."

"And dangerous. I had to pull you out once and you were no small thing. You lost your striped canvas shoes, which were exceedingly ugly anyway." Renie was humoring Judith, but without much grace.

Judith grinned at Renie. "You saved my life." She spoke with a trace of awe.

"Yeah, well, what else could I do? I'd have caught hell from our parents if I'd let you squelch around and sink in there. It would have put a real damper on the weekend." Renie was looking faintly embarrassed.

Judith resumed walking up the dirt road. "We've had some interesting adventures, coz."

"Life's interesting," Renie remarked, her patience restored. "That is, if you're paying attention. A lot of people aren't. I guess they're like Riley's nerds—just passing through."

"Maybe Riley had something there," Judith said, leaning her rod up against the porch. "It's too bad he had to convey his sentiments in such an ugly style."

Renie removed the trout from her leaf-lined creel. "Mainly, it's too bad he's dead. He might have changed some more, but for the better." She eyed the dead fish and frowned. "Poor Riley."

"Amen," said Judith.

* * *

After they had cleaned their fish, Judith put them in the icebox. "It was so warm today that this block really melted quite a bit. Maybe we should get some more in Glacier Falls tonight."

But Renie reminded Judith that the creamery where they bought the ice would be closed. "We're leaving in the late afternoon," she pointed out. "We'll have enough until then."

Judith was dubious, but didn't argue. "We're going to go home and leave this mess in Costello's inept hands," she grumbled as they changed into clean clothes for dinner. "I feel like a flop."

"Come on, coz," Renie said, pulling a Marquette University sweatshirt over her head, "nobody expects you to be the Queen of Crime. How many murders do you read about every day in the newspaper? Do you have a wild urge to solve them all?"

"Of course not," Judith replied from in front of the unadorned oval mirror above the bedroom dresser. "I never even give Joe advice about his investigations. But when I practically stumble over a body, especially of someone I know, I feel an obligation." She brushed her hair with a vengeance.

"You might as well forget this one," Renie said. "It's going to turn out to be somebody we never heard of, like maybe an outraged patron who felt he or she got stung buying a five-figure painting that looks like cat tuna. Or an aspiring artist who was fiendishly jealous and thought Riley stood in his way. Or hers. In these days of equality, you've got to give everybody a fair shake at being a homicidal maniac."

Judith looked in the mirror, seeing Renie's reflection behind her. "What if the killer is never caught?"

"That happens," Renie allowed, but she lowered her eyes.

"That's wrong," said Judith.

"That's life," said Renie.

"That bothers me," said Judith.

"I know," said Renie. "And *that* bothers *me.*"

NINE

The Tin Hat Cafe in Glacier Falls wasn't the newest eatery in town, it didn't aspire to excellence, and the tired waitresses acted as if they were doing their job as a penance. What atmosphere there was came from the clientele, rather than from the decor. The menu was limited, with six entrees that never changed. The special was always the prime rib. But the food was wholesome, the prices were modest, and the tables were clean. The floor was another matter.

The cafe was located at the corner of the only stoplight in town. The Tin Pants Tavern was next door, and the booths built against the wall that divided the establishments were known to rock on a Saturday night. Judith and Renie recalled one such occasion in their youth when they had driven into town with their parents, and a fist had come through the wall right next to Uncle Cliff's ear. Uncle Cliff had slowly turned around, gazed at the fist, and buttered it. The waitress had given him a free piece of apple pie.

Judith ordered the prime rib, medium rare; Renie went for the hamburger steak with mushroom gravy. Both dinners were complete, with soup, salad, roll, dessert, and coffee so strong that Renie attempted to stand her spoon up in it.

At almost nine on a Wednesday night, the cafe was nearly deserted. A pair of older men sat at the counter, drinking coffee and eating pie while they exchanged gripes about the decline in the logging industry. A young couple in the opposite booth held hands across the table and gazed into each other's eyes. At the front of the restaurant, three middle-aged women stood at the cash register, trying to sort out their bill.

Judith was studying their own bill when Renie hissed at her. "Look who's here—Dewitt Dixon and Mrs. Dixon. I recognize her from someplace—a gallery opening, maybe."

Judith tried to turn around and stare without being obvious. She failed. Dewitt waved and approached the cousins. Erica Dixon greeted Renie graciously and acknowledged the introductions to Judith with a bright smile. In her Escada separates and thigh-high Spanish boots, she looked as incongruous as a Rolls-Royce at a demolition derby.

"I just came from the airport," Erica announced in a piping voice that didn't go with her designer appearance and chic blond good looks. "I flew home this morning, as soon as I heard the news about Riley. It made all the papers in Europe, of course. He was highly respected over there, particularly in Italy and France."

Judith wasn't sure what protocol demanded when giving condolences to an ex-wife. "It's a terrible tragedy," she said, hoping to cover all the bases at once. "Won't you sit down?"

Dewitt glanced over his shoulder at the waitress, who was eyeing him as if she thought the Dixons were Bonnie and Clyde out on a holdup spree. "Maybe we'd better. I think they're about to stop serving. I haven't had dinner, but Erica ate on the plane."

"That was hours ago," Erica said, sitting next to Judith. "They served right after Greenland. We came the polar route."

Reluctantly, the waitress approached. Somewhat gleefully, she announced that the kitchen was out of everything but the salmon and the prime rib. Both of the Dixons requested salmon. Their soup arrived before Erica could shed her red-and-green-plaid jacket.

"I thought you'd checked out of the auto court," Judith said to Dewitt. "We didn't see your car around this afternoon."

Dewitt tasted his soup, which was chicken vegetable with thick noodles. "I had some business matters to attend to, here in Glacier Falls and also in town. But when Erica notified me that she was coming home immediately, I knew she'd want to call on Iris, so I kept my motel reservation. I picked Erica up at the airport around seven-thirty and drove straight up here. It's too late to go back to the city tonight."

"I'm exhausted," Erica declared, proving the point by going limp against the back of the booth. "It's been so hectic since I heard about Riley. Good heavens, it's already morning in Rome. I've been up for twenty-four hours straight."

Their salads arrived, and the Dixons had to fight to hold onto their soup bowls. The waitress stomped off to the front door and turned the cafe sign to "Closed." She shot a look of triumph at the four late diners, who were now the only customers left in the restaurant.

"By the way," Judith said as the Dixons tried to keep pace with their waitress, "we've got your cigarette case, Dewitt. You must have dropped it at the cabin when you stopped by last night."

Dewitt Dixon's imperturbable air was momentarily nettled. "My . . . ? Oh! Yes, I wondered where that had gotten to. It seemed like a small matter in the wake of Riley's death." Tackling his salad, he had again become in control. "I'm sorry I missed you two last night. I heard someone inside the cabin and assumed you were home, but it turned out to be Clive Silvanus. I hope he wasn't much of a bother. Clive took Riley's passing very hard. I felt obligated to see that he got back to the Green Mountain Inn safely."

The explanation was smooth. Judith decided against mentioning the peripatetic painting. If Erica's pride and joy was really missing, it wouldn't do for Judith to say so now.

Ironically, it was Erica who brought the artwork into conversational play:

"I was telling Dewitt on the way up here that I was so glad we'd purchased Riley's last landscape. It will be a fitting memorial. You know," she continued in her piping voice as the waitress removed the soup bowls and hovered over the salad plates, "I'm tempted to name the gallery after Riley. What do you think, darling?"

"Darling" looked like he was thinking of thunder. But his voice was calm. "Give yourself some time, my dear. You're reacting to the shock of the tragedy." With a sigh, he surrendered his salad plate. The waitress stalked off. "It would be appropriate to have at least one of Ward Kimball's works, you know. I've no objection to hanging his 'Summer Storm' from our private collection."

Erica looked mildly interested. "That's not one of my favorites. I wonder if he has anything tucked away I'd like better."

Renie was waving for coffee refills. The waitress ignored her. "Do you know Ward Kimball?" she asked, a covetous eye on the coffee carafe which sat on a hot plate behind the lunch counter.

"No," Erica replied, taking a tortoiseshell compact from her suede handbag and examining her eye makeup. "Ward was never one to exhibit himself along with his paintings." She closed the compact and turned to Dewitt. "You've met him, though, haven't you, darling?"

Dewitt's expression was blank. "Have I? Perhaps. Yes, some years ago, at an arts festival. He has a daughter, I understand. I've never seen her. She must be grown up by now."

"She's a lovely young woman," Judith remarked. "She paints, too."

Dewitt's eyebrows lifted. "Really? How extraordinary for a person with so little sight. Ward's talent must flow strongly in her veins."

"Actually," Renie put in, giving up on the prospect of more coffee, "Riley had been giving her lessons."

"How generous of him!" Erica exclaimed in her high voice. "And how typical. But that was Riley, great of heart, great of temperament. No one has had a greater impact on my life than he did," she asserted with fervor. "I was hardly more than a child, trying to sell sketches of Alcatraz in North Beach, when he came along and told me I wasn't an artist. He was right, of course." She let out a trilling little laugh. "I had an eye, but no talent. He urged me to become a critic, so I started writing articles for underground publications. Amazingly, people in the art world took me seriously. Then I met Dewitt." She gave her husband an arch smile that might or might not have been affectionate. Judith couldn't be sure. "He showed me a whole new world, from the collector's perspective. My family bought only what their decorator recommended. Dewitt educated me about the buyer's mind. I suppose you could say I've covered the gamut of the artistic community." With a self-satisfied air, she twirled a blond curl at her ear.

The salmon steaks, complete with baked potato and broccoli, arrived along with dessert, which was vanilla ice cream.

"I say," Dewitt called to the waitress, "if you please, miss, the ice cream will melt before—"

But the waitress had slammed back into the kitchen. Erica Dixon seemed undismayed at the prospect of mushy dessert. "Perhaps you're right about the gallery name, Dewitt. It would be different if I'd acquired a lot of Riley's work while we were married." She paused, glancing at the cousins. "How very rude. Did you know that Riley and I were married years and years ago? I'm not sure I made that clear."

The cousins acknowledged that they were aware of the brief marital interlude.

"Fourteen months, to be exact," Erica said, checking her salmon for bones. "Had I not been young and impulsive, I would have had the foresight to make off with all sorts of Riley's paintings. But at eighteen, all I wanted was out. What a pity. His early efforts were crude but compelling. Think how marvelous it would be to have just one or two—and then the contrast of the last landscape." She quivered at the mere idea.

"Contrast?" Dewitt curled his lip. "If you ask me, he regressed. 'Spring River' is all charm but lacks technical merit. The most I can say for it is that it's not ugly, like those wretched so-called portraits he was working on when he died."

" 'Spring River' is stunning," Erica declared, her gray eyes flashing angrily. "It's a departure for Riley. Yes, you might call it a regression, but I consider it a retrospective—it goes back to his earlier days, when everything about him was softer and more vulnerable. The technique is different, but it's exquisite. Honestly, Dewitt, you refuse to appreciate what's really there. When we look at that painting together, I'll show you the values I see."

Dewitt gave Judith and Renie a wry look. "Pardon us, ladies. My wife and I are engaged in a squalid artistic and domestic debate. We shouldn't air our differences in front of you. But in our defense, we've been apart for several weeks."

"That's okay," Renie said with a wave of her hand. "We're married, too. The important thing is that you're communicating. My husband, Bill, says that the trouble with most marriages is lack of intimacy. Now, he's not talking about physical intimacy, but—"

"Gosh, coz, look at the time!" Judith interrupted in a feigned panic. Fascinating as Bill Jones's theories might be, Judith didn't care to hear them secondhand from

Renie. "We'd better scoot before they throw us out. I mean, we finished eating a long time ago, and they probably think we're not going to pay the bill."

Pay they did, receiving no word of thanks from the grumpy waitress, who accepted their money at the cash register. A moment later, the cousins were out on the sidewalk.

Judith and Renie took advantage of the mild spring evening to walk off their dinner. Glacier Falls was tucked in a valley among the mountains. Logging had built the town, farming had sustained it, and tourism kept it alive. A brief flirtation with gold mining some thirty miles up the highway and sixty years in the past had brought glittering promises that were soon broken. Yet Glacier Falls continued to grow, albeit slowly, as families tired of urban congestion and preferred to commute.

Within two blocks, the cousins were out of the commercial district. The small, aging houses had the look of a company town, no doubt built by the logging firms back in the heyday of tall timber and high prices.

"I smell a sawmill," Renie said, sniffing at the fresh mountain air. "Is that one about a mile out of town still operating? We got some cedar shakes there years ago."

"I think so," Judith replied. Except for an occasional car and the barking of a dog, the night was very quiet. "I wonder if Riley wanted to move away because he intended to marry Lark. Maybe he was going to sell his place and divvy up the profits as a consolation prize for Iris."

"Why not just give her a couple of paintings? His property isn't worth more than one-fifty," Renie pointed out. "Real estate is still relatively cheap up here."

"True." Judith stepped into the street. There was no curb, nor had there been a sidewalk for the last block. The forest began beyond the next row of houses. Turning left, the cousins headed toward the small frame Catholic church. "Did you get the impression that Erica thinks Dewitt has Riley's painting in his possession?"

"It seems to be a given," Renie allowed. "Maybe he

does have it. Maybe Clive has ours, which isn't theirs after all."

"Maybe that's not our problem," Judith replied. "Maybe I didn't want a Riley Tobias in the first place. At least not an ugly one." But a little sigh escaped her lips.

The cousins strolled past the Catholic church, the Methodist church, and the foursquare gospel church. Each stood on a different corner of the same intersection. The local funeral home was situated on the fourth corner lot. Briefly, Judith thought of Riley Tobias, lying inside. She grimaced, then picked up the pace. Past the local Ace Hardware, the Bank of Glacier Falls, the John Deere outlet, and Buzzy's Burger Barrel went the cousins, making the loop back to Judith's car. They were about to get in when the Dixons pulled out just ahead of them. Judith could see the outlines of Dewitt's and Erica's heads through the rear window of the white Mercedes.

"I don't think they ate their ice cream," Judith remarked as she got behind the wheel.

The half-dozen large, handsome older homes of Glacier Falls were located in the last two blocks before the turnoff to the cabin. A local lumber baron had decorated his mansion with the Victorian gingerbread typical of the era. Another had gone in for the log-cabin look, which had weathered beautifully over the years. A third home, also constructed at the turn of the century, had undergone a complete renovation, and looked as if it belonged in a southern California cul-de-sac. Judith smiled to herself at the differences in taste—and in people.

Up ahead, the Dixons kept the pace at about a half mile. "Have they got kids?" Judith inquired, slowing for the bridge that crossed the river just above the falls that gave the town its name.

"I don't think so," said Renie. "How could Erica go running around Europe and open up galleries and be so well groomed and self-absorbed? Good grief, her fingernails are all the same length! How could she possibly have children?"

Renie's reply satisfied Judith. The car climbed the Sand Hill, then dipped down toward the river valley. At the Big Bend, the cousins passed the road that led to Ward Kimball's house. A half mile later, the Mercedes turned off at Riley's property. Obviously, Erica Dixon was going to keep her vow to offer condolences.

"Past Wife comforting Present Mistress while Future Bride languishes downriver." Renie ticked the three women off on her fingers, then swerved in the passenger seat. "Hey, look—Nella's back. The lights are on."

Judith hadn't noticed; she was too busy concentrating on turning into the dirt drive. "We'll stop by tomorrow," she said as Renie hopped out of the car to open the gate. "Maybe we can get some ice. Let's chip some off what's left and have a nightcap."

Five minutes later, Renie was hoisting her bourbon while the Coleman lantern cast dancing shadows on the knotty pine walls. "I wonder if Iris told Costello about Riley giving you that canvas. And if she let him know that Clive had been here."

Judith sipped appreciatively at her scotch. It had been a long day. Indeed, the past forty-eight hours had been tiring, physically and emotionally. "We don't know—and neither does Iris—if that painting really belonged to the Dixons. Only Erica and Dewitt could be sure of that, *if* they saw the canvas. Clive might have stolen it simply to add to the inventory. Dewitt might have taken it so he wouldn't have to pay Riley's estate."

But Renie disagreed. "Erica wants 'Spring River' as the centerpiece of her new gallery. There's no way she could show it off without Clive—or Iris—finding out about it. My guess is that Riley didn't give you 'Spring River.' If it's missing from the studio, then there are two stolen paintings. Sure, Riley could be impulsive, but nobody hands over a painting worth seventy grand on a whim."

Judith, however, shook her head. "No, coz. That doesn't wash. Iris seems to know what Riley had in the studio. She definitely said that only one canvas was missing. The more I think about it, the more I'm convinced that Riley gave me 'Spring River.' But you're right about one thing—it doesn't make sense for him to have done that. So he had to have a reason we can't fathom. He was even willing to let me take the painting off to the B & B. Why did he do such a crazy thing?"

Renie studied her bourbon glass. "Sheer perversity is the only answer I can come up with. But in stopping the sale, Riley was cutting off his nose to spite his face." She considered her words and shivered. "As it turned out, he did worse than that. He got himself killed."

A troubled expression crossed Judith's face. "Let's say he told someone what he'd done. Who could he have told? Almost anybody. Iris. Lazlo. Ward. Clive. Dewitt. Even Lark. We only have her word for it that she didn't see Riley yesterday. Now, who is the most likely person among the above? I choose Clive, for a couple of reasons." She stopped to catch her breath and take a drink. "Clive was Riley's agent and he needed to know where that painting was. Don't you think he came up here to broker the deal with Dewitt? No painting, no deal. And Riley had better explain himself. Also, who shows up *here* but Clive? What if he wasn't really drunk?"

Renie's eyes lighted up just as the single Coleman lantern died down. "You mean he was faking so he could pretend to pass out and stick around? But how could he be sure we'd leave?" She rose from the sofa to pump up the lantern.

"He couldn't. But he had to gamble that we would—and we did. As for Dewitt, he knew Clive had to be somewhere around here. If not at the Green Mountain Inn or Riley's, where else? Nella was gone, Dewitt knew he wasn't over at the auto court, and as far as I know, Clive wasn't acquainted with anyone else in the area."

"Except Ward Kimball." Renie sat down again. The lantern glowed brightly. Outside, a chorus of frogs began their nightly serenade.

"That's possible," Judith admitted, "but Dewitt would

look here first. He said he didn't really know Ward and Lark. Besides, they live a half mile away."

Renie had to admit that Judith's argument was convincing. "Clive finds out Riley gave you 'Spring River,' Clive learns Riley is dead, Clive decides to ensure his commission by getting the canvas back. But he doesn't give it to Dewitt. Not yet."

"Maybe he can't," Judith said in a faintly distracted voice. "Maybe it's a legal thing, with Riley dead. The estate, or . . ." Her words trailed off as she stared at Renie. "Clive lied," she said abruptly as her thoughts snapped into focus. "He told us he didn't talk to Riley yesterday. But if he knew about my gift, then Clive actually saw Riley."

The cousins gazed wonderingly at each other. An uncertain knock sounded at the door, making them both jump. It was after ten o'clock. Visitors seemed unlikely. But so did most of the things that had happened during their stay at the cabin.

Lark Kimball looked tired and distraught. There were scratches on her arms and leaves in her hair. She all but fell into Judith's arms.

"What happened, Lark?" Judith cried, leading the younger woman to the sofa. "Here, sit down. Yes, you're okay. Oh, my—what's going on?"

Lark struggled to catch her breath. "I . . . I've never come down the highway this far by myself. I was all right as long as I stayed on the shoulder—I could follow the gravel just fine. But once I turned off onto your drive, I became confused, like I did yesterday. I got off the trail. Then I ran into your icehouse and I heard voices. I knew I was getting close."

"But . . ." Judith began, to no avail. Lark kept right on talking.

"That tape—the one Riley made—it's gone!" Her face was pale in the lantern light.

Judith's first reaction was to suggest that she look harder. But Lark's search would be more thorough than that of a fully sighted person making a cursory perusal. "You're sure?" was all Judith said.

"Yes!" Lark's small hands twisted in distress. "I haven't touched it since you were at the studio earlier this evening."

Judith signaled for Renie to fetch Lark a beer. "Did your father know you had the tape?" Judith asked.

Lark shook her head. "Riley gave it to me Sunday. Dad hasn't been in the studio for weeks."

"Did you hear anybody come by after we left?" Judith inquired as Renie handed Lark a bottle of beer.

Again Lark shook her head. "I went into the house. Dad and I played a Bruckner symphony. He decided to go to bed early. Riley's death has upset him. I went back to the studio because . . ." She paused, gripping the beer can tightly and searching for words. "I wanted to hear Riley speak to me again. Alone. That's when I discovered the tape was gone, so I came down here to see you." Her face wore a questioning, if not quite accusing, expression.

"We didn't take it," Judith declared. "There must have been about a two-hour interval, when someone could have gone in and gotten it. Was the studio locked?"

"No," Lark admitted. "I knew when you left that I'd go back. I would have locked up then, for the night."

"Was the tape marked?" Renie asked, sitting down next to Lark on the sofa.

Lark didn't know. Her poor vision didn't permit that kind of scrutiny. She doubted it, however. "I'd left it in the recorder, so it was ready to be played again. Why would anyone come to the studio, listen to a tape they didn't know existed—and then steal it?"

"Was there anything else on that tape?" asked Judith.

Lark frowned. "I don't think so. I never fast-forwarded it after Riley's message ended." She touched her cheek with her hand. "Oh, dear! I suppose there might have been something on it. But what?"

The question baffled Judith as well as Lark. "The point is," Renie noted, "that someone must have figured the tape was important. Was anything else missing?"

Lark didn't know that, either. She had been so upset over the loss of the tape that she had fled the studio and headed straight for the road. "If the studio had been ransacked, I would have noticed. It felt the same, it smelled the same." She flushed suddenly, then turned away. "I'm very aware when things are out of place." Her voice was defensive, her manner strangely awkward.

Judith nodded, though the change in Lark puzzled her. "Maybe you should report the theft to the sheriff," she said. "It may not have anything to do with Riley's death, but it strikes me as odd."

Lark, however, refused. The tape was too personal. She wouldn't dream of confiding in a law officer, especially one as callous as Abbott N. Costello. Judith didn't much blame her, but felt the decision was unwise. She kept that opinion to herself, changing the subject to the arrival of Erica Dixon.

"Erica?" Lark was temporarily distracted from her latest loss. "She and Riley got along quite well, considering that they couldn't stay married to each other."

"They were friends?" Judith was surprised.

"Not friends," Lark explained. "I don't think they'd met since San Francisco. But last February, right in between snowstorms, Erica and Dewitt came up to see Riley about a painting. I wasn't at the studio then, but later, I met Erica when she came alone. She asked me about buying one of Dad's works, but when I told him, he said he wasn't interested in selling. She didn't press the issue. Besides, the sum Riley asked for his landscape was so high that even a wealthy collector would have had to think twice about another expenditure. Erica has to spend her money on diversity to get the gallery going."

Renie interjected a question. "You've never met Dewitt, I take it?"

Even before Lark answered, something flickered through Judith's brain. She leaned closer, anxious for the younger woman's reply.

"No." Lark now seemed more at ease. "That is, not officially. He came by the studio—Riley's studio—one day when I was working, but he didn't come in. I sensed someone was outside; then Riley told me it was Mr. Dixon."

The odd thought took form in Judith's mind: At the Tin Hat Cafe, Dewitt had said he'd never seen Lark, yet he had mentioned her poor sight. Judith supposed he could have heard from Riley or Erica or even Clive that Lark was blind, yet his manner had not rung quite true. A second realization followed the first, but Judith said nothing for the time being. As ever, she had to let logic take its course.

Judith couldn't judge how much beer was left in Lark's can, but the offer of a refill was a good excuse for bringing up a touchy topic. "Riley enjoyed his beer, I gather," she remarked in a conversational tone after Lark had turned down a second can. "We had some with him while we were at the studio yesterday."

"Yesterday!" Lark turned pale. "How can it be only yesterday?"

Judith made sympathetic noises but kept on track. "He wasn't much for the hard stuff, though, was he?"

Lark's attention seemed focused elsewhere. "No," she said at last, in a vague sort of voice. "He was a beer man. Wine occasionally. I never knew him to drink cocktails."

Renie shot Judith a curious look. "Did he drink much when he worked?" asked Judith.

Puzzled, Lark turned toward Judith. "Not really. He couldn't handle it, you see. If Riley drank more than three beers, he was out of it. You would never think that to look at him." She uttered a sad little laugh. "I mean, I couldn't *look* at him the way other people did, but I know he was a big man. Oh, my God, *where is that tape?*" The words tumbled out on a frenzied note.

The cousins commiserated some more. At last, they offered to drive Lark back to the Big Bend. She protested, but without conviction. It wasn't until they had seen her to the front door of her house that Judith remembered something Lark had said that didn't make sense.

"Our icehouse," Judith told Renie as they drove back down the highway. "We don't have an icehouse."

"She meant outhouse," Renie responded. "She was confused, upset. Or maybe she thought it *was* an icehouse."

"Does it *smell* like an icehouse? We put enough lye in there yesterday to eat up the first six inches of dirt." Judith noted that the white Mercedes was now parked over at the Woodchuck Auto Court. The Dixons apparently had concluded their visit to Iris. "Lark also mentioned hearing our voices. Now, we may not be a couple of whisperers, but we weren't exactly shouting, either. Have you ever heard anybody inside the cabin when you were at the outhouse?"

Renie admitted that she had not. "So what are you getting at?"

"Lark went the wrong way somehow," Judith said as they once again turned into the dirt drive. "She ended up at Nella's. How she managed to get back over here, I can't guess. Sheer luck, I suppose. I can't imagine what it's like to live in a world of shadows, but it must take a while to judge distances on unfamiliar ground."

"I feel as if we're groping around in the shadows," Renie declared, getting out of the car. "And what's this about Riley drinking only beer? That sounds like a typical alcoholic. Sure, in public he limits himself to a couple of cans, but in private he glugs down a quart a day."

Judith didn't comment. Renie was right, yet there was something about Riley's drinking habits that bothered her. In fact, everything about Riley bothered her. She was hardly surprised to find Iris Takisaki sitting on the porch steps, hugging a hooded cable-knit sweater around her slim body.

"I didn't think you'd be gone long," Iris said in a petulant tone. "It's going on eleven."

Judith and Renie squeezed onto the steps on either side of Iris. "What's up?" Judith asked.

Iris stared straight ahead, out beyond the river and into the blackness of the trees that marched up the side of Mount Woodchuck. "Riley's painting is still missing. Dewitt is threatening to sue me. Now what do I do?"

TEN

JUDITH WAS FRESH out of advice. All she could do was ask for an explanation.

"It's simple," Iris replied, now more glum than sulky. "Dewitt came to get the painting yesterday afternoon." She paused to let the meaning of her words sink in on the cousins. "Riley stalled him, according to Dewitt, saying that Clive had to be on hand to broker the deal. But Clive didn't show, according to Dewitt, so he told Riley he'd come back later. Which he did. You know that—you were there. But, of course, Riley had given you the painting by then. You didn't know it was Dewitt's, and then it was taken from here." She jerked her head in the direction of the cabin at her back. "I can't imagine why Riley pulled such a stunt, but he did. The canvas he gave you *has* to be 'Spring River.' Nothing else is missing."

Not for the first time did Judith try to think of a plausible reason why Riley would give her a painting he'd already sold. Again she failed to come up with a credible answer. "So Dewitt wants to sue for breach of contract?" She asked.

Iris seemed close to tears, though more out of frustration than sorrow. "Something like that. The man's a snake. Riley didn't like him, and it had nothing to do with the fact that Dewitt married his ex-wife. If I hadn't known Riley better, I would have thought he was afraid of Dewitt. But I can't think why."

The frogs had chanted their last encore; the brief silence was broken only by the sound of the rolling river. "Does Dewitt have that much influence in the art community?" Judith finally inquired of both Iris and Renie.

It was Renie who answered. "No. I can't think of any one person who has serious clout. We don't live in that kind of visual arts environment in this part of the country."

Iris was nodding agreement. "In fact, Erica is probably more influential than Dewitt. But Riley had no qualms about her. As far as I'm concerned," she went on a bit heatedly, "he was far too kind when it came to Erica. If she hadn't been such a rotten wife to him, he wouldn't have turned so sour on marriage."

"Have you talked to Clive?" asked Renie. "Not only was he here last night, but so was Dewitt."

"Really?" Iris turned from cousin to cousin. "Maybe Dewitt stole the canvas while Clive was passed out. But what does he do with a stolen 'Spring River'?" Apparently stymied, she twisted her hands together.

Judith slouched in her place on the steps. She could think of nothing to say to comfort Iris. Frustration hung on the night air, heavy as the mountain dew.

Iris sighed. "I can't believe that Clive would resort to chicanery. Why should he? If the canvas is sold, he gets his commission. I've always trusted Clive. Except . . ." She ran a hand over her sleek dark hair. "I trusted him because Riley did. But I know he's been actively, even aggressively, seeking new clients to represent. I hear the rumors in my business. Two weeks ago, I suggested to a local CEO that he hang a Rowena Farnham woodcut in his corner office. Rowena's fairly new on the art scene, she's very good, and it turns out that she's just authorized Clive to arrange a showing for her. I mentioned it to Riley, but he only laughed. He said art agents shouldn't put all their eggs in one basket. That's true, but Clive's flurry of activity bothered me."

"Why do you think he was looking for so many new clients?" Renie inquired as an owl hooted in a nearby tree.

"I don't know." Iris rubbed at her temple. "Maybe he thought Riley wasn't going to pull out of his slump."

"The bottom line is that you're still missing 'Spring River,' " Judith noted.

With an effort, Iris rose from the steps. "I'm missing more than that," she replied in a tired voice. The lantern light from the doorway illuminated her face as she gave the cousins a bitter smile. "I'm missing Riley. Very much."

Joe was in bed when Judith called from the auto court. Feeling a sudden surge of loneliness and a need for assurance that Hillside Manor hadn't floated down Heraldsgate Hill, she'd decided to phone home. Renie stayed behind, pleading the desire for an elaborate bedtime snack.

"No structural damage," Joe informed Judith. "The main thing was the rugs, but they'll dry. Besides, Sweetums looks good in a swimsuit. I cut a hole for his tail."

Judith smiled into the phone. She was only beginning to get used to having someone other than herself responsible for Hillside Manor. "The insurance will cover it, I gather?"

"Sure, except for a fifty-dollar deductible. Stop fussing. Caught the perp yet?" Joe asked, sounding much too chipper for eleven-fifteen at night.

"Not even close," Judith admitted. "Joe, did you really think I'd spend all my time up here sleuthing?"

"Why not? You love it. Why worry about an old dump on the river nobody uses anyway? Why bother with property you're paying taxes and insurance on? What's the point, just because it's in the middle of some of the most beautiful scenery in North America? Why would you even consider turning it into another B & B when you've already proved you could do it successfully once? Gee,

Jude-girl, don't ask me why you shouldn't be holding amateur detective night in the forest primeval. I'm just a dumb Irish cop."

Judith gulped. "Damn," she whispered away from the receiver. So Joe had been stringing her along, waiting for her to come up with the idea on her own. Or did he think she'd already had it before she left home? Had he condoned her taking part in the murder investigation in order to divert her from another B&B venture or to spur her on? Or was he merely putting her on? Still, the idea for converting the cabin was tantalizing; Judith just wished she'd thought of it first. "It's going to cost a mint," she said at last. "Ten grand, easy. We'd have to take out a loan. I just paid off the one on Hillside Manor last year."

"It's an investment," Joe said in that casual, mellow voice that never failed to make Judith tingle, even when he was speaking of mundane matters. "I can get it through the credit union. It'll be cheaper than a bank."

"Who'd run it?" Judith queried, her mind now racing. "It seems to me I ought to get it off the ground myself. Then there's the catering sideline. I couldn't leave town and let that slide. I couldn't leave *you.*" Her voice took on a plaintive note.

Judith could hear Joe moving around in the bed. She wished she were next to him, in the circle of his arms. "Worry about that stuff later," he said. "We're talking about a year, maybe two, down the road. What about hiring that Swedish carpenter of yours? You know, the one who remodeled the toolshed."

"Skjoval Tolvang?" Judith envisioned the aged but excellent craftsman. "I don't know if he'd want to work so far out of town."

"You'll find someone who can do a good job." Joe yawned, a not-quite-natural sound. "Now that you have a plan, you can start with the basics. Zoning, for instance. Wiring, plumbing, all that. Or have you already looked into it?"

"Uh—not yet. We've stuck to housekeeping chores so

far. But zoning shouldn't be a problem, with the auto court across the road." Judith could hardly believe she was serious.

"You've thought about the alternative—like time-share," said Joe on the end of another yawn. "The advantage is obvious. No on-site management, no heavy-duty labor, not to mention having the place freed up when the family wanted to use it. What do the relatives think? I suppose Renie's got some design ideas for the marketing end."

"Oh, Renie's got ideas," Judith said quickly, wondering how her cousin—and the rest of the family members—would react to such a radical proposal. Getting the aunts, uncles, and cousins to agree on where to dig a new outhouse hole had practically triggered a full-scale war.

"Good work. It sounds as if you two have spent your time wisely." Joe paused, and Judith wondered if those magic green eyes of his were dancing with mischief—or glittering with purpose. His voice dropped a notch. "Does the mist still rise up in the meadow at dusk? Do the stars seem so close you can almost touch them? Does the river croon you to sleep like a Nat King Cole ballad? Gee, Jude-girl, I haven't stayed overnight at the cabin since 1966." A low purr—or was it a growl?—trembled over the phone line to caress Judith's ear.

Judith wanted to rebuke Joe, but her heart was doing curious things. So were her knees. She held the receiver in one hand and braced herself against the wall of the phone booth with the other. They hadn't yet been married a year. There really hadn't been time for Judith and Joe to enjoy the cabin. Maybe Joe would like rusticating by the river, if only he had a chance to try it. Their one nocturnal adventure at the cabin had taken place in the autumn months of their engagement a quarter of a century ago. The couple had felt compelled to make a getaway from a soporific public-library lecture on the ramifications of the then-new Medicare program. At twenty-five, Judith hadn't much cared, but she and Joe had been forced to give Gertrude a convincing excuse for their late return. Judith had told her mother they'd gotten trapped in the reference section. Gertrude had retorted that they'd probably been stuck under "S"—for Smut. The memory—not of Gertrude's disapproval, but of crisp autumn leaves, a hint of frost, and the river turned to gold in the mellow sun—prevented Judith from chiding Joe.

"We'll be home by nine tomorrow night," she said in a meek voice. "Miss me?"

Her husband chuckled. "I haven't had time. I got home from that police-guild meeting at nine-thirty, and then it took almost an hour to pry your mother out of the can."

"Mother got stuck in the bathroom?" Judith's voice was strident with alarm.

"Not *that* can," Joe replied. "She'd opened up some chili and was eating it cold, straight out of the can. She got her fist wedged. Carl Rankers and I finally poured vegetable oil into the can and then we managed to pull her loose. She's mad as a hornet and swears she can't shuffle cards because her fingers are swollen."

"Oh, good grief!" Judith spun around in the phone booth. "She's okay, though? How long was she stuck? Did she phone you at the house or just screech?"

"She heard me pull the MG into the garage," Joe explained in his normal, casual tone. "Then she used her free hand to flash the lights on and off in the apartment. I don't think she'd been waiting too long. It was her mid-evening snack. She'd had pickled pigs' feet for dinner. Or supper, as your dear mother calls it."

Assured that Gertrude was all of a piece, Judith finally exchanged good-night kisses with Joe over the phone line. Renie, carrying a flashlight, was waiting on the dirt road.

"Where were you? I was getting worried."

Judith explained, at least about Gertrude. She'd save the B&B plan for morning. Renie was unmoved by her aunt's predicament.

"She did it on purpose, of course," Renie said as they locked up for the night.

Judith looked perplexed. "No—well—maybe. Because I left?"

Renie raised both eyebrows. "Because you left her with Joe."

"Oh," said Judith. *"Oh."*

"You're crazy," Renie said flatly as she dredged the breakfast trout in seasoned flour. "There's a world of difference between having a B & B in the heart of the city and one sixty miles away, up in the mountains. You've got the weather factor, with snow for more than three months of the year, the annual flood threat, and windstorms from October to April. You'd have to add more than two bedrooms, not to mention your basic plumbing and a couple of baths. New kitchen, wiring throughout, parking, and furniture that doesn't look like it was part of a post-Hiroshima clearance sale. Why, you'd have to tear the whole thing down and start over. Clear more land. Plant a garden. Make real trails, instead of using the old tree blazes my father hacked out. Then you get to the operation itself. Impossible. You're one person, coz, and you're not invincible. And what about the rest of us? Where do we come in?"

Judith was getting out eggs and juice. "Well, nobody comes up here much. Not even us. It seems a shame to let the place just sit and molder."

"Who knows how our offspring—Mike, Anne, Tony, Tom—will feel about it a few years from now? They're still kids, really. Someday they'll have families of their own." Renie turned the trout in the skillet of hot butter. "Not to mention the rest of the next generation. Cousin Sue's boys have already shown more interest than anybody, but that's because they're the oldest of the grandchildren."

"There's always the time-share possibility," Judith said, but her voice was already wavering, along with her will.

"Aaaargh! I can see the nightmare that'd cause." Renie stepped aside as Judith put the bread in the oven to make toast. "Ten grand? I say thirty, easy. Honestly, coz, I don't get what you're thinking of."

The excitement that Judith had felt earlier had been dampened not only by a night's sleep, but also by Renie's negative reaction. Under the stars, in the moonlight, with Joe parading plans over the phone, the potential of another B&B had seemed dazzling. By dawn's not-so-early light, it was more like a bad dream.

"Maybe," Judith mumbled, shaking salt and pepper onto the fried eggs, "it was a ruse."

"Maybe," Renie assented. Once again, she seemed much more alert at 8:30 A.M. than was customary. "He's devious, I'll give him that."

"He needn't worry," Judith declared, turning the bread over in the oven. "We're leaving today. We can hardly get into trouble in the next few hours."

Even as she spoke, Trouble was approaching in the form of Undersheriff Abbott N. Costello and Deputy Dabney Plummer. Judith and Renie had just sat down to breakfast when the law officers arrived at the door.

"Damn!" muttered Judith, getting up to let them in. "Isn't it a little early to start work?"

Apparently it was not. Costello and Plummer pulled chairs up to the table. The offer of coffee was accepted. From the looks of longing on both men's faces, it seemed that the offer of much more would not have been taken amiss. Judith started to weaken and suggest some toast, but a chilling glance from Renie deterred her. Indeed, Renie seemed to be eating very fast.

"We hear there's a missing painting," Costello said, his eye on Judith's plate. "We hear you got a freebie."

Judith waved her fork. "We don't have it now. It's been stolen."

Costello dumped a large quantity of sugar into his coffee. "You know who took it?"

With her mouth full, Renie shook her head. She seemed to give Judith an extra nod, as if urging her to do or say something. Judith complied as discreetly as possible.

"We know who was here while the canvas was in the cabin," she said. "But we have no proof, and somebody else might have come along, too. We're not even sure the painting we had was 'Spring River.' Riley didn't call it anything except a landscape. Have you asked Dewitt Dixon or Clive Silvanus?"

Costello erupted with his nasty chuckle. "Now, what kind of dumbbells do you take us for? 'Course we asked 'em. They claim ignorance, which is probably about right, since they strike me as a pair of idiots. You sound like that Takisaki dame. She seems to think one of them made off with the picture." He leaned forward, his hat almost touching Judith's shoulder. "Say there, where'd you get those trout?"

Renie swallowed hard, then leaned back in her chair. "What trout?"

Costello's eyes narrowed as he looked from Renie to Judith's plate, where the last of the four fish remained almost intact. "*Those* trout. You two been fishing?"

Judith suddenly realized why Renie had eaten so fast—and had urged her to do the same. "Us? Fishing?" Judith's black eyes grew very wide as she stared at the undersheriff. "Where?"

Costello gave her a scornful look. "I can write a citation for that," he snarled. "A hundred-dollar fine each, plus the possibility of thirty days in jail. How'd you like that?"

Renie burst into sobs. "How cruel! How monstrous! And all because we're sentimental fools! May Mary Most Holy defend us! And St. Izaak Walton protect us!" She crossed herself rapidly.

"What?" Costello appeared justifiably confused. "What are you talking about?"

Sniffling into her napkin, Renie seemed to be struggling for control. "Judith's late husband was an ardent angler. His greatest joy was reeling in those frisky rainbows. He died up by the Green Mountain Inn, near that riffle where the willows come forth in the spring. Just the day before yesterday we buried his ashes out there by the vine maples. To commemorate him, we fixed fish for breakfast." She hung her head. "We bought our little trout at Falstaff's Market on Heraldsgate Hill. I think it was flown in from Japan."

Costello wore a dubious expression; Dabney Plummer looked a trifle pale. "You buried some guy in the front yard?" Costello asked in a slightly scandalized voice.

Still wiping at her eyes, Renie stood up. "It's not illegal. It's our property. Come on, I'll show you. We even made a little cross of twigs to mark the spot."

"Never mind," Costello said hastily. "We're outta here." He practically ran to the front door, Dabney Plummer chugging along behind him.

"Izaak Walton was an Anglican," Judith said after the lawmen had left.

"I know *that.*" Renie munched on her fourth piece of toast.

"You could have gotten us in trouble. What if it *isn't* legal to bury ashes in the front yard? And Dan was too lazy to walk up to the Green Mountain Inn, let alone go fishing. Costello might have tried to prosecute us. Since when have you told such outrageous tales?"

"Since I had visions of that goon of an undersheriff confiscating our trout," Renie answered, now a bit cross. "Why should you always be the one with the big fat fibs? I thought I was pretty good."

Judith sighed, extracting a few bones from the white meat of her trout. "At least they didn't press us about who was here Tuesday evening. By the way, did you catch Lark's comment last night about how Dewitt watched her painting in Riley's studio?"

Renie had. The cousins wondered why Dewitt had lied about knowing Lark. "To be fair," Renie pointed out, "he said he'd never met her. And he didn't, not really."

After polishing off the rest of her breakfast, Judith pushed her chair back. "It also meant he was pulling the wool over somebody's eyes when he pretended to be surprised to learn that Lark was an artist. Who was he lying to? Us? Or Erica?"

"All of the above," Renie replied, "but only because we happened to be there. He can't give a damn about us. So why doesn't he want his wife to know? This gets goofier and goofier."

Judith agreed. While cleaning up from breakfast, the cousins debated the wisdom of ransacking Clive's room at the Green Mountain Inn or breaking into the Dixons' cabin at the Woodchuck Auto Court. They were convinced they might find the missing canvas in one of those places. But in the end, they vetoed both ideas as too risky. Instead, they decided to call on Nella Lablatt.

Nella was a woman not merely of an uncertain age, but of an unspecified century. She could have been born anywhere between the surrender of Geronimo in 1886 and the passage of woman suffrage in 1920. Nella wasn't coy about her age—she was absolutely reticent. Nor had she ever acknowledged her place of birth. As far as the cousins were concerned, she had been a fixture on the river for as long as they could remember—and, according to the real old-timers, quite a while before that. Nella was a pioneer, a legend, and, as she was wont to say, "The best damned postmistress Ike ever had until he treated me like Mussolini."

If she had been around in the so-called Gay Nineties of the last century, she was still there in the same decade of the twentieth. "Gay" had meant something quite different a hundred years ago, but Nella had kept up on all phases of life. She was plugged into a Walkman when Judith and Renie appeared at her door.

"Yo! Sir Mix-a-Lot," she shouted, pointing to her headphones. " 'Baby Got Back' is the bees' knees!"

The cousins smiled, somewhat thinly, and waited for Nella to finish bouncing around her living room. With a final flip of her fingers and hips, she yanked off the headphones and beamed at her guests.

"So what's happening? I hear you were with Iris when

she found the late Riley Tobias. Tough aggies, that." Nella growled out the words, looking angry. "You live long enough, you see everything. I've had a lot of neighbors croak on me, but Riley is the first one to get himself murdered." Shaking off such gloomy thoughts, she beamed again at the cousins. "How are you two? Talk about a sight for sore eyes! I remember when the both of you were knee-high to a jackrabbit." She pointed first at Renie. "You were the puny one, built like a bean." Then she turned to Judith. "And you, Tubby, I used to take you for a beach ball! Talk about round! Why, I could have rolled you all the way into Glacier Falls! What happened? You look better. Older, but better."

Judith blinked several times, trying to adjust to Nella Lablatt's rapid-fire delivery. It was said of Nella that the only thing she ever got out faster than the mail was her tongue. It was also said that she put out almost as fast as she got out. Or something like that. With five husbands to her credit, Judith had never doubted it.

"I suppose Iris told you about the prowler," Judith began.

Nella cut her short. "She sure did. That's nothing new around here. But murder is. I wish I'd been home Tuesday. I might have seen whoever it was that killed Riley." Her bright blue eyes studied the window that looked out onto the stand of cottonwood trees separating the Lablatt and Tobias properties. "I hear somebody stole a painting, too. I hope it's one of Riley's plug-uglies and not something nice. He really lost it this past year, you know. How about a pick-me-up?"

Judith declined; it was far too early for the cousins to imbibe. Nella had no such compunction. Her small, square figure toddled on tiny feet to a counter which had once served postal customers and was now a wet bar. "Why do you think Riley went sour?" Judith inquired.

"Conceit," Nella replied. The old post office safe apparently served as a liquor cabinet. "Riley thought he was God Almighty. Guess what, he wasn't." She leaned down to hear the combination of the safe click. The living room was a virtual museum in miniature of the past century. Every nook and cranny of the small space was filled with mohair chairs, a tweed sofa with chrome legs, a lamp base shaped like a Maxfield Parrish nude, a Danish-modern coffee table, crocheted antimacassars, knitted doilies, paintings by Riley Tobias and Ward Kimball—as well as prints by Andrew Wyeth, Georgia O'Keefe, and Roy Liechtenstein—Ansel Adams photographs, and a framed picture of Dwight D. Eisenhower with his front teeth blacked out.

"It's a shame," Nella continued, placing a champagne bottle and a tulip-shaped glass on the counter. "Riley was very talented. It's too bad he died, of course, but maybe it was just in time. Some people shouldn't live so long." Her round, pink-cheeked face beamed at the cousins, clearly indicating she didn't deserve to be numbered among the prematurely dead.

"You mean he was self-destructive?" Renie asked, gingerly sitting down in a Pennsylvania Dutch rocker.

Nella was quick of mind, but not always hasty in rendering opinions. She took a moment to consider Renie's question. "No—not that. But he'd outlived his talent, if you ask me. It happens. Take Madame Schumann-Heink. Remember how she went around giving farewell concerts for about ten years? No, of course you don't; it was before your time. But you get my meaning."

"Was Riley drinking a lot?" Judith asked. Pushing aside some magazines, a crossword-puzzle dictionary, and a pile of postcards featuring Venice, she settled farther back on the maroon Victorian love seat.

Nella closed the safe. "No, not him. A few beers, that was it. He was more the kind to drive other people to drink."

She poured herself a glass of champagne and offered a toast: "To Riley. He's with the Immortals."

Judith asked about Dewitt and Erica Dixon. Had Nella met them?

"Pair of snobs," Nella declared, adjusting the waistband

on her magenta sweat suit. "But nice enough, once you get past the phony-baloney. Mrs. Dixon knows her gardening. I showed off my early bulbs when she was here last month."

A sudden thought struck Judith, but she held her tongue. It was Renie who posed the next question: "What about Clive Silvanus?"

Nella drained her glass. "Shifty. But he's done well by Riley. He brought me some of his momma's recipes. Chitlins, okra, grits—all that Southern stuff. Not bad. I canned the okra."

Nella, the cousins knew, was an infamous canner. Over the years, the shelves in her icehouse had been filled with everything from candied carrots to calf's brains. Much of it looked revolting, but Nella's diet was a testimony to longevity.

Judith was reminded of the need for ice. But Nella only laughed, her square little body jiggling inside the sweat suit. "Goodness, I haven't had ice in there for years, not since Kenmore and I got our first Crosley. Or was it Crosley I bought the first Kenmore with? I forget."

Thankful that Nella hadn't numbered an Admiral and a Magic Chef among her husbands, Judith allowed that they would probably get along without more ice. "In this warm weather, it melted faster than we expected," she explained. "We've got beer and eggs and butter and milk and juice, but they should keep."

Nella brightened. "Juice? Come out and see my rhubarb juice. The color's something to behold, like pink pearls. Goes good with champagne, too."

Obediently, the cousins trooped after Nella, through the compact kitchen and the enclosed back porch, then down the stone path. The icehouse was six feet by eight feet, lined with shelves and crammed with cartons. The array of jars was dazzling in itself, but what caught Judith's eye was a canvas leaning against a stack of paraffin boxes.

"What's that?" she asked, staring at the painting.

Nella was taking a quart jar from a middle shelf.

"What? Oh, that. One of Riley's pictures. Pretty, huh? But wait till you see this rhubarb juice!"

Judith, however, was transfixed by the canvas. So, it seemed, was Renie, who stood at her elbow. Soft pastels created a flowing river that seemed to move among the boulders. Sunlight dappled the ripples, highlighting the pebbles beneath the surface. On the bank, graceful ferns appeared to sway in a gentle breeze. To Judith's untutored eye, the painting had a Monet-like quality. A rainbow of colors filled the canvas—muted green, purple, pink, brown, yellow, and blue, melting together as if fresh from Mother Nature's palette. The style was hauntingly familiar, though Judith couldn't place it in recent memory. Perhaps she'd seen an early Tobias like it in his living room, or at Ward's house, or even at Nella's.

"How did you get that?" Judith finally asked in awe.

Nella was turning the blue-tinged jar in her hands, letting it catch the sunlight streaming through the open door. "You cut up the rhubarb, put it in a flat-bottomed saucepan, and add just enough water to—"

"No, Nella," Judith interrupted. "I mean the painting. It's absolutely breathtaking."

As she glanced at the painting, Nella's improbably smooth forehead creased a bit. "Yes, yes, it's very nice, as I said. Riley had his moments. But canning's an art, too. One of the secrets is to make sure your fruit is underripe—" She broke off, cocking her head. "What's that? I heard someone call me."

Nella's hearing was obviously keener than that of the cousins. Judith thought she heard an unusual noise, but it was more of a loud hum than a voice. Neither she nor Renie heard Nella's name called out until they were at the door of the icehouse.

"It's Lark Kimball," Nella said. "Wait here. I'll go get her." She scooted down the path and around the side of the house to the front door.

"Well?" Judith gave Renie a meaningful look.

Renie turned slightly, glancing over her shoulder at the canvas. " 'Spring River'?"

"I'd bet on it," Judith replied. "Now *that's* worth five figures—if anything is that doesn't have three rooms and a roof."

A droll smile played at Renie's mouth. "Well, this is as good a place as any to ditch it. If that's what somebody did. It's sure not the painting Riley gave you. Where did this one come from?"

Judith shrugged. "Damned if I know. Another present?"

Renie's answer was cut off by the appearance of Nella, with Lark Kimball on her arm. "Ward dropped Lark off for a visit on his way up to the Green Mountain Inn. I want to give her a jar of chokecherry jam. Come, Lark. There's no step."

The cousins exchanged greetings with Lark; then, on a sudden whim, Judith followed Nella and her latest guest back into the icehouse.

"Lark," Judith began, realizing that three made a crowd in the little structure, "don't think this is an idiotic question, but do you know what 'Spring River' looked like? I mean, could you see it well enough to recognize it, or did Riley describe it to you?"

Lark's smile was both patronizing and tolerant. "I know what it looked like. My fingers make up for much of what my eyes miss."

"Of course." Judith took Lark's hand. "Tell me, is this 'Spring River'?"

Lark bent down, her face almost touching the canvas. She peered at the painting for a long time, then slowly ran her dainty fingers over the surface. Renie leaned forward in the doorway. Nella scanned a bottom shelf, looking for jam. Judith stood directly behind Lark, who traced delicate blue flowers, slim green reeds, subtle soft ridges that evoked the river's flow.

It dawned on Judith that she hadn't checked for a signature. Indeed, the canvas might be marked on the back. Perhaps there was no mystery to its identity. She was about to say as much when Lark turned away from the painting, gazing, more or less, at Judith.

Lark surprised all of them by bursting into a merry gale of laughter. Even Nella, with a pint jar clutched in her hands, looked up. "How funny!" Lark said at last, between giggles. "Whyever did you think that was 'Spring River'? It's not even one of Riley's works." Her laughter subsided, and the long pale lashes dipped on her cheeks. The golden hair lay in soft tendrils around her face. "I did this. It's mine."

ELEVEN

"I CALL IT 'Morning,' " Lark explained to her astonished listeners. "It's one of a series. I finished 'Dawn' last winter. I'm working on 'Midday' now."

Judith's jaw dropped; Renie gaped; Nella handed the pint jar to Lark. "Here, dear. Try this on whole wheat toast." Nella gazed benignly at the cousins. "Well, I *thought* it was Riley's. He brought it over here last week." She turned to Lark. "It's very nice. It certainly reminds me of Riley's paintings when he was much younger. You could actually see things in them, instead of blobs and daubs. But then, I'm no art expert."

"Why," Judith asked as Nella guided Lark out of the icehouse, "did Riley bring that canvas to the icehouse in the first place?" A glance at Lark's clouded face told Judith that the younger woman was wondering the same thing.

"Oh," Nella answered in less than her usual assured manner, "he said something about the weather getting warmer and that he wanted a cool place to store the picture while it dried. Does that make sense, Lark?"

"No," Lark responded. "It would dry more quickly where it was warm, of course. Besides, I finished it almost a month ago. Tempera doesn't take that long to dry under any conditions."

"Artists are peculiar people," Nella declared, opening the back door for her guests. "Present company excepted." She gave Lark's arm an affectionate squeeze. "Even your father can be odd sometimes. I thought about marrying him once, but that was before I got rid of Delmar and took up with Crosley. Or was it Kenmore? I forget."

Judith waited for Nella to help Lark sit down on the love seat. Some of the postcards and the crossword-puzzle dictionary fell on the floor. Judith stooped to pick them up. "Haven't you wondered where your painting was?" she asked Lark.

Lark's reaction was one of bafflement. "I assumed it was at Riley's studio. I finished it there, under his tutelage. Why should I think it was gone?"

Briefly, Judith berated herself. She wasn't used to walking in the shoes of a person with severely impaired sight. Lark's world was very different. So much could not be taken for granted. "Why do you think Riley put 'Morning' in Nella's icehouse?"

Lark's frown deepened. "I can't imagine. I've got 'Midday' at my father's studio. He brought it home the day Riley died. I let Riley send 'Dawn' to his brother, Yancey."

Renie, who had been leaning against a Queen Anne breakfront crammed with china and souvenirs, gave a little start. "Was it a birthday present?" she asked.

A wistful smile played at Lark's lips. "How did you know? Riley, as usual, had forgotten to get his brother a gift. He asked if I'd mind if he sent my painting. I said I'd be pleased—especially if Yancey enjoyed it."

"Did he?" inquired Renie with a quick glance at Judith.

Lark was looking forlorn, her hands tucked inside the sleeves of a baggy pink cardigan. "I don't know. Riley hadn't heard from Yancey for a couple of months. Neither of them were much at writing letters, and you know how Riley hated the phone."

The glimmer of an idea was forming in Judith's mind. "When was Yancey's birthday? March?"

Lark inclined her head, obviously trying to remember. "Yes. March fifteenth. The Ides of March—that's how I can remember it."

The conversation turned to more mundane matters. Judith flipped through the postcards from Venice. Renie admired Nella's fancywork. Lark expressed her delight over the chokecherry jam. Nella showed off her latest tapes, which ran the gamut from rap and reggae to Rodgers and Hart.

"How was your trip?" Judith asked, realizing that she and Renie had neglected to inquire about Nella's latest visit to her relatives.

At the wet bar, Nella was removing the cork from the champagne bottle. "Fine, lovely, wonderful. Lark—how about a bit of bubbly?"

Lark requested sherry instead. Nella rummaged around in the safe and came up with a bottle from Portugal.

"Your family must be scattered all over," Judith remarked. "Where did you go this time?"

Nella was looking at her watch. "Now, girls, it's after ten. Surely you won't refuse a dollop of sherry. This is good stuff. You wouldn't want to waste it in a casserole."

Reluctantly, Judith and Renie gave in. "I remember some of your grandchildren," Judith continued doggedly, still trying to pin Nella down about her travels. "They used to spend summers up here. Do they live close by?"

"They're all over the map," Nella replied blithely. "Great-children, too, and now four great-greats. You name a city, even a country, and I can point to some of my own." She handed out the sherry glasses. "Tell me about your boy, Judith. He must be almost ready for college."

Judith winced. "He should have been done with college by now. Kids these days take their time. Mike's majoring in forestry. With any luck, he'll graduate this term. And if miracles still happen, he'll get a job."

Lark sipped her sherry, then gave a little sniff. "Why do

parents always insist that their children get jobs? Dad constantly harps about me going to work. Why can't mothers and fathers just be satisfied to let their children *be?* Riley thought that life was a full-time job, and I think he was right."

Judith raised her eyebrows; Renie bristled. But Lark wasn't finished:

"It's fine for somebody like Iris to dash around, making herself important as a color consultant. But for people who really want to get something out of life, a job just gets in the way."

"Maybe Iris likes to eat," Renie pointed out with bite in her voice.

The argument cut no ice with Lark. "Iris is a leech. She sponged off Riley, and spent her own money on herself. All those clothes and that condo in town." Lark looked disdainful.

Nella, who was now sitting cross-legged on the floor, scowled over the rim of her champagne glass. "Lark, don't be mean-minded. Iris was very fond of Riley. I went to see her after I got home last night and she cried all over me. Have a little heart, honey. What have I been telling you?"

Lark's fine molded chin jutted. "You don't listen, Nella. You're just like Dad. You treat me as if I were a helpless child! My God, I'm thirty-two years old; I'm a woman with real emotions! Why can't you people understand that being almost blind only means that you can't see well, not that you can't feel deeply?"

Judith glanced at Renie, who responded with an almost-imperceptible nod of her head. The cousins tossed off their sherry. "It sounds to me as if you two buddies need to talk privately," Judith said, hoping to strike an ameliorating note. "We'd better get back to the cabin and clean the downspouts. Say, Nella, have you got a ladder we could borrow?"

Nella did, and the request seemed to break the spell of hostility. Five minutes later, the cousins were coming up their dirt drive, carrying the ladder at each end.

"So what's your reaction to the birthday present?" Judith asked as they positioned the ladder at the near side of the cabin.

"Mixed," Renie replied. "Yancey hated it, according to the letter. But he thought Riley had painted it. Now why would Riley pass Lark's work off as his own?"

"I put that notebook of Clive's in my purse. I want to check something before I answer that." Judith stepped on the first rung, testing the ladder's stability. "You better get a broom. I think there's an old one under the house." She waited while Renie crawled around, hit her head, swore, and finally reappeared with a much-abused broom.

"That's a mess," Judith declared. "Still, maybe it'll work." She started up the ladder, but froze on the third rung from the top. Her gaze was fixed on the window into the loft.

"What is it?" Renie demanded.

Judith dropped the broom and hurriedly climbed back down. "It's Clive Silvanus. Quick, let's head him off at the Dutch door."

"Ah declare," Clive said, looking flustered but not unduly alarmed, "Ah hope you have seen mah LaGrange College ring, class of 1965?"

"Afraid not," Judith answered tersely. "How did you get in, Mr. Silvanus?"

"Just call me Clive." His mustache twitched as he smiled at the cousins. "And then call me Clever." Reaching into the pocket of his tan polyester pants, he hauled out a big ring loaded with keys. "It's a wonder Ah don't walk lopsided. But these do come in handy now and then. You were nowhere to be found, so Ah thought you wouldn't mind if Ah came in to look for—"

"We do mind, kiddo," Renie interrupted. "You're damned lucky we didn't swat you with that old broom out there. We also mind that you're lying through your teeth. You wouldn't be looking for a notebook, would you?"

Clive evinced surprise. "A notebook? Now that you mention it, Ah do believe Ah did misplace mine somewhere." He started to exit the cabin, but Judith and Renie formed a barrier. "Excuse me, ladies, but Ah must be on my way. It is with regret that Ah must consider mah class ring lost. It meant a lot to me."

The cousins stood firm. "Don't you want your notebook?" Judith asked, going eyeball-to-eyeball with Clive. "We found it under the bed in the loft. Why don't you tell us how it got there?"

Clive chewed at his upper lip, threatening to devour his mustache. His eyes darted around the cabin, as if he could find a logical explanation in the knotty pine paneling. "Ah was in a daze? Ah was fleein' snakes? Ah never met a ladder Ah didn't climb? Oh, shoot!" He pounded his fist into his palm and shook his head. "What difference does it make? You wouldn't believe me anyways."

"Try us," urged Renie, looking more pugnacious than usual. "Here's a hint—were you searching for a painting Riley gave my cousin?"

Now Clive's expression of surprise was even more exaggerated. "Riley *gave* that picture away? Well, now! And here Ah thought it had been misplaced!"

"So you took it back," Judith said in a reasonable tone. "Where is it?"

Clive was looking more uncomfortable by the second. His mustache seemed to droop with the rest of him. "That's hard to say." He ran a finger inside his shirt collar, while beads of perspiration popped out on his forehead. "Did Riley tell you what that painting was called?"

"No," Judith replied honestly.

Clive gulped. "Then let's call it 'Missing.' " He staggered a bit, then gave Judith a beseeching look. "Ah don't suppose you've got any of that fine bourbon left? Ah could use a drink."

Grudgingly, Renie poured out the last shot from the pint bottle. "No ice," she said in a sour voice. "We're almost out of that, too."

Clive Silvanus had sat down on the sofa. He loosened his brown striped tie and unbuttoned the top of his beige shirt. "Ah'm flummoxed," he mumbled, taking a big pull on the bourbon. Neither Judith nor Renie asked why; instead, they waited for their uninvited guest to explain.

"Riley told me he'd given you that painting for safe-keepin'." Clive's eyes were pleading, looking not unlike those of a puppy who expects to get swatted with a rolled-up newspaper. "After the poor man got himself killed, Ah got worried. No offense intended, but Ah didn't think this was a very good place for keepin' a painting worth seventy thousand dollars. Ah came over here and pretended to get a bit tiddly, and hoped you two might go out for a spell. You did, and right after that, who should show up but Dewitt? He told me Iris couldn't come up with the painting he'd bought for his wife's gallery. So naturally, Ah thought that somehow Riley had given you Dewitt's picture. It wasn't hard to find in this little place. Ah felt obligated to hand it over to Dewitt."

The cousins stared at Clive Silvanus. Outside, birds chirruped and the river rolled. The silence inside the cabin was unsettling. Indeed, Clive seemed more than unsettled: He seemed to be growing despondent.

"Why," Judith asked, still speaking in a reasonable tone, "do you think Riley gave us a painting that belonged to the Dixons?"

Clive frantically scratched his bald spot. "Ah told you, Riley did odd things. What matters is that the Dixons got their painting." Despite the assertion, gloom settled in over Clive as he drank the dregs of his bourbon and apparently tasted despair.

In the old pine deck chair, Renie was looking puzzled. "Wait a minute, Clive—what did you mean when you said we should call the painting 'Missing'?"

"What?" Clive looked as perplexed as Renie. "Ah don't know—Ah spoke out of turn. These last few days have made a mess of mah nerves." He stood up, his legs wobbly.

Judith retrieved Clive's notebook from her purse, but not before she had checked one of the notations. Clive accepted the notebook without enthusiasm. Making commiserating noises, Judith saw their guest to the door. After Clive had made his heavy-footed way back down the road, she turned to Renie.

"Well?"

"Something's missing, but it's not the painting Riley gave you," Renie replied. "Want to bet that Nella has a seventy-thousand-dollar painting in her icehouse, right next to the rhubarb juice?"

Judith sat down on the couch. "Here's what I think, coz. Riley had lost it. Lark is very talented, and Riley knew it—even if she doesn't. Let's assume that Hong Kong collector who bought 'Autumn Images' never saw the painting itself—he or she knew only that it was a Tobias, which it no doubt was. But what if A.—for Anonymous?—did see Lark's work, loved it, and thought Riley had done it? Riley doesn't let on, sells Lark's 'Dawn' as his 'Spring Meadow,' and says he's given her painting to his brother as a birthday present."

"Ah!" Renie angled one leg over the arm of the deck chair. "But in reality, he sends his own failure to Yancey, who hates it. Then he gives you his ugly version of 'Spring River.' Meanwhile, he hides Lark's 'Morning' canvas in Nella's icehouse until Dewitt comes to collect it. But Riley got killed before Dewitt showed up."

"But he didn't," Judith protested. "Dewitt *did* see Riley Tuesday afternoon. Riley said he had to wait for Clive." She lifted her eyebrow at Renie in a significant gesture.

It took a moment for Judith's insinuation to dawn on Renie. "Riley might have meant what he said . . . Clive *is* the moneyman. But if Dewitt knew what he was buying—and if the painting he saw was in Nella's icehouse—how would Dewitt know that, though?"

Judith smirked at Renie. "Maybe Riley told him. Dewitt wouldn't want us to know that he knew. Not if he was the one prowling around Nella's about the time Riley was killed."

"So is Clive lying or being duped?" Once again, Renie

looked perplexed. "Did Dewitt take Riley's canvas—*your* canvas—under false pretenses?"

"That I don't know," Judith admitted. "At this point, I'm more interested in opportunity than motive. Clive saw Riley, Dewitt saw Riley, everybody saw Riley. Even Lark could have been there at some point, maybe while Ward was looking for her."

"You're right," Renie said, her brow clearing. "The only person who is definitely out of it is Erica Dixon, because she was en route from Europe."

Judith was wearing a sly expression. "Was she?"

"Huh?" Renie frowned at her cousin.

Picking up Clive's empty glass, Judith carried it to the sink. "We could use some more water. Maybe we should call on Iris." She spoke almost absently.

"Back up," Renie urged, getting out of the deck chair. "What about Erica?"

"It's just one of my crazy ideas," Judith said. "I may be wrong, so let's skip it for now." She bent down to get the empty bucket out from under the sink.

"Oh, no, you don't!" Renie gave a mock kick in the vicinity of Judith's rear end. "You've pulled this crap on me before. Give, coz, or you'll be wearing that bucket on your head instead of carrying it in your hands."

Judith sighed. "Okay, but don't you dare laugh. Remember how I was asking Nella about her trip? She evaded me like crazy. I tried to pin her down about where she'd gone, but she managed to divert the conversation. On top of that, I noticed that those postcards from Italy—the ones she had on the love seat—were blank." Judith waited for Renie to catch on.

"Meaning they weren't from someone? They're souvenirs?" Renie made a face. "Are you trying to say that Nella—not Erica—went to Europe? Whoa!"

"What if neither of them went abroad? I can't think of a motive for Nella, but Erica might have wanted to get her mitts on more of Riley's paintings. She admitted as much," Judith reminded Renie. "So maybe Erica coerced Nella into taking her place on the trip to provide an alibi if a theft—or worse—was in the works."

Renie leaned on one of the stools next to the small counter that divided the kitchen from the living room. "Too weird, coz. What would Erica do? Offer a bribe? Blackmail Nella? Haven't we got enough suspects without adding Erica and Nella to the list?"

Judith's lips tightened. "You can't go by the numbers. The killer could be anybody. Oh, I know, I know. It doesn't make any sense." She headed for the door. "But you've got to admit it's a bit queer. Why won't Nella say where she was? How do we know Erica was out of the country? We only have her word—and Dewitt's—for it."

"That," Renie replied, "can be checked. You'd better call Joe."

"Not yet," said Judith. "Besides, I'm supposed to be planning Mountainside Manor."

"You've already got a name for it?" Renie locked the door.

"Shut up," said Judith.

"I just did," said Renie.

Judith gazed at the lock on the Dutch door. "Why bother?"

"What about the downspouts?"

Judith shot Renie a rueful look. "With any luck, somebody will steal them."

"Why?" Renie inquired.

"Why not?" said Judith.

Iris Takisaki was up to her perfectly plucked eyebrows in paperwork when the cousins arrived. "Insurance forms, obituaries, correspondence—if the usual demands of death weren't enough, Riley let things slide." She tapped a stack of mail with a silver ballpoint pen. "Some of this goes back to March. He should have hired a secretary instead of relying on me. I've got my own career. I used to tell him that, but he'd just give me that big grin and say he didn't trust anybody else."

Judith and Renie expressed sympathy for Iris's burdens. She was sitting at a deal table in the living room, the sunlight filtered by half-closed blue blinds. The cluttered area looked in more disarray than usual, with file boxes stacked in one corner, several cartons in another, and portfolios on every possible surface. It appeared that Iris had even begun to clear out the studio. Several wrapped canvases were lined up against one wall. The box of paints the cousins had seen earlier now reposed next to the hearth.

"I want to get everything done as quickly as possible," Iris said, following the cousins' gaze around the room. "Personal, professional, whatever, it's all got to be organized and taken care of. I'd like to have this place on the market by June first. I never want to see it again after that." She slammed a ledger shut for emphasis.

Judith expressed surprise. "I thought you liked it up here on the river, Iris."

Iris let out a big sigh. "I did. But it's got too many horrible memories now. I told myself I could change my mind and be sorry if I sold the property right away. But summer is the time to find a buyer, and frankly, I'd like to put all of this behind me." She waved a hand at the room, but she obviously meant much more than four walls and a picture window.

It was Renie who broached the subject of Riley's recent sales. Iris evinced interest. "I recall something about autumn," she responded. "Lots of brown and orange and gold. Riley let me see what he was working on as long as I didn't make a pest of myself. As far as I know, Mr. Kwan bought it sight unseen, which isn't so unusual. What's your point?"

"Was it ugly?" Renie asked point-blank.

Iris looked affronted. "Ugly? No, of course not. But," she added, her expression turning thoughtful, "it was rather discordant. Much of his last work was, you know."

"Clive said 'Spring Meadow' was sold to an art dealer in mid-March, but he didn't tell us who," Judith put in, stretching the truth about their source of information. It wasn't a lie, she told herself: Clive's *notebook* had told her and Renie about the sale. "Do you remember that one?"

"Vaguely." Iris remained pensive. "I don't know who bought it—it was a 'blind' sale." She grimaced slightly. "No, I'm not poking fun at Lark—she might think me cruel, but she's wrong. What I mean is that the buyer wanted to remain anonymous."

"Would Clive know who it was?" Judith asked, more from curiosity than from a sense of sleuthing.

Iris considered. "Probably not. Such sales are very discreet. At those prices, the purchaser deserves his or her privacy. Riley was pleased, of course. At least for a while." She shook her neatly coiffed head. "He was so up and down. Life with Riley was never smooth." Her smile was tinged with sadness.

Allowing for a brief, tasteful pause, Judith went on. "What we're trying to say is that Riley told Clive he had in fact given me 'Spring River.' But why do you think he'd do such a thing when it was already sold to the Dixons?"

Iris got up from the cane-backed dining room chair in which she'd been sitting. "He liked to tease people. Sometimes, he even liked to set up situations that pitted one person against another. Though I don't know why he'd involve you, Judith. You're outside the art community. That wasn't Riley's way." With a wistful shake of her head, Iris fiddled with the onyx fish amulet that hung at her breast. "I suppose we'll never know, will we?"

But Judith wasn't one to give up when it came to seeking solutions. "Maybe," she allowed, wondering if Iris should be given a look at Lark's painting in Nella's icehouse. She decided against it, afraid that the hostile feelings between Iris and Lark might only cloud the issue.

Sitting on a hassock by the fireplace, Renie looked up from the box of paints she'd been perusing. "Has Dewitt paid for his painting yet?" She nudged the box, but found it too heavy to move.

Iris was lighting a cigarette. "I've no idea. You'd have to ask Clive."

Figuring that was a hopeless idea, Judith didn't comment. She switched conversational directions to the murder investigation. Iris scoffed.

"That idiot of a Costello doesn't know anything. He's all finished with the studio, so I'm free to clean. It was a halfhearted effort, if you ask me. Everything about that undersheriff is ineffectual. Costello insists Riley was drunk when he was killed, which sounds preposterous. But given that, anyone could have strangled him with that wretched picture-hanging wire. Yes, there were fingerprints." She paused to blow out a cloud of smoke. "Riley's, mine, Lazlo's, Ward's, Clive's, Dewitt's, probably yours. And Lark's." She pulled deeply on her cigarette and lifted her eyebrows at the cousins.

"Lark's." Judith ran her tongue over her lips. "Do you think Lark saw Riley the day he was killed?"

Iris was at the liquor cabinet. "Would you like a drink? I don't usually indulge before noon, but it's getting close and I'm a wreck. Martinis?"

"Vodka for me," said Renie, giving up on her attempt to move the heavy box of paints out of the way. It was easier to move the hassock.

"I'm okay with gin," said Judith, her brain still whirling with the logistics of switched canvases. The autumn painting had fetched forty grand, sight unseen. Mr. Kwan of Hong Kong had wanted a Riley Tobias work, and Judith figured that was what he'd gotten. As far as she knew, Lark hadn't painted any autumnal scenes. But the first of the "Spring" paintings had been switched, with Lark's shipped to the anonymous buyer and Riley's sent to his brother. Then the Dixons had come along, and Judith had been the recipient of the real Riley Tobias work. Meanwhile, Riley had hidden Lark's canvas in the icehouse, awaiting delivery. Did Clive know about the switch? It appeared not, or else he wouldn't have given Dewitt the wrong painting. The real question was, did the Dixons know?

Judith heard almost nothing of the conversation between Renie and Iris. They were back to harping on corporate ignorance, with Iris complaining about the need to create a palette of colors for individual companies, and Renie griping about the difficulty of adhering to those same guidelines in graphic design.

Iris busied herself with bottles, glasses, and a shaker, all of which were stored in an eighteenth-century Portuguese armoire. Apparently mistaking Judith's blank expression for boredom, Iris returned to more personal matters. "I don't know what to think about Lark. She had a terrific crush on Riley. He was very sweet with her, as far as I could tell. I think Ward disapproved. Oh, not at first—he felt Riley would make a better teacher, if only because he wasn't her father." She poured out the gin martinis first and handed a glass to Judith. "Except," she added with a strange, bemused look on her oval face, "he was."

TWELVE

JUDITH ALMOST DROPPED her martini. *"What?"* She gaped at Iris.

Iris mixed vodka and vermouth with efficiency. "You never guessed?" She shook her head sadly. "Oh, Riley was a lot younger than Ward's wife. Maybe that was what appealed to her. I wouldn't know—it was before my time. Naturally, Ward was furious. But he'd waited so long to have a child. It's possible he couldn't have any of his own." She stopped talking long enough to give Renie her drink. "Then, when Lark was born blind, Mrs. Kimball—Felice, I think her name was—felt so guilty. And Ward couldn't reproach her. The tragedy was too dreadful. So they pretended the child was his. To compound the disaster, Felice died a few years later. What good would it have done to advertise the truth? Despite her betrayal, Ward had loved his wife. Lark was the cherished legacy from Felice, and it didn't matter who had fathered her."

"Oh, my!" Judith's exclamation was very soft, but nonetheless deeply felt. "Does Lark know?"

"Certainly not." Iris sat down again in the cane-backed chair. "What good would it do to tell her now?

Especially with Ward so ill. Really, he's been a wonderful father."

"But Riley knew?" Renie queried.

Iris nodded vigorously. "Of course. How else would I know?" She bit her lip and frowned. "Oh, dear, I shouldn't have told you. Honestly, I don't know what got into me! All these years I've guarded this secret as if it were my own, and now . . ." She buried her face in her hands.

"It's the strain," Judith offered in consolation. "The truth can't hurt Riley now, I suppose. Though Ward and Lark should still be protected."

Iris looked at Judith between her fingers. A twisted smile played at her lips. "Oh, yes—Lark must always be protected! I wonder what it's like to come into this world and have everyone offer themselves as your personal shield for as long as you live."

Renie gave a little snort. "I don't think Lark looks at it that way."

Putting her chin on her fists, Iris stared out through the slits in the blue blinds. The midday sun was shining directly on the river. The snowfields on Mount Woodchuck seemed to have shrunk in the past twenty-four hours. But Iris didn't seem to be taking in the scenery. Nor did she respond to Renie's remark.

"Shall I fix some lunch?" She was sitting up straight now, her usual brisk manner back in place.

To Judith's surprise, Renie declined. "We've got some stuff at the cabin we ought to eat up before we head home. Thanks, though, Iris."

Sipping their drinks, the three women turned to less volatile matters than Riley's death, missing artwork, and the Kimballs. Real estate seemed a safe topic; they discussed current property values in the country versus in the city. Judith, however, couldn't resist one pointed question:

"Once you sell this place, will the money go into Riley's foundation?"

Iris's face was expressionless. "No. He left me this property. In fact, I own it now. Some years ago, he signed a quitclaim deed. That's why I don't have to hold off for probate or anything like that."

Judith nodded. "That seems fair. You helped keep it up; you lived here, too. You did a lot for Riley. In many ways, you . . . uh . . ." Judith decided to quit while she was ahead. "Twenty years is a long time," she amended.

Now Iris gave Judith a droll look. "There *is* such a thing as a common-law wife. I could qualify, I guess. But it's not necessary. Except for a bequest to his brother, Yancey, everything else Riley acquired goes to the foundation. It'll be wonderful for aspiring minority artists."

Renie was cradling an eighteenth-century creamware potpourri holder in her hands. "What," she asked, "about Riley's personal collection? He has some nice things, like this."

"A good question." Iris smoothed a stray strand of hair away from her forehead. "It's occurred to me that wherever the foundation is ultimately housed, there should also be a museum. Small, of course. Most of the pieces Riley owned were works he admired tremendously. Many of them inspired him in some way. A few were gifts, but all the same, I think that, along with selected paintings and sketches of his, they would make a fitting tribute."

"That sounds like a good idea," Judith commented. "It also sounds like a lot of work. Who's in charge of the foundation?"

Iris carefully set her martini glass on the dining room table. She gave the cousins a self-effacing look. "I am."

"We should drink the rest of the juice," Judith argued as she and Renie crossed the road to the Woodchuck Auto Court. "Why do we need to buy pop?"

"You drink the juice," Renie retorted. "I'm dying for a cream soda. I'd forgotten that I don't like martinis, even ones made out of vodka."

Kennedy Morton was waiting on a customer at the filling station. The cousins went into the office, where Renie delved into the old-fashioned cooler, searching for cream soda. She found a bottle, rather than a can, and appeared very pleased with herself.

The proprietor entered, shaking his head. "People expect too much. Just because I got gas doesn't mean I got tools. I sent that bozo up to Gary Johanson at Green Mountain. Gary knows more about fixing cars than I do." He glanced at the bottle Renie was holding. "That'll be a buck-ten. You need an opener?"

Renie didn't. She paid for the soda, then followed Judith out into the midday sun. "That was a real bombshell about Lark," Renie said, keeping her voice down, since several of the Morton children were tumbling about in the grassy area by the rental cabins.

"It sure was." Judith, however, sounded a bit vague.

"I didn't know what to make of it," Renie went on. "I was kind of surprised that Iris is head of the foundation, too. But I suppose it makes sense."

"Yes, it does." Judith was even more remote. Renie realized they were walking in a circle.

"Buzz, buzz, here's your coz." Renie jabbed at Judith's arm. "What are you doing, jumping into a quandary?"

But Judith merely gave a slight nod in the direction of the little cabins. "Erica Dixon. She's in the doorway. See, you can just make out her white slacks."

"White slacks! Women who wear white slacks should stand on a pedestal with an inscribed plaque at their feet. They must never eat. I couldn't keep white slacks clean for a—"

Erica emerged, interrupting Renie's harangue. Judith called out a greeting. "Are you and Dewitt staying on for the funeral Saturday?" Judith asked as Erica came around the white Mercedes in her white slacks and a black silk blouse.

"We might as well." Erica looked glum. "This is a fine mess, if you ask me."

Four curious faces had slipped up behind Erica. Judith recognized Velvet, Giles, and Rafe. They were joined by a slightly older girl who might or might not have been of school age. It was she who tugged on Erica's white slacks.

"Hey, missus, can we sit in your car? It's pretty and I'm Skye."

Erica glowered at Skye and her siblings, then tried to pull free. She failed. "The car's locked," she said firmly. "Now go away. Please."

Amazingly, the children obeyed, but Erica's formerly pristine slacks now bore several brown marks. Renie snickered behind her hand. Judith tried to cover her cousin's lack of tact by responding to Erica's original complaint:

"You mean the 'Spring River' debacle? I thought Clive had handed it over to you and Dewitt."

Erica rolled her eyes. "Clive! He doesn't even know where the painting is! I refuse to ask Iris. She tries to be polite, but naturally, she resents me. And that Philistine of an undersheriff doesn't seem to care about art! He says the studio at Riley's is full of pictures. Why not just take another one and be done with it?" Erica threw up her hands.

Renie had regained control of her better self. "Gee, I guess we were mistaken. Did you see 'Spring River' in progress? I hear it was . . . intriguing."

"Of course I saw it." Erica gave Renie a petulant look. "It wasn't quite done, but I could tell it was one of the best things Riley had painted in years."

Renie assumed her middle-aged ingenue air. "Interesting. I've heard people talk about 'Spring River' as if Riley had painted it with his lips. Tell me, Erica, did you and your husband see the same picture at the same time?"

Erica was beginning to wilt, from either emotion or the full sun. "No, we didn't. We each made a trip up here. Oh, we came together once, but Riley wouldn't let us see anything but sketches. Then I drove up in early April to see the work in progress, and a couple of weeks ago, after I'd left for Europe, Dewitt came back to finalize things. Riley was almost finished by then." She was fingering her cheek, gazing off in the direction of the gas pumps.

Renie pressed on. "Did your descriptions of the painting agree?"

Erica Dixon made an impatient gesture. "Certainly. Dewitt had to admit that Riley's last landscape had a lyrical quality. My husband realizes he has to put petty jealousies aside when it comes to a serious investment in art."

Back on the grassy patch, the four Mortons had joined hands and were playing something resembling Ring-Around-the-Rosy. Or the Bataan Death March, given the number of punches and kicks that were being exchanged.

Judith's and Renie's gazes locked briefly. It was obvious that they were thinking along the same lines. "So," Judith remarked in a casual voice, "you came up here to discover that Dewitt hadn't yet taken possession of 'Spring River'?"

Erica removed a pair of expensive sunglasses from the pocket of her black silk shirt. "That's right. And Clive insists he can't find it. We don't know whether to sue him or the estate. Dewitt urges caution, but as soon as we get back to town, I'm calling our attorney."

A pickup truck with three teenagers in the back pulled into the filling station. Their radio blared Nirvana. Judith wondered if Nella Lablatt would come out and join them.

"At least you haven't paid for it," Judith shouted over the din.

"What?" Erica yelled back, her piping voice very shrill. "But I have! That's what's so aggravating. I've spent seventy thousand dollars for nothing! Wouldn't you be wild?"

"I'd be broke," Judith muttered, but of course Erica couldn't hear her. The cacophony rose to headache-making proportions. With a nod at Erica, a shake of the head for the pickup, and a gesture to Renie, Judith started for the road. Two minutes later, the cousins were safely within their own gate, entering the cabin.

"Erica's out a bundle," Renie commented.

"And Iris hasn't seen the money." Judith gave Renie a sidelong look.

"Meaning Clive has it? But who's got the Tobias?"

"Dewitt," Judith answered promptly. "But I wonder where. Maybe he dropped it off in town on his way to pick up Erica at the airport."

"So what happens to Lark's canvas?"

Judith didn't feel qualified to answer that question. Making luncheon suggestions was more in her line at the moment. "We have hot dogs and that's it," she said, temporarily giving up on theories. "Do you want to eat at the Green Mountain Inn?"

"No." Renie sighed. "We ought to make good our threat to clean out the icebox. And do likewise with the downspouts. Which comes first?"

In a fit of virtue the cousins opted for labor before leisure. To further enhance their work ethic, they washed windows, too, inside and out. It was after one-thirty when they finished. Renie held up four skinny hot dogs and made a face.

"Where did Falstaff's keep these? In the pet-food section? Maybe we've earned lunch out after all."

Judith was leaning against the linoleum-covered kitchen counter. "We haven't earned anything, coz. I feel like a flop. Joe's pulling my chain about another B & B, Mother got stuck in a can of chili, my house may be under water, and I haven't got the foggiest idea who killed Riley Tobias. The only thing this trip has accomplished is getting Dan out of the basement."

"Maybe he enjoyed the ride." Seeing Judith's long face, Renie immediately regretted her flippancy. "Hey, remember that friend of my mother's, Mrs. Jorkins, who used to take her son, Will, for a Sunday drive? Except Will lived in Wisconsin, so she drove his framed eight-by-ten picture around every weekend?"

A faint smile touched Judith's lips. "Yeah, I remember. Mrs. Jorkins is dead, too."

"But Will isn't. He teaches at the University of Wisconsin. I forget which branch." Renie set out a kettle for the hot dogs.

Rousing herself from lethargy, Judith got busy with carrots and celery sticks. "I guess I'm still bowled over by Iris's revelation about Lark. I wonder if Nella knows."

"She would if anybody did." Renie scooped water out of the fresh bucket they'd brought from Riley's well. "The question is, how does it figure into the murder?"

Tossing carrot peelings and celery leaves into the garbage, Judith gave Renie a rueful look. "I haven't gotten that far. I'm still working on why Riley would propose to his own daughter. At least I've got a plausible answer to that one. Maybe."

Renie juggled hot dog buns. "Gee—I almost forgot about that! 'Weird' doesn't begin to describe it. That's sick." She paused, a knife hovering over the butter dish. "So what's your explanation?"

"It's not a satisfactory one." Judith put the celery and carrots into a tall glass. "I'd guess that Riley was stringing Lark along. Let's say that he had indeed lost it. Or at least gotten off on the wrong track. Along comes Lark, who is very talented. Whether she's Riley's or Ward's daughter doesn't matter in this context—she could inherit her gift from either of them. But she's more than good, she's brilliant. She may not know that. Ward would, but he's overly protective. Perhaps he doesn't want her paintings exposed to the dog-eat-dog art world. Riley, however, takes advantage. He sells them as his own. It's as good as a cash cow. Lark paints; he makes a bundle. Clive can't tell the difference. He's the moneyman. But Riley has to keep Lark at the easel, under his thumb. Am I making sense?"

Renie looked disturbed. "I'm afraid so. Ugh, I don't like it. Riley was so convincing when he talked about painters seeking Truth. I hate to think that he didn't just paint a lie, but was actually living one. It's possible, I suppose."

Judith began to set the table. "There was a chance Ward might see Lark's work out in the world and recognize it. But Ward's not a well man. In the natural scheme of things, Riley would have outlived Ward. He might have counted on Ward pegging out very soon." Judith flung herself onto the chair as Renie speared hot dogs out of the kettle. "Now think about it, coz. It's one thing for Ward to be outraged because Riley seduced his—Ward's—daughter. It's something else for Riley to lead Lark on if she was in fact *his* daughter. What do you suppose those two men were really quarreling about?"

"Whew!" Renie handed Judith the mustard. "This gets uglier by the minute." She chewed at her lower lip. "It sure doesn't get any clearer."

Judith took a bite of hot dog. "Think motive. Ward might not be Lark's biological father, but he's been a father to her, if you know what I mean."

Renie gazed with unblinking brown eyes at Judith. "I do know. But not as well as you do."

To her dismay, Judith flushed. The subject of Mike's father was still touchy. She and Joe had not felt it was yet time to tell Mike the truth. He had grown up believing that Dan McMonigle was his father, and perhaps it was best to leave well enough alone. The priority was for Mike to accept Joe first as his stepfather. The rest might—or might not—come later. "Let's leave my problems out of this. Ward must have been absolutely wild about Riley's seduction. In fact, it makes me wild, too. We're talking incest, coz. That's nasty."

"Not as nasty as these hot dogs. Do they look a little green to you?"

Judith gave Renie a look of reproach. "Knock it off. Can't you ever take life seriously?"

Renie's brown eyes danced. "Not when I'm eating. Go on."

"Next, we've got Iris. She gets the property, which is, frankly, minimal, and not worth killing for. But she's head of the Riley Tobias Foundation. What does that mean? Does that enable her to dispose of Riley's estate at her whim? Is it a power trip?"

"We can discount Iris," Renie said. "We were with her when she found Riley. Besides, Iris knew Lark was no real threat, at least not in the long run."

Judith nodded over her glass of orange juice. "Remember what that tape said—'*Be* my lover, my etc.' Riley was urging Lark to do something in the future. At least you could interpret it that way. Lark claimed they were lovers. What does that mean? They snuggled? They kissed? They *canoodled?* In less explicit days, it didn't necessarily mean they were jumping in and out of the sack."

"True," Renie agreed. "So we cross out jealousy and insert money and possibly power as far as Iris is concerned. What about Good Ol' Clive?"

"We already talked about him, as well as Dewitt and, by implication, Erica. A failing artist wasn't worth as much to Clive Silvanus as a dead genius. And Clive was reportedly seeking out new clients." Judith snapped off a carrot stick.

"Something else bothers me," Renie remarked, lavishly salting her celery. "Why would Erica—who seems like a shrewd cookie—permit seventy grand to be paid out for a painting she hasn't got?"

Judith gave up trying to get any more catsup out of the squeeze bottle. "Maybe she gave her husband carte blanche while she was in Europe. *If* she was in Europe. As for the Dixons' motive, individually or collectively, I don't know. They purchase a very expensive painting from an artist who used to be married to Ms. Dixon. Money exchanges hands, the artist is murdered, and the painting supposedly disappears. What's the connection with Riley's death? Maybe . . ." Judith bit her lip, not quite ready to spin out the thought that was beating at her brain.

"You're forgetting Lazlo Gamm," Renie reminded Judith.

"It's not hard. Lazlo is a phantom. I'd dismiss him entirely if I wasn't sure I'd seen him hiding behind the Berkmans' A-frame." Judith sighed. "There's another fine point. While we were at Riley's just now, I was marveling at his collection of art objects. Everybody has gotten robbed around here—except Riley. Yet he was accustomed to leaving the floor unlocked despite having a fortune sitting around the house. What kind of thieves would steal our old Victrola but pass over a seventeenth-century bronze of the Three Graces? Doesn't that strike you as odd?"

Renie, who had been struggling with the cap of her cream soda, finally got the bottle open. "Now that you mention it, yes. But Riley rarely left the place. Maybe that explains it."

"Maybe." Judith didn't appear convinced.

Taking a deep swig of soda, Renie sighed appreciatively. "Speaking of Riley's place, I noticed something over there just now." For once, she looked unusually diffident. "It's probably dumb, but you know that box of paints?"

"Right. What about it?"

Renie set the soda bottle down. "There wasn't any orange."

Judith peered closely at Renie. "No orange?"

"Not the color or kind of orange we saw under Riley's body. To dry that fast, it had to be tempera. Oil and acrylic take longer, especially oil. Riley hadn't used watercolors in years. He was working in acrylic, if you recall."

Judith did, vaguely. She didn't, however, possess Renie's professional expertise on the subject. "So elucidate, coz. What are you getting at?"

Renie gave an uncertain shake of her whole body. "I don't know. Except that there was no reason for Riley to spill tempera paint on the floor. It comes in jars, usually, which shouldn't have been open. Where did that orange tempera come from? You've got the logical mind—you figure it out."

But Judith couldn't. The cousins returned to ruminating. Renie asked Judith if she even faintly considered Nella a suspect.

Judith wore an exasperated look. "I never considered Nella. Not for that. I'm just curious about why she's so disinclined to talk about her trip. Nella's never been the evasive type. If," Judith continued, speaking more slowly, "she went to Europe and gave Erica an alibi, then I'd have to figure Erica is the guilty party. But a motive eludes me, and I certainly don't see Nella in collusion with a murderer. Not knowingly, at any rate."

"I think you've gone round the bend on that theory," Renie declared. "Passports have pictures. How could Nella pass as Erica? There must be a fifty-year age difference. And they don't look at all alike."

"There's such a thing as forgery," Judith pointed out. "Eat up, coz. You're right, we have to call on Nella again."

As usual, Renie needed no urging when it came to eating. Ten minutes later, the cousins were back on the shoulder of the highway, heading for Nella Lablatt's house and returning the ladder. Midway, they saw Iris getting into a green Acura. Judith waved.

"I'm off to Glacier Falls," Iris called. "I have to make the final arrangements with the undertaker."

Judith nodded. Across the road, the four redheaded children were gathered next to the Mortons' mailbox. "Sweet-Stix, Sweet-Stix, give us Sweet-Stix!" they called.

Iris got into her car and reversed out of the drive. The cousins kept walking, the ladder between them. The children went running off toward the cabins, chasing their dog. The dog ran, disappearing around the side of the filling station. Chickens squawked and the children cut short their chase. Glancing behind her, Judith saw them swarming over the Dixons' white Mercedes. She imagined there would be lots of brown patches left on the gleaming finish when they were done.

Nella Lablatt was doing aerobic exercises to a videotape. "Almost finished," she shouted as the cousins came through her open front door. "Want some more sherry? Or is it time for a blast from the past?"

"Huh?" Judith stepped over the threshold with Renie in her wake.

Nella didn't respond, but huffed and puffed in time to a vigorous young hunk on the screen. "Sex," Nella shouted. "Sex sells anything. Even . . . health." The video ended, and Nella shook herself. "I sent a picture to Photo-Date last month. I haven't had an answer yet. Do you know that there are a hundred thousand people over a century old in this country? And that number is growing by the day. Not," she added hastily as she switched off the VCR, "that I qualify. But it's interesting, huh? How about that sack?"

"Sack?" Judith looked startled.

"Right," Nella replied, removing the tape. "Sack. It's an old-fashioned drink, and I've got some. Care to try it?"

"Why not?" murmured Judith. "Can you get in the bag by getting into the sack?"

"You can if you drink enough," Nella responded cheerfully. "Originally, it came from Spain and the Canary Islands. It's a wine, I guess you'd call it." She had gone to the wet bar, where she seemed to have stored an endless array of bottles, domestic and imported, humble and exotic. "All that exercise makes me thirsty. The secret of drinking is moderation. I never have more than four glasses of three different things a day."

"Really." Judith spoke with awe. Her own private peak had already been reached. If achieving Nella's advanced age—whatever it might be—involved such rigorous rules of imbibing, she figured she'd just as soon have three scotches in a row and pass out permanently. A hot cup of tea would have served her better.

"We're curious, Nella," Judith said, reluctantly accepting a glass of sack. "Did Lark take her painting home with her?"

Nella squatted on a footstool. "Nope. Ward came to collect her and she didn't want to explain to him about Riley bringing it over here. In fact, she told me I could have it." Nella gestured with her glass at the wall where President Eisenhower's photograph hung. "I think I'll pull that thing down and put Lark's picture there. I'll have to move those samplers, though."

Judith's gaze tracked the pair of samplers with their homely cross-stitched verses. She wondered how Nella would react if she knew that Lark's "Morning" had fetched an asking price of seventy thousand dollars. She also wondered if she should tell Nella the truth. But prudence advised her to keep quiet—for now. The cousins could be wrong about Riley substituting Lark's painting for his. And if they were right, Judith might trust Nella, but she wasn't so sure about anybody else along the South Fork.

"Can you lock your icehouse?" Judith asked.

Nella looked surprised. "Sure. It's been broken into a couple of times. Thieves love my quince jelly. Why do you ask?"

"If you've got room, you might put Lark's painting in the safe," Judith said. "I'm not exactly certain, but I think someone might want to steal her canvas."

Nella seemed undisturbed by the idea. "Well, they take everything else. Why not that? If it'd make you feel better, I'll put it in the post office safe. Really, it's quite roomy. In the old days, I had to keep all sorts of parcels there. Tools, clothes, even small appliances. At Christmastime, I'd run out of room. I always felt like Mrs. Claus. And Herman thought he was Santa. Or was that Delmar? I forget." Nella drank deeply from her glass of sack.

"Say, Nella," Judith began, tasting her wine and finding it very dry and probably potent, "we heard something startling today. Did you ever pick up on any rumors about Riley and Ward's late wife?"

"Felice Kimball?" Nella laughed. "Heavens, no! Felice was so prim and proper that she wasn't sure I was fit company. Too fast for her, I guess. Anyway, Riley would have been young enough to be her son. Who's been spreading stories about poor Felice? She's been dead for over twenty years. She passed away about the same time that I lost Seldon, my last husband."

Judith's brow furrowed. Something was wrong. She wasn't quite sure what it was, but for the first time, she saw a glimmer of light. Certain images flashed before her mind's eye, disconnected, seemingly irrelevant, yet somehow leading her in a logical, if as yet unclear, direction.

"Did you and Lark resolve your argument?" Judith inquired, wanting to steer the conversation on a different course.

Nella nodded emphatically. "That girl needs a mother to talk turkey to her. Sometimes I try to fill the bill. Lark finally listened up. What's to be gained by her and Iris feuding now that Riley's dead?"

Renie was discreetly trying to dump her drink into a potted fern. "So there was a feud between them?"

"Ohhh . . ." Nella's eyes roamed around the knotty pine ceiling. Renie hastily emptied her glass. "Maybe that's too strong a word," Nella continued. "They never had words, that I know of. But Iris couldn't warm to Lark, and Lark just plain didn't like Iris. The Old Green Monster, if you ask me."

"Jealous of Riley's affections?" asked Judith, wishing she had Renie's nerve. In her place on the love seat, she didn't have access to a potted plant.

"Typical," Nella replied. "You know what men are—they think all the women are crazy about them. And if they play around a bit, no harm done. Doesn't mean a thing. I caught Crosley in bed with Mrs. Burgess once, and I threatened to shoot them both." She frowned, and shook her head. "Or did I catch him with Herman? I forget."

Eventually, the talk had moved on from straying spouses and masculine failings to preserves, petit point, and paintings. The cousins helped Nella move Lark's canvas into the safe. Feeling relieved, they started to make their farewells. Judith, however, could not quite give up on her theory about Nella's recent vacation.

"I noticed those postcards of Venice on the love seat," she remarked as the three women stood on Nella's front porch. "I haven't been to Italy in years, but I thought Venice was sadly decayed and awfully dirty. I wonder how their plans are coming to keep the city from sinking."

Nella took a flyswatter from a nail and swung with vigor. Her victim, which was actually a mosquito, found itself splayed against a cedar shake. "You can't go to Europe and not expect to find old things. Most of those churches and castles and such are older than I am." She laughed richly and replaced the flyswatter. "You met the Morton kiddies? Aren't they something? I lost track of how many they got. You wouldn't think he had it in him. Or that he had it in—"

"I liked Venice," Renie interrupted. "I loved the gondolas. I was never so relaxed in my life."

Judith waited for Nella's reply, but when it came, it had nothing to do with murky canals and singing gondoliers. "You two used to have a lot of fun going down the river on old inner tubes. Didn't you get your butts full of bugs one summer?"

Judith allowed that had indeed happened, and in the process, had cured them of inner tubing. "The river was too low that year," she said, mentally running up a white flag. "We'll see you, Nella. Thanks again for everything."

Despite having been forced to give up prying about Nella's travels, Judith felt triumphant. "You see? She won't say where she's been. Doesn't that strike you as suspicious?"

"So?" Renie followed Judith around the wooden gate. "Even if Nella went to Europe instead of Erica, does that necessarily make Mrs. Dixon a killer?"

"No," Judith admitted. She punched her fist into her palm. "Damn! I wish we could sneak into Nella's and find her passport."

"She may not have one. If your theory is right, she used Erica's, or a phony variation of same."

"I know, I know." Her small victory fading fast, Judith stood next to the cabin with her hands on her hips. "Okay, we've got four more hours. What should we tackle next?"

"What—or who?" Renie asked. "We've done about all we can do to this place. The work that's left is mostly structural. Unless you want to drive into Glacier Falls and get new gutters."

"I'll leave that for Mike," Judith said. "He may have

time after—*if*—he graduates." She turned to Renie. "Did you notice if the Dixons' car was at the auto court?"

"Yeah, I think the kids were still horsing around there. Why?"

Judith sat down on a moss-covered stump, the remnant of an autumn storm that had left a large cedar threatening to crash into the roof. "I can't figure out a motive for Erica, unless she stood to gain financially by Riley's death. You know, an insurance policy or something he made out to her when they were married. But Riley was broke then, and probably didn't have any insurance. Plus, I got the impression that Erica came from money. Remember her remark about the family having a decorator? She also referred to the seventy grand as money *she'd* spent—not *we.*"

Renie leaned against an alder tree. "That's right. Maybe Dewitt doesn't have any money of his own."

"You're the one who knows him," Judith pointed out.

"Not well. I don't think Dewitt and I have ever talked about anything except art and design. Until now, that is."

Judith got up from the stump. "Let's talk some more."

Renie didn't argue. They were back at the wooden gate when they heard screams, followed by a crash. Then there were more screams. The cousins ran out to the road, frantically looking in both directions.

At the edge of the Woodchuck Auto Court's property, they could see the white Mercedes lying on its side in the ditch. Erica Dixon and Carrie Mae Morton were both screaming, their arms waving wildly, their legs pumping over the tarmac.

Judith and Renie tore down the highway, raced across the road, and leaped into the breach.

THIRTEEN

JUDITH AND RENIE weren't sure what was more miraculous: that the Morton children hadn't been seriously hurt in their attempt to drive the Mercedes, or that Erica Dixon hadn't strangled all four of them for tampering with her expensive car.

There was also the hostility which had arisen between the Mortons and the Dixons. Kennedy Morton told Dewitt Dixon that if he and his fancy-pants wife hadn't left their keys in the car, the youngsters wouldn't have been tempted to go for a spin. Erica Dixon shrieked at Carrie Mae Morton that her passel of brats had no respect for other people's property and were damned near as dumb as their parents. Meanwhile, the would-be auto thieves had crawled out of the Mercedes and were playing in the middle of the highway. Nella Lablatt hurried from her yard, where she had been weeding, and shooed the foursome back to their own property just as a school bus lumbered along and chugged to a stop to discharge more Mortons.

Iris Takisaki had also joined the group, which was turning into a crowd. "What happened?" she asked, looking startled.

The cousins explained. Iris stared at the Dixons, who

were still engaged in verbal combat with the Mortons. Erica's piping voice had risen to a squeak; Carrie Mae was growing hoarse. Iris marched up to Dewitt, who was nose to nose with Kennedy Morton.

"Hold it!" she cried, wedging herself between the two men. "Dewitt, open that trunk!"

Shocked, Dewitt took three steps backward. "What are you talking about? Our car is ruined! We'll have to get a tow truck!"

But Iris didn't budge. "The side of the car may be damaged, yes, but you can still open the trunk. Do it, or I'll call the sheriff instead of AAA."

Again Dewitt refused. Iris's diversion had created a calming effect on the others. Erica watched her husband curiously; Carrie Mae hugged some of her children; Kennedy Morton stalked off toward the filling station, where a black Corvette had just pulled in; the other Morton offspring were dancing around the Mercedes.

Iris proved to be just as stubborn as Dewitt. Finally, it was Erica who gave in. She opened the driver's side of the Mercedes and removed the keys from the ignition. But Iris was wrong: The trunk had been jammed by the accident.

"Have you got a crowbar?" Iris shouted the question at Kennedy Morton, but he either didn't hear her or chose to ignore the request. Instead, he fawned over the Corvette and its owner, a suntanned young man who looked as if he'd just come in from the beach at Malibu.

Iris whirled on Dewitt. "You say you haven't received a painting from Clive! I say otherwise! I don't know how you got it, but you did! Don't you dare threaten me! I'll countersue for defamation of character!"

Angrily, Iris started back across the road. Nella trotted after her. Carrie Mae had a parting shot:

"I got an axe, Iris, honey! It's the one I use on the chickens when I get tired of wringing their necks."

But Iris paid no heed. With Nella at her side, she disappeared among the young cottonwoods that lined the other side of the highway.

All seven Morton children went to the shoulder of the road, standing a few feet from the battered car, which lay in the ditch like a beached whale. "Sweet-Stix!" they cried. "Sweet-Stix! Give us Sweet-Stix now!"

"I'll give them something," Renie muttered while Dewitt called from the phone booth for a tow truck and Erica extracted insurance information from Carrie Mae. "And I thought raising three kids was a pain in the backside!"

Judith, however, wasn't in the mood to discuss childrearing. "Do you think Iris wanted to see if the painting Riley gave me was in the Dixons' trunk?" she murmured.

Renie shrugged. "Could be. But we know better. I think."

"Right," Judith replied, still in a low voice. "At least we know where Lark's version is. But Riley's canvas could be in the trunk."

Renie gave Judith a curious look. "Wouldn't Erica have seen it?"

"I don't know." Judith spoke out of the side of her mouth as Erica approached the cousins. "I'm wondering if he's got anything in there—and that's why he wouldn't open the trunk."

Still puzzled, Renie couldn't press Judith further: Erica Dixon was upon them, flushed with anger, blond hair disheveled.

"Now we couldn't leave this horrible place if we wanted to," she said with regret. "Dewitt felt we should wait until after the funeral, but I said it was pointless. What's so hard about an hour's ride from town to Glacier Falls?" She snorted and stared at the disabled Mercedes. "Well, he got his way. Now we're stuck."

"It's not exactly Dewitt's fault that the Morton kids wrecked your car," Judith pointed out in a reasonable tone.

With a heavy sigh, Erica brushed at her unruly hair and resettled her sunglasses on her thin nose. "It was *his* keys they stole. The little wretches took them right out of our room. They've been in and out of there like so many mice. I did *not* leave my keys in the car." She glared at Dewitt, who had bolted from the phone booth and was looking frazzled. "Excuse me, I have to call my lawyer."

"You're suing the Mortons?" Judith was surprised, though she realized she shouldn't be. It seemed to her that rich people rarely had any compunction about wringing money from poor people.

But Erica's thin eyebrows shot up. "The Mortons? What for? They do have insurance—they have to, they're in business. I told you, I'm suing Clive Silvanus. The man's a crook." She dashed into the phone booth and shut the door.

Dewitt Dixon, however, had other ideas. He had come charging back across the grass to the driveway, where he began shouting at his wife. "Stop that, Erica! You don't know what you're doing! You're going to cause serious problems!"

But Erica ignored him. Judith and Renie watched while Dewitt Dixon's usual aplomb disintegrated. Erica, whose temper was already frayed, pounded on the telephone. It was obvious that she was having trouble making a connection. The Morton children wandered back from the road, looking as if they were plotting their next round of mischief.

"Your car's busted," Thor announced to Dewitt Dixon. "You got another one?"

Glaring at the youngsters, Dewitt turned on his heel and started back toward the rental unit. But his annoyance was exceeded by his distress. He wheeled around, then strode purposefully back to the phone booth. Erica was yanking on the receiver and swearing a blue streak.

"Erica! Wait!" Dewitt wasn't giving up.

Neither was Erica. She gave the booth a swift kick, then must have gotten a dial tone. She had also put ideas into the Mortons' curly red heads. They rushed the booth, practically knocking Dewitt over. Surrounding the glass and wooden structure, they, too, kicked, screamed, and pounded. Erica Dixon erupted from the booth, fists and hair flying.

"You little monsters!" she raged. "Go away! Leave me alone! Stop that!"

Dewitt started pulling Mortons off his wife. Or perhaps he was hauling Erica away from her attackers. The cousins found it hard to tell, but decided to intervene before somebody actually got hurt.

Judith got hold of Giles and Velvet; Renie wrestled Skye and Rafe to the ground. The Dixons finally subdued Shanna, Thor and Jade just as Carrie Mae came back out of the Morton living quarters with a howling little Fabio in her arms.

"Now you've done it!" Carrie Mae exclaimed angrily. "You woke up Fabio! We've got a right to throw you out of here for disturbing the peace!"

Giles was trying to bite Judith's arm. Velvet, however, had decided to cuddle. She wrapped herself around Judith's knees and began to hum.

Another argument ensued. Kennedy Morton was nowhere to be seen, and Judith didn't much blame him. She thought it best to escape. Letting go of Giles, who was still gnawing away, she tried to loosen Velvet's grip. But Velvet had taken a fancy to Judith.

"I like you," she cooed. "You're nice." Velvet tossed her head in Erica's direction. "She's mean. She won't give us candy. If you give us some, we'll like you even better. We treat people who give us candy real nice."

"Sorry, Velvet, I don't have any," Judith said, wincing at Giles's persistent tooth attack. "Can you get this vampire off me?"

Velvet giggled, but to Judith's relief, managed to pry Giles loose. Renie, meanwhile, was sitting on Skye's and Rafe's legs.

"Can we go now?" she asked plaintively.

Putting the renewed brawl behind them, the cousins fled across the highway. Renie didn't bother to ask why Judith headed not for the privacy of their own driveway, but up the road, toward the Green Mountain Inn. She did, however, have another question for Judith:

"What was that crack you made about Dewitt's trunk being empty?"

"I was referring to luggage," Judith replied as a county truck filled with sand lumbered past, "as in what Erica brought back from Europe. If she went in the first place."

Renie kicked at a pebble on the shoulder of the road. "Oh, *that.* You're really hung up on Erica's travel itinerary, aren't you? I wish you'd just call Joe and be done with it."

Judith shook her head. "I don't want to pester him. It's after three o'clock, and he probably couldn't get the information out of INS until tomorrow anyway. Besides, if Nella used a phony passport, the records would show that Erica did indeed go abroad. So what's the point?"

"There isn't any, as far as I'm concerned," Renie muttered. "Erica has no real motive. Nobody saw her the day Riley died, and with half the neighborhood running in and out of his studio, that seems odd."

"She might have been the prowler Iris saw," Judith pointed out, raising her voice to be heard over a trio of motorcyclists. "Murderers are often risk-takers."

"So why are we going to talk to Clive Silvanus?" Renie stopped shouting as the cyclists slowed and turned in to the Green Mountain Inn. "Or am I assuming wrong about our stroll?"

"Your assumption is correct," Judith responded primly.

At the front of the inn, the owner and operator was working under the hood of an out-of-state car. It took Gary Johanson a moment to focus on the cousins. Meanwhile, the bikers had already gone inside. The only other vehicle parked in the small lot was a black Infiniti. Judith hadn't noticed it before, and wondered if it belonged to Clive.

"That's right," Gary Johanson said, wiping his hands on a dirty rag. An angular man of forty, Gary had thinning brown hair and keen brown eyes. "Mr. Silvanus has been keeping it out back. We try to reserve the front for the restaurant and the grocery. I keep the cars I'm tinkering on over by the shed."

"He's here, then," said Judith.

But Gary shook his head. "No, he went for a walk up to see Our Lady of the Stumps. He left about ten minutes ago. I guess he needed to cool down after that squabble he had with that guy from down the road. You want to wait? Dee's got cherry pie this afternoon."

Judith's ears had pricked up at the mention of a squabble. "Who do you mean? Dewitt Dixon?"

Gary shook his head. "I don't know the guy's name, just that he's staying at the Woodchuck. He was here yesterday, too, having breakfast with Mr. Silvanus. Kind of smooth, or what do you call it? Suave?"

"That's Dewitt all over," Judith murmured, though he'd been neither smooth nor suave during the latest debacle with the Mortons. "What were Dewitt and Clive fighting about?"

Gary didn't know. "It was more of an argument, out back." He nodded toward the shed. "Dee was busting her brains, trying to think up an excuse to eavesdrop, but I told her to knock it off. How come women always have to know everything?" Gary seemed genuinely perplexed by the idea. "Now what about that pie?"

The cousins debated briefly, then decided to make the short hike up to Our Lady of the Stumps in the hope of meeting Clive along the way. It had been a long time since they'd viewed the wood carving in the huge, burned-out cedar snag. Hansel Gruber had been part of the local art scene early in his career as a wood-carver, and Our Lady had been one of his first so-called "natural" works. In those days, Gruber had carved for carving's sake, creating beauty out of trees, logs, and stumps wherever he found an appealing setting. In their youth, Judith and Renie had made several pilgrimages with their fathers to Our Lady of the Stumps. On the last trek, some thirty years earlier, they had all sat down on a log to admire the carving and discovered they were keeping company with a five-foot garter snake. Much to the amusement of Donald and Cliff

Grover, the cousins had run shrieking and screaming all the way back to the highway.

The Jimmy-Jump-Off Creek Road was a dirt track that took off just before a small bridge about fifty yards up from the Green Mountain Inn. It rose steadily through thick stands of ferns, vine maples, and devil's club for almost a quarter of a mile. Then it branched off: On the left stood the ruins of a sawmill, and across a meadow, an ancient cabin that had been converted into a rambling, ramshackle house; to the right, the road narrowed down to a trail that led to the wood carving.

At the fork, Renie nodded in the direction of the dilapidated house. Smoke trickled out of a tin chimney, but otherwise, there was no sign of life. "Hippies in mid-life crisis?" she asked.

"Maybe," Judith answered. "I wonder how much stuff they have in there that belongs to us."

The trail continued to rise, though the grade was easy. The greenery thickened, with large clumps of salmonberry, thimbleberry, and blackberry bushes. A stand of second-growth timber grew tall, blocking out the sun. The cousins could hear birds and unidentifiable forest animals chattering among the branches. The sound of the creek was distant, spilling down the mountainside out of sight. Judith and Renie walked for half a mile, but with no sign of Clive Silvanus.

"Communing with Art or Nature doesn't strike me as Clive's style," Judith noted. "You don't suppose he plans on trying to get Hansel Gruber as a client, do you?"

"He'll have some problems," Renie replied. "Gruber's been dead for at least five years."

A simple sign made of cedar with the words "Our Lady of the Stumps" burned into it pointed the way to the carving. The remnant of the once-great tree stood some twenty feet off the main trail, in a grottolike setting among the new growth. The old-timers told how the cedar had been struck by lightning on the eve of the loggers' first foray into the forest at Jimmy-Jump-Off Creek. The gods were angry, they liked to say, and sent the storm as a warning.

Undaunted, the sawmill owner clear-cut the rest of the stand, but left the charred giant in peace. Years later, Hansel Gruber created his own memorial to the forest in the jagged, twenty-foot snag.

Our Lady was larger than life, shown from the hip with the Babe at her breast, and one arm thrust over her head. Her facial features were crude yet poignant. The veil seemed to float around her, as if caught on a gentle wind. As ever, the cousins were awed.

Renie was the first to break the silence. "You know how you remember most things as bigger than they really were. That's not true with this carving. It's even more overpowering now than it was when we were kids."

Judith agreed. They wandered around the stump, taking in the wood sculpture from different angles. Judith also cast her glance among the trees. She could see no sign of Clive Silvanus.

"We couldn't have missed him," she said, trying in vain to make out fresh footprints in the ground by the cedar stump.

"He must have changed his mind," Renie said. "Maybe he walked up to the ranger station. It's not that far."

"True." After a final perusal and a silent prayer, the cousins started back to the main trail.

"Gruber did the columns in the lobby of the First Northwest Bank Building downtown," Renie noted. "They're sort of like a totem pole, but less rigid artistically."

"I know. I've been there." Judith pulled a face. "They were the ones who foreclosed on our first house. It's too bad Gruber didn't carve a picture of Dan putting the mortgage money on a ninety-to-one long shot at the track."

"There's a Buddha about halfway up the one column," Renie remarked. "He looks a lot like Dan when he sat around in his underwear, eating Ding-Dongs and watching the demolition derby."

"What underwear?" Judith replied, then stopped at the fork in the road. Across the meadow by the sprawling shack, she could see three people; one of them resembled Clive Silvanus.

Renie followed her cousin's gaze. "Well. Do you suppose one of the hippies is an artist in residence?"

The cousins pulled back just enough to avoid the trio's direct line of sight. They waited in silence for several minutes before Clive started across the meadow. Shielding her eyes from the sun, Judith peered more closely at the grasses, which she recalled as once being crisscrossed by deer runs. Only a single trail remained, yet the meadow was curiously flat in the middle. Judith frowned as the hippies went back inside the house. Clive was whistling when he hit the road. He jumped when the cousins popped out from behind a stand of sword ferns.

"My! You startled me! The woods are alive with the sound of city dwellers!" Clive had his beige sport coat slung over his shoulder. "You out enjoyin' the fine spring weather?"

Judith smiled thinly. "Yes, we are. And you?" She nodded at the hippie establishment. "I take it you're getting reacquainted with the counterculture of the past?"

Briefly, Clive looked unsettled. Then he beamed at the cousins. "Ah once considered becomin' a hippie mahself. But mah daddy wouldn't hear of such a thing, so Ah decided on bein' a preacher instead. But that didn't work out, so Ah got a job fetchin' and haulin' for the local art museum. One thing led to another, as they say, and here Ah am." He looked very pleased with himself.

The diversion in conversational tactics cut no ice with Judith. "So what did the hippies tell you? That they didn't take 'Spring River'?"

Something flashed in Clive's eyes even as his round face fell. "That's what they say. What do you think?"

Judith shrugged. "They may be right. Iris seems to think the Dixons have it."

Clive began to walk down the road. The cousins fell in step beside him. "Iris is wrong. She's a smart lady, mind you, but this time Ah do believe grief has unsettled her brain. If Dewitt had that painting, his Little Woman wouldn't be actin' like a bear in a buzz saw."

"She would if she didn't know he had it," Judith pointed out, just for the sake of argument.

Clive's laugh was nervous. "Now, now, what are you tryin' to say?"

"You said yourself that you gave Dewitt the painting that Riley had given to me," Judith commented innocently, "So what's the problem?"

"Ah didn't exactly say that." Clive's soft mouth closed like a sponge.

Renie gazed up at Clive, almost tripping over a root in the process. "Level with us, Clive. The painting Erica wants is the one that's missing, right?"

Halting in mid-step, Clive wagged a finger at Renie. "You are puttin' words in mah mouth, little lady." He cast a sympathetic look at Judith. "Ah understand why you might be upset because your Tobias went the way of all flesh. But it would behoove you to keep out of this sticky business. Maybe Iris will make it up to you. Ah'm just moseyin' along, a simple Southern boy in the slow lane of life."

They were almost to the highway. The sound of the creek grew louder as it reached its passage under the bridge to the river. Judith decided to play her trump card: "Erica plans to sue you."

Clive stopped dead in his tracks. His pale face turned absolutely ashen. "*Sue me?* Whyever for?"

"It's simple. Erica has paid out good money for a painting she doesn't have." Judith's tone was noncommittal.

Clive bristled and resumed walking. "That's between her and Dewitt. Ah don't believe in gettin' mixed up in married folks' hassles. And mark mah words," he went on as they reached the main road, "if Erica sues, she's the one who'll end up behind bars. Or worse." His gaze roamed to the thick green clumps of thistles, devil's club, and nettles that grew along the edge of Jimmy-Jump-Off Creek. Judith knew the lushness of the scene could fool the uninitiated. Clive's voice turned ominous. "Oh, my—Erica is a foolish woman! Doesn't she know there's a killer on the loose?"

FOURTEEN

JUDITH WAS DEBATING the efficacy of Truth. Fortunately, for Renie's sake, she was keeping the argument to herself. By the time they reached the cabin, Judith still hadn't come to a conclusion. She said as much to Renie:

"If we confessed that we knew where Lark's 'Morning' was, what would happen?"

Renie paused with her foot on the bottom porch step. "Erica and Dewitt would insist on taking possession."

Judith clung to the staircase railing. "What would happen to the canvas Riley gave me?"

Renie considered. "It'd disappear. As it's already done, it seems. At least as far as Erica is concerned. Then, eventually, some private collector in Europe or Asia or somewhere else out of the country would pay big bucks and hang it in his billiard room."

"And?" prompted Judith.

Renie grinned. "Clive and Dewitt would split the profit. With Riley dead, they might get fifty grand apiece, maybe more."

"Do you think they've already made thirty-five each?"

Renie's grin widened. "Erica's seventy grand, which

hasn't gone into the estate? Sure, why not? It's a neat scam."

"It sure is. And it's *logical.*" Judith was silent for a long moment. Then she sprang away from the porch. "Come on, let's go prove that Honesty Is The Best Policy." Judith walked briskly to her car. She was opening the door when Lazlo Gamm appeared from around the curve in the dirt road.

"I bring you greetings," he said in his melancholy voice. "We met before, under happier circumstances."

Nonplussed, Judith gathered her composure and closed the car door. "That's right. And the next time we saw you, you ignored us. Tell me, Mr. Gamm, is it harder to land your copter up at the hippies' meadow than at the one over at Riley's?"

The question seemed to surprise Renie more than Lazlo. "Not really," he responded, hands deep in the pockets of yet another beautifully cut Armani suit. "If anything, the meadow up the road is wider."

Judith leaned against the car, arms folded across her breast. Renie had come around from the passenger side to stand by the trunk. She was still looking flabbergasted.

"I don't get it," Judith said pleasantly. "What do you do with that copter, Mr. Gamm? Hop from one natural landing site to another around here? Where do you sleep?"

Lazlo Gamm's big brown eyes grew even more mournful. "Why do you ask? What does it matter? Who cares what happens to poor Lazlo?"

"But we do," Judith asserted. "That's why we ask."

Apparently appeased, Lazlo Gamm removed his hands from his pockets and gestured in a lugubrious manner. "I sleep up at the campground, by the ranger station. I have a very fine tent and an excellent sleeping bag. Four walls hem me in, reminding me of my extreme youth under the Communist regime. My father was a Freedom Fighter. We fled my homeland on a moonless night. So now I steer my copter where my whimsy takes me. I am like the down of the thistle, floating, flying, landing, resting. Whither poor

Lazlo? Wherever his heart must take him." He looked as if he could cry.

Renie had finally regained her aplomb. "Your heart seems to have brought you to an unlucky spot this time. Have you been around here for the past three days?"

His big brown eyes looked very innocent. "Of course. I could hardly leave, under the circumstances. I might be wanted."

"Yes, you might," Judith agreed. "By the sheriff, for instance. Has Abbott N. Costello talked to you?"

Lazlo Gamm looked aghast. "The sheriff? No, of course not! Why would he?"

For once, Judith was at a loss. She had no idea how to proceed with Lazlo Gamm. Certainly, it appeared that he had left Riley's meadow at least two hours before the artist was killed. But there was no reason he couldn't have taken off and landed at a different site nearby. On the other hand, Judith had no motive for Lazlo.

"Look, Mr. Gamm," she said in her most down-to-earth manner, "you seem to be the wild card in this crazy deck of characters. Do you mind if we ask why you came to see Riley in the first place?"

Not only did Lazlo seem not to mind, he seemed elated that someone should care. His wide smile changed his long face for the better. "Naturally you should ask! I have intruded upon your property. You have a right to know if I mean you harm. Why did I come to see Riley?" The smile was fraying around the edges. "I didn't." The smile began to wither. "I came to see a young lady." The smile disappeared.

The image of Lazlo Gamm as Judith had first seen him skulked across her mind's eye: the Armani suit, the leather briefcase—and the big bouquet. "You brought those flowers for her, not for Riley," Judith said in mild amazement. "Did you give them to her?"

Sadly, Lazlo shook his head. "Riley didn't want me to. Oh, he pretended otherwise, but I could tell he was annoyed. I was crushed. Still, he promised to see that she got them."

"She did," Judith assured him, ignoring Renie's impatient, querying look. "I'm sure she's been enjoying them very much. Why don't you call on her?"

His big brown eyes scanned the web of vine maples that formed an arch over the dirt road. "It's been difficult. Riley gave me the wrong directions. He said she lived a few houses upriver. But it turns out to be *down*river. I went there today, but she was busy."

Enlightenment was dawning on Renie. "Lark Kimball?" She glanced at Judith for confirmation. "So that's why you were hanging around the Berkmans' place. You were searching for Lark!"

It was Lazlo's turn to look baffled. Judith intervened. "The Berkmans have the A-frame next to us on the upriver side. We saw you there yesterday. So what did you do, land up at the meadow off the Jimmy-Jump-Off Creek Road, then take the copter down to . . ." Judith's memory raced along the highway. ". . . that empty field at the Higby farm next to the Kimballs?"

"Higby?" Lazlo still seemed bewildered. "That is possible. They are older people, kind and receptive to the hundred dollars I gave them for use of the field. Are you sure Lark got the bouquet? I didn't have the nerve to ask her father."

"Quite sure," Judith replied in a warm tone. "You must give her some time, Mr. Gamm. Her grief is very fresh."

Lazlo had become mournful. "That's why I stayed on. To comfort her, you see. I will certainly remain for the funeral. Perhaps then she will turn to me and seek consolation." Despite his words, Lazlo Gamm looked pessimistic.

"That's very kind," Judith assured him. "Is there something we can do for you?" She was still mystified about his unexpected appearance at the cabin.

But Lazlo merely gave that slow, agonized shake of his head. "No one can help poor Lazlo. I wandered in here simply to explore. I must do something to use up the time until Saturday."

Given Lazlo Gamm's melancholy mien, his explanation seemed adequate. Moments later, he was meandering aimlessly along the riverbank. Judith and Renie got into the car and headed out.

"Okay, Sherlock," said Renie, "how did you figure that one out?"

"The bouquet," Judith replied simply. "I've been bothered all along about seeing those chrysanthemum petals on Nella's walkway. Mums don't bloom until late summer or early fall. In fact, there weren't even any chrysanthemum shoots coming up in that bed. So that meant that somebody with out-of-season flowers had been over there. If it wasn't Lazlo himself, it had to be Lark, trying to find her way to our place. Don't you remember the scent of flowers in her studio?"

Renie did, vaguely. "So Riley did in fact pass the bouquet on to Lark?"

"Right. Which means," Judith continued with a hint of dismay in her voice, "that Lark did indeed see Riley the afternoon he was killed."

Renie was craning her neck to get a look at the Higby farm. "The copter's not there now," she remarked. "I wonder where he's parked it this time."

"Probably across from the campground in back of the ranger station," Judith answered, slowing to make the turn into Ward Kimball's place. "They've got an actual landing pad, as I recall."

"Lazlo seems innocent," Renie remarked.

"He sure does." Judith eased the car into the parking spot next to the Volkswagen bus. She turned and raised her eyebrows at Renie. "He also has a motive."

Renie stared at Judith. "Lark?"

"Right." Taking the keys out of the ignition, Judith unfastened her seat belt. "Lazlo's reputation as a Romeo may or may not be deserved. But it sounds to me as if he is genuinely smitten with Lark. Want to bet who bought 'Dawn'?"

Renie stared some more. "But that would mean Lazlo knew Lark was a talented painter in her own right."

"That's right," Judith said, giving Renie half a beat to let the concept sink in. "Get out, coz. We still have some sleuthing to do."

Ward Kimball was outside, planting geraniums in big terra-cotta containers. He smiled and waved when the cousins got out of the compact.

"Are you on your way back to town?" he asked as Judith and Renie sidestepped geranium pots, fertilizer, and a couple of spare garden tools.

"In an hour or so," Judith replied. "We plan to eat dinner on the way home." She gave Ward an uncertain smile. "Since we're heading back soon, we thought we ought to make a confession. Where's Lark?"

Ward gestured toward the studio. In the spring sunshine, he looked healthier and happier. Judith wondered if the demise of Riley Tobias, along with the warmer weather, hadn't contributed to Ward Kimball's well-being.

"I can't pry her loose from there," he said with a little shake of his head. "I tired to talk her into signing a teaching contract for next year in Glacier Falls, but since Riley died, she's more determined than ever to paint. Maybe she feels she has to keep up the tradition."

Ward started toward the studio, but Judith put a hand on his arm. "The family tradition?" she asked quietly.

Ward blinked. "Yes, I suppose. I certainly haven't done much the last few years. But Lark never took her work seriously until she began studying with Riley. I suppose I owe him something, really. I've been pretty hard on the poor fellow, I'm afraid." He gave Judith a sheepish look. "Maybe I was jealous."

"Jealous?" Judith kept her voice very soft. "Of what, Ward?"

Ward frowned into the blue sky, his face weather-beaten but his color good. "You know, it's odd that you ask that.

I'm not entirely sure. Riley was a superb artist, but so was I." He spoke unaffectedly. "Maybe I felt that Lark took my talent for granted. Children often do, you know, and I think that's good. They shouldn't have the burden of going around saying, 'There's my father, the famous artist,' or 'Meet my mother, the world-renowned nuclear physicist.' Parents should just be parents, and in Lark's case, her lack of sight has been enough of a burden." He gave Judith a self-deprecating smile.

Judith, however, was suffering from mixed emotions. "So you were jealous of her admiration of Riley?"

"I think so." Ward gestured sharply with one hand. "Oh, I was very angry with him about his intentions. He led her on, and it wasn't fair. I wouldn't be surprised if he talked about marriage. But Riley wasn't the marrying kind. Look at poor Iris. Look at Erica, for that matter. No, Riley would have broken Lark's heart. I couldn't allow that." Suddenly his face sagged, and all the previous buoyancy drained away. "I couldn't stop it, either. But somebody did."

"Yes," Judith replied in a flat voice. "Somebody did indeed." She stepped back, waiting for Ward to summon Lark.

Renie watched him cross the lawn to the studio. "Zilch," she murmured. "Is he into thirty years of denial?"

"It's possible," Judith whispered. "Maybe he never believed his wife was unfaithful."

"Nella didn't believe it, either," Renie noted. "Could it be that Iris is the one doing the denial bit? Has she woven herself a fantasy?"

But Judith could only shake her head in a doubtful manner. Lark was coming out of the studio, holding Ward's arm. She greeted the cousins without enthusiasm. Ward led them all inside the house, where he offered a lengthy list of beverages.

But Judith declined, wanting to come to the point quickly. As succinctly as possible, she recounted the story of Riley's gift, the strange behavior of Clive and Dewitt at the cabin, Erica's pique over paying seventy grand for nothing, and finally, the discovery of Lark's painting in Nella's icehouse.

"You didn't tell me about that," Ward said to Lark in rebuke.

Lark made an impatient gesture. "Why should I? It seemed unimportant. Riley must have had his reasons for taking the canvas to Nella. I told her she could have it."

"But she can't," Judith declared, leaning as far forward as possible on the soft leather sofa. "Don't you understand? That painting *is* 'Spring River.' At least as far as Erica Dixon is concerned. I'm willing to bet that your 'Dawn' is hanging in some collector's house at this very minute. Riley did a terrible thing, Lark. He passed off your wonderful works as his own." Judith stopped just short of accusing Riley Tobias of using Lark Kimball for his own selfish ends.

But the point was not lost on Lark. She reacted by jumping out of her chair and screaming, "No! That's terrible! How could you! Riley was the most honest man I ever met!"

Ward stood up and went to Lark, but she rebuffed him with a swing of her elbows. "Go away! You don't want to believe anything good about Riley! You hate him because I loved him! And because he usurped you as the dean of Northwest artists! Now he's gone, and there's no one to take his place!"

The expression on Ward Kimball's face was one of weariness, confusion, and hurt. Judith felt something wrench inside her; then she spoke quietly but firmly.

"That's not true, Lark. There *is* someone to take Riley's place." Judith paused, watching Ward's puzzled reaction and Lark's defiant face. "It's you, Lark. *You* are the new dean of the Northwest school. Take it and run."

Lark Kimball wasn't convinced, but at least her hostile attitude disappeared. Judith didn't mention Lazlo Gamm's name or press her point about Riley's duplicity. Recalling her annoyance with Lark for failing to see Riley's flaws, Judith realized that what had really angered her was the younger woman's poor judgment of character. She had once made the same mistake. The important thing now was for Lark to learn from experience and look to the future.

Lark had loved Riley. But she also loved her work. She knew that it was good. The passion so evident in Riley Tobias was also obvious in Lark. Her goals were nebulous. She had never considered exhibiting her paintings, and was incredulous that anyone would pay money to own a Lark Kimball canvas. She was sure that Judith was mistaken about the collector. And she was adamant in her belief that Erica Dixon wouldn't give seven cents, let alone seventy thousand dollars, for a "Spring River" signed by Lark Kimball.

"There's one way to find out," Ward asserted, no longer on the defensive with Lark. "Take Erica to Nella's and let her see if the painting in the safe is the one she bought."

Lark, however, remained dubious. "When Erica finds out Riley didn't paint it, she'll change her mind."

"At least you'll know if that's the canvas she viewed when she visited Riley's studio," Judith pointed out. "If she says it isn't, then she's stuck with the one he gave me."

The Kimballs got into their Volkswagen van and followed the cousins back down the road. Ward and Lark went directly to Nella's; Judith and Renie pulled into the auto court. A man with a tow truck was grappling with the Mercedes. His audience consisted of Dewitt Dixon and all eight Morton children, including little Fabio, who was sitting in a red jump seat.

Dewitt did not look approachable. He was grim-faced, trying to ignore the squeals and shouts of the Mortons in general and of Thor in particular, who was shooting at him with suction darts. Two had already stuck to the seat of Dewitt's tailored trousers, and another had lodged on the back of his head. He seemed not to notice.

Parking at the edge of the driveway, Judith waited while Renie went in search of Erica Dixon. Less than a minute passed before Erica came out of the motel unit, her toilette rejuvenated.

"I don't get this," she said, leaning in the open window on the driver's side of the car. "Your cousin says you have a painting to show me."

Judith nodded. "We do. You want to drive or walk across the road to Nella's?"

Erica frowned. "Nella's? Since when did she start peddling pictures? Is it something she crocheted?"

Judith had no opportunity to answer. Erica turned on her heel and started for the road. Renie got back in the car and the cousins drove the short distance to Nella's.

Nella Lablatt had Lark's painting in the middle of the living room. Lark was pale; Ward looked proud; Nella was mixing margaritas at the wet bar.

"If you feel a tequila, you'll feel just fine," said Nella by way of greeting. "Hey, Erica, you want a cutting of dogtooth violet?"

Erica gave a start, not at Nella's offer, but at the sight of Lark's canvas. "My God!" she exclaimed. "It's 'Spring River'!" She rushed across the room and knelt to examine the painting. Or, it occurred to Judith, to pay homage. Except for Nella's swizzle stick stirring up a storm, the room was silent. It was Ward Kimball who spoke first.

"Riley Tobias didn't paint that, Erica. Lark did." His voice was very quiet.

Erica whirled on her haunches, almost upsetting herself. "What? That's crazy! I saw Riley working on this!"

"Working?" Judith asked, also speaking softly. "Or looking?"

Awkwardly, Erica stood up. "What do you mean?" Confusion enveloped her face. "Oh! Well—I didn't actually see him apply brush strokes, if that's what you're saying. But Dewitt did. He told me so, and he wouldn't . . ." Her voice trailed off in perplexity.

"I assure you," Ward said, assuming the dignity of venerable artist as well as proud parent, "Lark painted this. I will also attest to the fact that"—his voice caught and his gaze flickered at his daughter, who remained motionless—"Riley inspired as well as taught her. In that sense, this painting is indeed a legacy of Riley Tobias."

Erica stopped staring at Ward and looked again at the painting. She sighed. "It's stunning. I said so before it was completed, and I'll say it again. But I couldn't think of paying seventy thousand dollars without the Tobias imprimatur. I want a refund."

"From who?" Judith interposed. "Clive? Iris? The estate? Who made that check out, Erica? And who was the payee?"

Erica tore her eyes from the canvas and stared at Judith. "Dewitt wrote the check. I assumed it was made out to Riley." Suddenly she looked confused. "But it was dated yesterday . . . and Riley was already dead . . ."

"You'll have to sort that out as best you can," Ward said calmly. "As for Lark's painting here, we didn't say it was for sale."

Erica's face fell. "Now just a minute, Ward! I made an offer on this picture, and even if I did it under false pretenses, I still want it. How about seven thousand?"

Ward's eyebrows lifted imperceptibly. He gazed at Lark, who was still immobile. "That's a considerable difference," he said mildly.

"It's also one hell of a price for a newcomer," Erica snapped. "Take it or leave it."

Ward was still watching Lark. She must have sensed his eyes on her, for at last she moved. "We'll take it if you agree to buy the rest of the series," Lark said quietly. "There will be three more, though the first one seems to be owned by an anonymous collector. Riley and Clive sold it for sixty thousand dollars."

Erica gulped, but to her credit, she didn't fall down foaming at the mouth, which Judith would have done in a similar situation. "I'll have to see the other works in progress," she said.

"You can see 'Midday' right now," Lark replied. "It's halfway finished."

"All right." Erica waved her hands. "I'm not agreeing to buy them all, not with the first one God-knows-where. But I would like a chance to view the companion piece to 'Spring River.' "

"It's not 'Spring River,' " Lark said stiffly. "It's 'Morning.' Don't confuse me with Riley."

Nella had come from behind the bar and was handing out margaritas. "No chance of that, kiddies. Your stuff is a lot prettier than Riley's, Lark. His last few pictures looked like bird doo to me. Drink up, we're celebrating."

Resignedly, Judith accepted her drink and licked at the salt on the rim of the glass. Ward and Lark were now seated on the love seat. Erica was pacing the room, her eyes glued to Lark's canvas. Judith wondered if she was calculating the value of her investment.

"To Lark," Nella said, hoisting her glass. "And to Erica, too. You're a smart cookie, kiddo. You won't be sorry you bought Lark's pictures." She beamed. "Just think, I almost replaced Ike with that masterpiece. I'm glad I didn't. I'd have missed the old geek."

Lark suddenly looked guilt-ridden. "Oh, Nella! I forgot I offered to give you that painting! I'm sorry! I'll paint you a special one, of your garden."

Nella sat down in the rocker. "Now wouldn't that be nice? I'd like that. We'll spend an afternoon going over all the flowers and leaves, and the rocks, too. I've dried and pressed some of the special ones over the years, so you can study those. Maybe you can paint it to size, so I won't have to worry about where it'll fit."

Judith pressed her lips together to keep from laughing at Nella's concept of creativity. She sought out Renie to see her reaction—but Renie wasn't there. It dawned on Judith that her cousin had been among the missing for several minutes.

No one else seemed to notice that Renie had disappeared. Under the influence of Nella and the tequila, the little group had grown quite matey. For all of her material trappings and self-assurance, Erica Dixon showed a proper respect for Ward Kimball. Lark warmed to the topic of her painting and described "Midday"—not in color and perspective, as a fully sighted artist might have done, but in texture and perception.

Judith went over to the window by the wet bar to check on the tow truck's progress. There was no sign of either truck or car, so she assumed the Mercedes had been hauled away. She was about to rejoin the others when she tripped over Renie. Judith stared.

"Hi," said Renie in a small voice, struggling to get up. "I was looking for my purse."

"Your purse is next to the potted fern. The potted fern is next to the potted guests. Have a drink and join us. Yours is sitting on the bar."

"I'll pass," Renie replied, dusting off her sweatshirt. "We'll talk more later." Casually, she strolled over to the footstool and sat down.

"Well, where have *you* been?" Nella asked brightly. "You didn't get your drink."

"Sorry," Renie responded. "I have to watch my salt intake. I tend to bloat." She gave Nella a wide smile. "I was admiring your crewelwork by the bar. I've no knack for that sort of thing."

"Don't be crewel, as Elvis used to say." Nella burst into laughter. "Now *there* was a singer," she went on, doing her own bit of rock 'n' roll in the rocking chair. "These new groups are well and good, especially Pearl Jam, which is my favorite, but how they dress! Grunge, they call it. As far as I'm concerned, they look just like three out of my five husbands. I forget which."

The talk turned to fashion, music, hair dos and don'ts, and, eventually, Riley Tobias. After a second margarita, the mood became maudlin. Judith and Renie offered their excuses. They had to pack up and get ready to head home. Nella insisted they have "one for the road," but the cousins declined. One had been enough for Judith, and Renie was quite satisfied with none at all.

"Well?" Judith inquired when they reached the car. "Lucky you—Nella left the safe open when she got out Lark's canvas. What did you find there, coz?"

In the passenger seat, Renie was looking smug. "No passport," she replied.

"Okay," Judith said, humoring her cousin as she made the tricky reverse out of Nella's drive. "What, then?"

"Five marriage licenses. Birth certificates for all of her children. Three divorce decrees. Two death certificates for the husbands who died. I forget which." Renie gave Judith an impish look. "And Nella's birth certificate."

"And?" Judith drove through the open gate to the family property.

Renie now gazed straight ahead. "That's it."

Judith glared at Renie. "So why the cat-in-the-cream look?"

Turning in her seat as Judith pulled up next to the cabin, Renie rolled her eyes. "Oh, coz, come on! You're the super sleuth! But there," she added in mock reproach, "I'm being unfair. I forgot to mention the part about Nella's birth certificate. She was born in Revelstoke, British Columbia."

Judith turned off the ignition with an impatient, jerky motion. "Big deal. It's a crime to be a Canadian?" She opened the car door and gave it a kick. "Are you sure you weren't under the bar swigging tequila?"

"Coz." Renie was wearing her aging-ingenue look again. "It *is* a crime. At least if you're impersonating a United States postal official." Over the roof of the car, she blinked four times in a row.

"Oh!" Judith's hand flew to her mouth. Then she laughed. "Oh, oh! Nella took FDR's appointment under false pretenses! Oh! That's funny!" She laughed even harder.

"Right," Renie agreed with a grin. "What do you bet Nella's big secret about her trip was visiting relatives up in

British Columbia? Maybe some of her kids moved back there. Whatever, she doesn't want anybody to know she isn't an American citizen."

"Maybe she was naturalized," Judith argued.

"Then why weren't her papers in the safe? Everything else was."

"But she hasn't been postmistress for years," Judith said.

"She gets a Federal pension, I'll bet. Social Security, too. Somehow Nella must have fallen through the immigration cracks. With all her changes of husbands and names, it probably wouldn't be hard to do," Renie observed. "And what's the big deal? I'm sure she did as good a job for the Stars and Stripes as she would have done for the Maple Leaf."

Bemused, Judith started toward the front porch of the cabin. "You're right, it does explain her reticence. Maybe we were wrong about Erica not being in Europe."

"Maybe *you* were wrong," Renie declared. "I'll bet Erica brought Nella those postcards as a souvenir, in thanks for starter plants or something. And the Dixons didn't want anyone looking in their trunk because . . . they didn't want anyone looking their trunk." She lifted her hands in an offering to the obvious.

Judith gave Renie a pat on the shoulder. "Match point, coz. I liked the part about your purse. Nice ruse."

"It was all I could think of. Anyway, none of them heard me." Renie chuckled as they went inside the cabin. "I might as well have been out in the icehouse stealing Nella's rhubarb juice. But a lost purse is always a valid excuse."

"Right," Judith agreed. Suddenly she froze, one hand on the counter that divided the kitchen from the living room. She stared at Renie. "What did you say?" But before Renie could reply, Judith waved a hand. "Never mind, I just had a weird idea. Let's get our stuff together. It's going on five and I want to get out of here before I decide I'm going crazy."

For once, Renie didn't press Judith for an explanation. The open road lay ahead, and so did dinner. After their relatively meager lunch, the cousins were looking forward to a full meal somewhere between the cabin and home. They packed their suitcases, put the few leftovers into the picnic hamper, and looked for any items they might have missed. The curtains were pulled, the stove was checked, and the door was padlocked. Their final stop was under the vine maples, where they said a prayer for Dan McMonigle.

"Well," Judith said as they got into the car, "we did everything we set out to do this trip. Except catch a murderer."

"That wasn't on our agenda," Renie reminded Judith. "Let's just be thankful that our mothers didn't catch the murder on TV. Otherwise, they'd have been driving us nuts with calls about our safety."

Judith gave a faint smile as she turned the key in the ignition. "Mine was probably too busy soaking her hand after the bout with the chili can last night. And yours doesn't watch the news, so that—" She broke off, frowning at the dashboard. "Damn. The key's stuck. At least nothing is lighting up."

"You probably jammed the wheels," said Renie. "Give it a jerk."

"The jerk's out under the vine maples," Judith replied, but her frown deepened. "Oh, dear—I shouldn't have said that. I've hexed us."

Showing mild concern, Renie leaned forward as far as her seat belt would allow. "You were annoyed with me when you pulled in. You shut the engine off too hard. Just jiggle the key and it'll free up. Trust me. Bill has taught me everything I know about cars."

Judith gave Renie a baleful look. "Bill knows as much about cars as I know about Freudian psychology."

"True." Renie gave her cousin a mischievous look. "But then, my husband is not a Jung man."

"Cut it out," Judith grumbled, wrestling with the ignition. "I'm not in the mood for your wretched puns. Damn,

I wish Mike were here. Unlike our husbands, past and present, he *does* know something about cars."

"Oh, right," jeered Renie. "I remember two winters ago when he and Kristin drove up here at night to do God-knows-what, and they locked the keys in this very vehicle. You had to get Carl Rankers to drive you all the way . . ."

But Judith wasn't listening. "Do you suppose it's the battery?"

Renie considered. "Bill would say it's the grommitz. He always says that."

Grommitz or not, the compact wouldn't start. Heaving a sigh of resignation, Judith opened the car door. "We'd better call Gary Johanson. Let's go over to the auto court and use the phone. I'm too tired to walk up to the Green Mountain Inn."

Again Renie offered no argument. But as they reached the highway, they noticed Dewitt Dixon arguing with Kennedy Morton. The debate was short-lived: Morton slapped a greasy rag against his palm and strode off into his little office. Dewitt stood by the gas pump, apparently still fuming.

"Is your car going to be okay?" Judith asked after hauling Renie across the road. "Cars are sure a trial. Mine won't start."

Dewitt turned slowly and glared at Judith. It was obvious that he didn't care to share troubles. "Bodywork on a Mercedes is always costly," he said in a cold voice; then his eyes sparked and he stormed over to stand toe to toe with the cousins. "You meddled! You ruined everything! How could you? I hope you enjoy your hideous painting! It cost me plenty!" Turning on his heel, he started back toward the motel.

"Whoa!" Judith called, hurrying after him.. "Where *is* my hideous painting? *I* don't have it."

Dewitt took three angry steps before he stopped abruptly and spun around. "You don't?" He looked astonished as well as incredulous. "Then who does? It's gone. It's been gone since yesterday."

Renie put a hand on his arm. "It's true, Dewitt. Judith hasn't seen Riley's canvas since you and Clive took it out of the cabin Tuesday night. Where did you put it?"

Dewitt gestured over his shoulder. "In the motel room, under the bed. I knew Erica would never look there. She's afraid of mice." The color had drained from his face.

Judith glanced over at Nella's house, wondering if Erica was still there, filled with triumph and tequila. "What did you tell your wife?"

Dewitt swallowed hard. "Nothing. Yet. I don't know where she went."

The cousins decided to leave Dewitt to his own devices. And to Erica. But Judith wasn't satisfied. "Who could have taken the blasted thing now?" she muttered as they started for the phone booth.

"Clive, in a double cross?" Renie suggested.

"Maybe," Judith replied, but sounded dubious.

For the first time, they noticed that a glazier's truck and a phone-company van were pulled up in front of Riley Tobias's house.

"Alexander Graham Bell is calling," Judith remarked. "Let's see if Iris is having a phone installed. If it's new, it might work better than this relic at the Woodchuck."

Iris, however, was outside, supervising replacement of the window Judith had broken with the falling ladder. Suffering a twinge of guilt, Judith hailed Iris.

"Don't fuss," Iris said. "It's covered, except for a small deductible." She sighed, gesturing at the workmen's vehicles parked in front of the house. "Wouldn't you know it? They all come at once, and make you wait until the end of the day."

"Right," Judith agreed, wondering how Hillside Manor was faring under the care of Arlene Rankers. Hopefully, the flood problem would have been resolved by the time Judith got home. "You've having a phone installed?"

Iris nodded. "I may have to be here to help show the place after I put it on the market. I didn't want to stay incommunicado." She made a wry face. "Besides, it's an added selling point if I make this house as up-to-date as possible."

The glazier was putting the finishing touches on his handiwork. Renie cocked her head as the lowering sun struck the new window. "Do you think the studio will add or detract from the sale?"

Iris shrugged. "Who knows? I don't expect to find another artist who'll want it. But it'd make a great guest house. Of course, there's no plumbing." She excused herself as the glass man came forward, ready to deal with the billing process.

"Looks good," Renie remarked absently. "Gosh, it'll be strange to have a new neighbor after all these years with Riley."

"Probably some Yuppies," Judith replied with equal vagueness. Her gaze was on the studio door. "Who drank?" she asked, seemingly out of nowhere.

Renie's gaze narrowed. "If it wasn't Riley, it had to be Iris. Or Lark," she added with a grimace.

Judith moved to the door. "I'm afraid so. It seems unlikely in either case, but alcoholics are so deceptive. To look at them, you'd often never know."

"Just like murderers," said Renie, following her cousin into the studio.

Judith turned to Renie, giving her a quizzical look. "Oh, no. Alcoholism is a disease." She bit her lip and gazed around the artistic setting that had made up Riley Tobias's life. And death. The outline of the body had been erased, though much of the spilled orange paint remained. "Drinking is no crime. It's an affliction. Murder is another matter." Judith bent down and lifted up the floorboard under which the empty bottles and the single beer can had been stashed. They were still there. "Hmm. I thought they might have been removed by now."

Renie was keeping one eye out for Iris. "By anybody we know?"

"Probably. But a bunch of empty bottles aren't evidence of anything except drinking." Judith circled the studio twice, her black eyes darting into every nook and cranny. She reminded Renie of a mother panther, checking her lair for danger. Judith paused by the garbage can that stood next to the house. "When's the pickup around here?"

Renie shrugged. "How do I know? We've never been on the route. We either hauled our garbage home or buried it behind the cabin."

Judith lifted the heavy plastic lid. She peered into the can, then gingerly picked through the top layer of debris. "Nothing," she said, then noticed another bin at the corner of the house. "Aha!" she exclaimed. "This is for recycling. There must be a half-dozen empty beer cans on top."

"And only one under the floorboard." Renie didn't sound impressed. "So what's your conclusion?"

Judith replaced the hinged lid on the recycling bin. "I'm guessing but there was a reason to ditch that poor lonely can. Fingerprints, maybe. Or the lack of them. Undersheriff Costello can sort that out. What matters now is that I think I'm on the right track," she declared with a determined look at her face. "Come on, coz. We're heading for the hippie hangout."

“WHAT ABOUT THE phone?” Renie demanded as the cousins waited for Iris out by the fence with its esoteric, eclectic decorations treasured by Riley Tobias.

Judith chewed on her lower lip. “Maybe you’re right. We ought to get Gary to solve the car problem first. We never know when we’re going to need a quick getaway.”

Renie was pacing nervously around the well. “You’re sure about this?”

“Ninety percent,” Judith replied. “There’s one thing I’d like to check out before I start shooting my face off. But it’s pretty straightforward, really. If Abbott N. Costello weren’t such a dope, an arrest might have been made two days ago.”

Iris Takisaki came out of the house just as the glazier pulled out of the driveway. The phone-company van followed almost immediately.

“They’re gone,” she said in relief. “How do you feel about a martini?”

Judith smiled and shook her head. “No, thanks, Iris. We’ve got a sixty-mile drive ahead of us. If we can get my car started. That’s why we came—to inaugurate your new phone.”

Iris laughed. "Why not? Come on in, and we'll see if it really works."

It did. Gary Johanson told Judith he'd be down as soon as he finished his dinner. He always ate early, he explained, before the regular customers arrived at the inn's restaurant.

Iris was smiling at the mauve Trimline phone. "That's a relief. I didn't mind when Riley was here, but since he's gone, I've felt isolated without a phone."

"You ought to meet my mother," Judith murmured. She started to sit down on the sofa, then gave their hostess a piteous look. "Fix yourself a drink, Iris. You're got a funeral to face the day after tomorrow. What Renie and I could really use is some crackers and cheese. We may not get dinner until late, unless Gary uses witchcraft to fix my car."

"I've got Brie," Iris said. "Let me go out to the kitchen and rustle up some crackers, too. Do you want the cheese warmed?"

Renie thought that sounded great. She rubbed her stomach as Iris headed for the kitchen. She rolled her eyes as Judith began opening drawers. She sat down with a thud when her cousin waved a contract at her that was signed by Dewitt Dixon and Clive Silvanus. She leaned back in the contour chair and sighed as Judith shook the contents of a brown paper bag under her nose.

"Now what?" murmured Renie.

"Now we eat Brie," Judith replied. "Or would you rather have Sweet-Stix?"

An hour later, Gary Johanson still hadn't shown up to start Judith's car. The cousins were getting anxious. Iris kept assuring them that they weren't imposing on her, but shortly after six, Clive Silvanus arrived.

"Oh, good Lord!" Iris exclaimed, seeing Clive on the back porch. "I forgot Clive was taking me to dinner in Glacier Falls! He thought the two of us should go over material for Riley's eulogy." She rushed off to admit her caller.

Renie glanced at Judith. "Well?"

Judith stood up. "Let's go so they can head out for dinner. We can wait for Gary by the side of the road."

"But—" Renie's protest was cut short by the reappearance of Iris, with Clive in tow.

"Tin Hat or Thai?" Judith asked, waving hello to Clive.

Clive, as usual, was dressed in varying shades of brown, his beige-and-taupe tie neatly knotted, but his tan slacks rumpled. Fleetingly, Judith wondered how he'd feel if he knew his scheme with Dewitt had been sabotaged.

"Ah thought we'd try that little steak place up from the traffic light," Clive said as Iris dashed into the bedroom, presumably to get ready. "Iris says it's hash-house food, but Ah say, what's wrong with hash?"

"Nothing," Renie replied, "unless you make it like Cousin Sue. She put her goldfish in it once."

Clive blanched. The cousins made their farewells, calling out to Iris, who returned a muffled "Good-bye" from the bedroom.

It was still daylight outside, so the cousins ambled back and forth along the shoulder of the road. Traffic was somewhat heavier than usual for a Thursday night, perhaps due to people getting a jump-start on the weekend. Ward Kimball's Volkswagen bus no longer stood in Nella's drive. Over at the auto court, three new arrivals were parked in front of the little cabins. There was no sign of the Dixons. Perhaps they were inside, doing battle over Dewitt's deception. Except for Kennedy Morton, who was pumping gas into a white Mazda Miata, the rest of the family was nowhere in sight. Judith figured they were probably eating, though what and how, she didn't want to know.

The cousins didn't recognize the old rust-red beater Gary Johanson drove from the Green Mountain Inn. "My latest fixer-upper," he said, sticking his head out the window. "Where's your car?"

Judith and Renie led the way up the rolling drive. Gary went to work. The cousins watched hopefully. Gary slid off the seat and crouched under the dashboard. Gary hit his head. Gary swore. Gary ducked under the dashboard again. Gary got out of the car, looking glum.

"These Japanese jobs can be tricky," he announced. "I'm a Detroit man. Now, if it were something simple like Iris's problem the other day, all I'd have to do is jiggle the key around and free up the wheels. She could have done that herself. But this"—he jabbed a thumb at the blue compact—"has got me stumped. You got towing insurance?"

Judith did. Gary told her to have the car taken to Fast Freddy's Auto Repair in Glacier Falls. But he warned her that they wouldn't be able to do anything until the morning. It was, after all, past six-thirty. Freddy might be fast, but he didn't do overtime.

Chagrined, Judith offered to pay Gary, but he refused. "You're a neighbor. We'll figure out a way to get back at you." He gave her a diffident grin and backed down the drive.

"Great." Downcast, Judith tried to figure out a better solution than the one Gary had offered. "I really don't want to spend another night up here. I'd rather have the car towed all the way into town, pay the extra mileage, and somehow get back to Hillside Manor tonight."

Renie, however, was puzzled. "I don't get it, coz. I thought you intended to solve this murder case. Are you slipping?"

"I wanted to tie up the loose ends, drive home, call the sheriff—the *real* sheriff—and let him sort it out. I'm not really sure, coz. I've only got a glimmer." Judith sighed as they started out for the phone booth at the auto court. "Most of all, I don't like the conclusions I'm drawing. I'd rather not stick around for the last act."

"You can't order up a murderer du jour, like soup," Renie pointed out. "I can follow your rationale—or your logic, as you'd put it—but I agree. You may be way off base this time. Either you're not telling me everything you know, or I'm being dense."

Judith gave Renie a rueful look while they waited at the edge of the road for a lull in traffic. "I'm probably not very convincing. But this isn't a situation where there are so-called clues that jump out at you. I'm sorting through fragments to make the big picture. What strikes me as unusual about this case is that the murder was so simple. Yet it's the innocuous, everyday things that seem to point to the killer. If I were a painter, I'd find Truth in tiny specks of color, not in great, bold splashes."

Reaching the other side of the highway, Renie gave a little shiver. "Frankly, I'll be glad to get out of here. I wasn't particularly nervous when we didn't have any inkling of the murderer's identity. But now, it's spooky."

The people at the towing service in Glacier Falls could scarcely believe that they had to make two trips to virtually the same place in one day. They'd be happy to take Judith's compact all the way into the city. But renting a car was not so easy. They had only one vehicle at their disposal, and it already had been leased to the Dixons. Nor could both cousins ride in the tow truck: There was room only for the driver and a single passenger. Judith requested the tow truck; she and Renie would sort out their own transportation later.

"Joe?" suggested Renie. "Bill? Joe and Bill? Bill and Joe?"

Judith looked at her watch. Dusk was settling in. "It's almost seven. Joe ought to be home. Still . . ." She frowned. "I hate to ask him. He's probably been chasing mass murderers all day and coping with Mother and Arlene the rest of the time."

Renie nodded. "Thursdays are horrid for Bill. He's got a lecture hall of over four hundred students, a graduate seminar, a division meeting, and about four private counseling appointments. Plus, it's his turn to air the hamster."

Judith looked impressed. "Wow! I didn't know Bill ever took care of the family pet."

"Only when the kids are gone and I'm out of town. The last time he did it, the hamster bit him. Or was it the other way 'round?" Renie looked vague.

Judith snapped her fingers. "I've got it! We'll borrow one of Gary's beaters. We can have the tow truck haul it back." She started walking briskly up the road.

"Hey, hold up!" Renie called. Judith stopped and turned around. "What about the hippies?"

"Forget the hippies." Judith waited for Renie to catch up. "Maybe a word of warning to the sheriff will suffice."

"You really think Clive is in cahoots with them?" Renie asked as they walked past the cyclone fence that guarded Trent and Glenna Berkman's property from the road.

"He's up to something," Judith said. She, too, was feeling ill at ease. The cousins walked faster. "I think Clive *and* Riley were in cahoots with them. Somewhere along the line, they struck a bargain with the hippies—a regular bribe to keep them from pinching Riley's art. Carrie Mae Morton mentioned that they were well heeled, at least by her standards. Since Riley was the only one around here who never got robbed, how else do you explain his good luck? He certainly had a lot of stuff worth stealing. I'll bet Clive was up there paying them off—or else calling it off, now that Riley's out and Iris is in."

Gary Johanson wasn't keen on letting the cousins borrow a beater. None of the four he had parked by the shed was really roadworthy. He'd rather they took his new pickup or Dee's Honda Accord. But Judith and Renie wouldn't hear of that. The trio stood under a tall hemlock and tried to come up with another solution.

"Say," said Gary, "what about Iris's Acura? She won't need it until the funeral on Saturday."

Judith wasn't so sure. "She might have to go into Glacier Falls tomorrow to finalize the arrangements."

"That Southern guy can take her," Gary countered. "Didn't he go off to dinner with her a while ago?"

"Yes, but . . ." Judith chewed on her lower lip. The darker it got, the more nervous she became. "I don't suppose they'll be gone long. We'll have to wait for Iris to come back with the car keys and ask her permission."

Gary loped over to the inn. "Hang on. I've got her extra set of keys. She left them in case the other one got broken off in the ignition. I forgot to return them, with all the excitement about Riley getting killed. Iris must have been too upset to miss them." He opened the door to the inn and reached inside. "Here, they were up on the board. Leave her a note. I'll explain." He eyed the cousins sympathetically. "Frankly, you two look beat."

"We just want to get home," Renie said. "Maybe it's finally hit us that there's a killer loose around here."

Gary gave a short, mirthless laugh. "Tell me about it. Dee and I have been sleeping with my .22 under the bed the past two nights. Who says all the crime is in the big city? We got plenty of it right around here."

Slowly, Judith closed her hands around Iris's car keys. "I'm not sure this is a good idea." She looked at Renie. "Do you think I could get Dooley and his chums to drive up here tonight and return the Acura?"

"You can if you give Dooley fifty bucks," said Renie, referring to Judith's former newspaper carrier, who had recently passed his first driver's test. "Now that he's given up Police Auxiliary work and taken up with girls, he might look upon it as an adventure. I'll split the cost with you."

Having settled the matter of commandeering Iris's car, Judith thanked Gary, who offered to drive them back to the cabin. The tow truck was just pulling into the dirt drive. The cousins removed their belongings from the compact's trunk and gave directions to the auto-repair shop at the foot of Heraldsgate Hill. After the defunct car had been dragged out of the driveway, Judith and Renie lugged their suitcases and the picnic hamper over to Riley's house. Judith slipped a note under the door and they were off.

"Phew!" Judith exclaimed as they raced past the Woodchuck Auto Court. "I feel better already! I was getting pretty antsy."

"Me, too," Renie agreed. "Maybe we can still stop for dinner someplace. Now that I'm not scared, I'm starving." She settled back in the comfortable seat as they took the curve by Ward Kimball's house. "Music. We need music to settle our nerves." With a flick of the wrist, Renie opened the glove compartment.

"We're chicken, coz," Judith said as the car began to make the Sand Hill climb.

Renie, however, scoffed. "Don't be silly. It's not 'chicken' to avoid getting ourselves killed. Tonight, you talk over your ideas with Joe. Tomorrow, you call the sheriff up here. On Saturday, we bow our heads and say a prayer for Riley. Come Sunday, I'll fix fried chicken with cheese spaghetti and you bring our mothers. Bill and Joe can watch whichever NBA teams are still dunking for dollars. All this will be behind us and life will go on."

Judith, however, didn't respond. A sense of failure, as thick as the darkness which now enveloped all but the ribbon of headlights, had settled over her. "I don't like giving up," she finally asserted. "Or giving in."

"You aren't," Renie argued, shoving a sturdy plastic cassette case back into the glove compartment. "You're only being sensible. And safe. Joe will be delighted."

"Joe." Judith sighed. Maybe Renie was right. If Joe had used reverse psychology, it had worked. She glanced at her cousin. "What happened to the music?"

"I can't read the labels on the tapes in the dark. I couldn't see them anyway without my glasses." Renie made one last stab at the glove compartment. "Here, this is a loose one. Let's try it and hope it isn't something Nella would like."

They were coming down the steep grade of the Sand Hill. Renie, who was particularly inept with anything mechanical, fiddled with the cassette, putting it in backward the first time. At last, after poking several buttons, the cousins heard the soft whir of the tape.

No sounds of a symphony, no thudding bass of a rock group, no brassy notes of a Broadway hit filled the inside of Iris's Acura. Instead, Judith and Renie heard the voice of Riley Tobias:

"This is my version of a love letter. I'm not clever with words . . ."

Judith applied the brake and pulled the car over to the side of the road. She stared at Renie.

"We're going back."

Renie's jaw dropped; then she saw the determined look on her cousin's face. "You're crazy," she murmured. "Okay, let's go."

SIXTEEN

UNDERSHERIFF ABBOTT N. COSTELLO was off duty. He could be beeped, however, if there was an emergency. Judith said that was indeed the case. It might take a while, the voice at the other end of the bad connection informed her. Even if Costello could be contacted immediately, it would take at least forty-five minutes for him to get to the vicinity of the Woodchuck Auto Court.

"Where do we wait?" queried Renie. The cousins had already returned Iris's car and were standing outside the phone booth. "Nella's?"

Across the road, the lights in Nella's house glowed invitingly, but Judith shook her head. "I don't think that's a good idea."

"With the Mortons?"

This time Judith grimaced. "Mortal danger is one thing—the Mortons are another." She turned around to gaze at their homely house. "On the other hand, I do have a question for the kiddies. Wait here and watch for Iris and Clive. I want to see what happens when he brings her home."

Renie complied. Judith returned within three minutes. "Well?" asked Renie.

"I was right." Judith scuffed at the gravel along the roadside. Before she could say more, a car coming from the direction of Glacier Falls slowed to make a turn. But instead of taking a right to Riley Tobias's house, it pulled left into the Woodchuck's drive. The cousins drew back into the shadow of the phone booth.

Dewitt and Erica Dixon emerged from a small sedan. Erica's tone was waspish as she spoke to her husband. "Go ahead, take credit for it! If your reputation as a shrewd collector means more to you than I do, maybe you'd just as soon go it alone. I may love you, but I'm not sure I trust you!" She stomped off toward their motel unit.

Dewitt doggedly followed her. "Don't be ridiculous, Erica! Would I try to hoodwink my own wife? I'm glad you bought Lark's painting. Maybe it means you're finally over Riley . . ."

The door closed behind them. The cousins stared at each other; then Judith said in a whisper, "Dewitt did hoodwink his own wife. He knew all along that Lark painted that picture. He saw her working on it. And I'll bet he and Clive were trying to pull a fast one, but maybe Dewitt chickened out after Riley was murdered and put a stop payment on the check. Erica's check. I'll be darned." Judith chuckled to herself.

Overhead, a sprinkling of stars dotted the sky. The moon was rising over Mount Woodchuck. In the distance, the river was only a faint murmur. Now that they were no longer headed home, nervousness again attacked Judith and Renie. Their eyes grew wary; their feet were restless; tension settled over them, heavy as the spring dew.

More cars, RVs, trucks, and vans cruised the highway. Fifteen minutes passed before another vehicle slowed down. It was a false alarm. The Buick from Oregon pulled into the auto court to discharge two cheerful seventy-year-olds whose goal was no more nefarious than finding a comfortable bed for the night. Judith and Renie resumed their watch.

Five minutes later, the headlights of a larger conveyance

shone, then turned into Nella's driveway across the road. Renie gave Judith a curious look.

"Ward?" she whispered, though her voice couldn't have been heard over the sound of a passing mini-van.

Judith peered into the darkness. "Ward. And Lark." She stood motionless as Ward Kimball assisted his daughter from the Volkswagen bus.

"What do we do?" asked Renie, still speaking softly.

"Nothing." But the pair didn't go into Nella's; instead, the Kimballs circled around to Riley's Tobias's drive. Cautiously, they went along the side of the house, apparently heading for the studio. "We wait for Costello."

"But . . ." Renie's face puckered in confusion. "Shouldn't we stall them?"

"No." The firmness of Judith's tone was not arguable, even for Renie.

Another five minutes passed. Judith's watch told her it was after eight o'clock. Restless, Renie paced the tarmac. "I wonder if Fabio would give me some strained peas," she mused.

"You're allergic to peas," Judith remarked a bit testily.

"Who cares? At this rate, I'll die of starvation before a reaction can set in." Renie seemed oblivious to logic.

Another car slowed, then turned into Riley's drive. Judith recognized Clive's Infiniti. The minutes passed like dead weight. Finally Clive, ever the Southern gentleman, got out and rushed around to open the door for Iris. He walked her to the door. They chatted; then Iris went inside. Clive returned to his car.

Renie grabbed Judith's arm. "Coz!" she cried, heedless of anyone hearing her. "We've got to stop him!"

"It's okay," Judith said, fobbing off Renie's clutching hand. "Let's go."

Renie was clearly all at sea. "This is crazy," she muttered. "What about Costello?"

"He'll be along shortly," Judith replied, then added under her breath, "I hope."

Iris was surprised to see her guests. "What happened? I

just found your note. But my car is outside. Did it stall again? You were welcome to it, really. I plan to spend tomorrow doing the rest of Riley's paperwork."

Judith and Renie were in the little entry hall off the kitchen. "It's a long story," Judith said. "Why don't we take you up on that drink offer?"

Iris led them into the living room. It appeared that she was already making order out of chaos. Much of the clutter had been cleared away, file folders rested in cardboard boxes, and two packing crates stood ready for whatever contents awaited them.

"Clive is going to help me with some of this tomorrow," Iris said, mixing martinis, two gin and one vodka. "He's really quite helpful."

Judith was standing by the window that looked out onto the studio. The edifice was dark, but she had a feeling it wasn't empty. Lark wouldn't need light to find what she was looking for.

"Clive's a hard worker," Judith remarked. "I mean, I assume he is, since he did so well by Riley."

Iris presented the cousins with their drinks. "His manner is deceptive," she said, sitting down in a zebra-striped chair. "If there was some way I could keep him on, I would. But that's pointless. The works that Riley kept for himself should go to the foundation."

"Of course." Judith raised her glass. "To Riley."

Iris and Renie followed suit. "I miss him," Iris said. Her dark eyes wandered around the living room, coming to rest on one of his early works, a view of morning mist rising from a stand of evergreens. "As maudlin as it sounds, he was the only man I ever loved."

Judith inclined her head. "Is that right, Iris?" She heard a noise outside. Neither Iris nor Renie seemed to notice. "In that case," Judith asked, keeping her voice even, "why did you kill him?"

Iris didn't move. She sat in the zebra-striped chair with the martini glass clutched in her long, slim fingers. Judith also remained motionless. Only Renie turned on the sofa, then twisted around as if watching for someone to come in through the back door.

"I understand you married a policeman the second time," Iris said in a conversational tone. "Is that what gives you such peculiar ideas, Judith?"

"Oh, maybe." Judith started to sip at her martini, thought better of it, and sat up straight in the cane-backed chair. "I used to be a librarian, as you may recall. The job gives you an inquiring mind."

Iris stood up, cradling the drink against her breast. "Inquiring, but not necessarily imaginative." She moved slowly to the armoire which housed the liquor. "I'm surprised that you'd come up with such fantasies. You saw Riley working in the studio. You were with me when I found the body. And why on earth would I kill him?"

Judith kept her voice as casual as Iris's. "For a lot of reasons. He may not have been in love with Lark, but he probably did intend to marry her. That in itself could have driven you to murder."

Iris laughed, a not-quite-musical sound. "How absurd! I told you, Riley was Lark's father." She opened the door of the armoire. "Are you accusing him of incest?"

"No." Judith's voice had taken on a sad note. "Riley wasn't Lark's father. You made that up, to mislead us. It was a stupid mistake, Iris. Maybe your only real mistake. Lark is thirty-two years old. Riley didn't come up to this part of the world until six or seven years after Lark was born. You were so anxious to debunk an affair between Riley and Lark as a motive that you invented an outrageous—and impossible—lie. All things considered, it wasn't worthy of you."

Looking relaxed as well as amused, Iris smiled at the cousins. "In groping for a motive, you haven't done badly. But you realize it's utterly impossible for me to have killed Riley. The undersheriff knows that—you're my witnesses."

"Not witnesses," Judith said firmly. "Dupes. We just

happened to be there. Otherwise, it might have been Dewitt or Clive. You sneaked back here from the Green Mountain Inn, got Riley to have another beer or two, coaxed him into standing in front of his easel—and strangled him." Judith ignored the scornful look on Iris's face. "That easel was very sturdy because it held large paintings, though you made sure it would support his weight by propping the heavy box of paints behind it. Then you spilled tempera paint all over the floor. It's not as slippery as oil or acrylic, but it did the job. Riley's body couldn't fight gravity. While we were over at Nella's, looking for your nonexistent prowler, Riley was slowly sliding to the floor. That's how you found him, and I've got to admit, it sure fooled me. We were a perfect pair of saps to make a perfect alibi. It's a terrible shame, Iris. I always liked you a lot."

Iris had put her martini glass down on a shelf in the armoire. She was reaching for a jar of olives with her left hand when Judith realized she had opened a small drawer with her right. The gun appeared before either of the cousins could move to stop Iris.

"I'm all alone here now," Iris said calmly, pointing the gun first at Judith and then at Renie. "Someone is bound to break into this place and try to steal some of the art objects. Who could blame me for shooting a couple of intruders, especially when they stole my car?" She smiled blandly at the cousins. "Having the phone installed proves I was frightened. In the wake of Riley's tragic death, I might also be hysterical."

It occurred to Judith that there never was a woman less inclined to hysterics than Iris Takisaki. The calm she exhibited was far more terrifying than any emotional outburst. Judith tried to think and listen at the same time. There was another noise outside. Judith caught her breath; then her heart sank. She heard Ward Kimball's Volkswagen van drive off down the road.

"It wasn't just jealousy that made you kill Riley," Judith said, aware that the only hope was to stall for time. "With

Riley dead, you have control of his foundation. Are you accountable to anyone?" There was no response from Iris. She merely moved two steps closer to Judith and Renie. "You could do as you pleased with his fortune and his works of art. Oh, you might go through the motions of an office and an exhibit and maybe even a few crumbs to starving minority students now and then. But Riley had accumulated considerable wealth. You'd be a rich, independent woman, Iris."

Iris gave a toss of her carefully coiffed head. "I'm already well off. And extremely independent." Her voice was tinged with scorn.

"Like hell," Renie said. "You may lead a comfy lifestyle, Iris, but you're not really independent. You doted on Riley, and felt he should reciprocate. Maybe he only wanted Lark because, as his wife, she could go on painting pictures under his name. But keeping up his artistic reputation was more important to him than you were. He intended to ditch you as soon as Lark said, 'I do, I paint.' Riley used both of you. Lark might never believe that, but you knew it, and that's why you killed him."

Iris glared at Renie, but she also kept Judith within full view. "And how could I overcome a man as big and strong as Riley?"

Judith tried to eye her watch. Over half an hour had gone by since she'd called the sheriff's office. "I already said it—you got him drunk," Judith replied. "It wouldn't take much, given his lack of capacity for liquor. You drank right along with him, but you hid your beer can under the floorboard. You couldn't risk fingerprints being found. Of course, you're used to drinking, aren't you, Iris? You've got quite a collection out there under the studio floorboards."

Iris's nostrils flared. Her fine features took on a grotesque aspect as she raised the gun. "You're a pair of meddlers! All your nice manners and neighborly ways are just a sham! You're really a couple of nasty bitches!"

Renie glowered right back at Iris. "And you're a Camp

Fire Girl? At least we haven't murdered anybody. Give it up, Iris. The sheriff's on his way."

To the cousins' dismay, Iris laughed. "The sheriff! You mean that dunce Costello? He's probably lost in the wrong county. Come on, let's go out to the studio. I don't want to make a mess in the living room now that I'm getting it straightened up."

Trying to stand, Judith realized her knees were weak. She held onto the back of the chair to steady herself. Renie went first, out the front door. The meadow was shrouded in mist. Fleetingly, Judith wondered if they dared make a run for it. But Iris was too close behind them. She might miss one of them, but she'd get the other.

The studio seemed very cold. Iris ordered Renie to turn on one of the lights, then told Judith to start the CD player. "Turn it up," she commanded as Wagner's *Ride of the Valkyries* poured from the speakers. Judith winced at the volume.

"No one will hear anything over that," Iris shouted as she held the gun in both hands. Judith was no expert on firearms, but Joe had taught her enough to recognize a Smith & Wesson .36 Chief Special. "Now I shoot you," Iris announced in a loud but controlled voice. "Then I switch off the music and toss a match onto those old paint rags in the corner." She gave a slight lift of her shoulders. "By the time the volunteer firemen get here, there won't be much left of you or the studio."

Horrified, Judith backed away from Iris and bumped into Renie, who was standing next to the new window. "You wouldn't do that! Nella and the Mortons will see the fire right away! And what about your cock-and-bull robber story?"

Iris appeared unconcerned, though her voice was showing signs of strain as she continued to yell above the Valkyries' wild cries. "Thieves fall out. A couple of days ago, didn't Clive and Dewitt think you were hiding a seventy-thousand-dollar painting? Let Costello try to unravel it. It won't matter to me. I'll be halfway to Glacier Falls, going to see the undertaker." She aimed the gun at Renie. "You've got an awfully big mouth, Mrs. Jones."

"And about now, it could eat an elephant." Renie appeared unnaturally composed. Judith's heart was pounding too hard to let her brain figure out why.

It was the brilliant light flooding the room that distracted Iris just as she was about to pull the trigger. Her attention shifted a fraction too long; Renie came down hard on the floorboard that covered the empty liquor bottles. The two-foot plank flew up, knocking Iris off-balance. Judith fell on top of her, trying to grab the gun. A shot went off, lodging somewhere in the rafters. Renie had scurried around to help Judith, getting an armlock around Iris's neck. She squeezed, hard. Iris screamed, turned purple, and slumped onto the floor. Wagner's Valkyries raged on.

The gun fell from Iris's hand. Judith pushed it aside. "Thank God for the sheriff," she murmured, going limp.

"The sheriff?" gasped Renie as bodies hurtled into the studio. "It's not the sheriff, coz. It's the TV reporters. I think we just made the eleven o'clock news."

Undersheriff Abbott N. Costello arrived two minutes later with Dabney Plummer and three other deputies. So did the entire Morton clan, the Dixons, and Nella Lablatt. The television crew had been so busy setting up equipment and giving orders to one another that Judith and Renie were able to escape in the confusion. Had Iris not been half-conscious, she, too, might have gotten away. Through the studio windows, the cousins saw an aggressive female reporter trying to interview her.

"Clearly," the reporter was saying, more into her microphone than to Iris, "the studio of the internationally acclaimed artist Riley Tobias has once again been a scene of wanton violence. What is your reaction to this latest outrage?"

"My attorney!" croaked Iris, struggling to sit up. "I want my attorney!"

"An understandable reaction, given the social ills that beset contemporary society," the reporter said smoothly, if loudly, over the music. "Would you care to comment on how it feels to . . ."

Judith turned away, almost colliding with a young man uncoiling a length of orange cable. Costello and his men had rushed past the cousins, either not recognizing them or not caring. Somebody turned off the CD player, but the night was still filled with unnatural sounds.

Nella, wearing a voluminous pink bathrobe and gold lamé bedroom slippers, stood on tiptoes to get a better look. "What's happening? Is somebody else dead?"

The four oldest Morton children shrieked with delight and charged toward the studio. Kennedy Morton darted after them, shouting.

Judith tried to steer Nella out of harm's way. "There's really nothing to see. I'm afraid Iris killed Riley." She spoke very quietly, lest Nella succumb to shock.

But Nella merely snorted. "Iris! Can't say as I blame her, in a way. Riley gave her a bad time. A woman should take only so much. Then she's got to draw the line."

Dumbfounded, Judith said nothing. Costello came back out of the studio, with Dabney Plummer at his heels. This time, the undersheriff noticed the cousins.

"You two again! You put in the call? What for?" He was scowling under his hat. "You had the gall to use the word 'emergency,' and all these dumbbell reporters hear it on the radio band and come a-running! Sheesh!"

Judith explained, aware that some of the TV personnel had formed a circle around them. "It appears that Iris Takisaki murdered Riley Tobias. When my cousin and I confronted her with the accusation, she pulled a gun on us and threatened to kill us. Luckily, we disarmed and subdued her before she could carry out her intentions. We'd like to file a complaint."

Costello looked skeptical. "This sounds screwy to me. You two gave her an alibi. Got any proof?"

"We can make a statement," Judith said calmly. "The

important thing is that Ms. Takisaki is placed under arrest."

"I don't have a warrant." Costello made as if to walk away.

Judith grabbed him by the sleeve of his jacket. "Now just a minute." She stood close to him, almost treading on his shoes. "You've got a murderer in there," she said between clenched teeth. "You've got the press all over the place. You've got two people who will testify that the suspect was about to assault them with a deadly weapon. You've got a chance to be a real hero. And if you don't act fast, you're going to get egg all over your face, and the next thing you know, you'll be sitting outside the Tin Hat Cafe with a tin cup." Judith gave Costello a little shake. "Get it?"

Her words seemed to sink in. Looking surly, Costello pulled free of Judith's hold, but he marched off to the studio, where his other deputies apparently were questioning Iris. More TV correspondents, along with print and radio reporters, had arrived, apparently drawn by information on the police band.

Wearily, Judith drew Renie aside. "We'll probably have to go into the county seat to make our statement and file a complaint. Maybe they'll give us a ride home."

"Maybe they'll give us dinner," Renie said, but she didn't sound hopeful.

Judith uttered a lame little laugh. "I couldn't figure you out in the studio, coz. At first I thought you were being reckless with Iris because you were hungry. Then I realized you saw those TV people arrive before she and I did."

"I saw them pull in when you turned on the CD player. Iris's back was turned and she couldn't hear them over the music. I knew it wouldn't take long before they made themselves known to you and Iris. Journalists are pushy."

Judith sighed. "Thank God for that."

A few feet away, Nella Lablatt and Carrie Mae Morton were engaged in animated conversation. Dewitt and Erica Dixon were being interviewed by a rival TV station. More people had shown up, including the seventy-year-old couple from Oregon who looked pleasurably excited. Their overnight stay at the Woodchuck Auto Court had turned out to be more entertaining than they'd anticipated.

A hush fell over the crowd as Undersheriff Costello emerged from the studio with Iris in handcuffs. Her carriage was proud; her expression, defiant. She didn't look at the cousins.

Over by the fence, a group of reporters had gathered around Dabney Plummer. At last Plummer was speaking. Judith and Renie stared.

"What's that all about?" Renie asked of another, passing deputy.

The broad-shouldered man gave Renie a curious look. "What do you mean? It's a press briefing." He frowned at Renie. "Dabney Plummer is our official spokesperson."

Judith and Renie were speechless.

A moment later, Costello hustled Iris into the backseat of his patrol car. The Morton children crowded as close as possible. Costello and the square-shouldered deputy also got in and drove off with a squeal of tires, flashing lights, and the siren's wail. Judith expected the Morton kiddies to be impressed.

They weren't. Standing close together, their faces downcast, they began to chant:

"No more Sweet-Stix! No more Sweet-Stix! No more Sweet-Stix now!"

Carrie Mae Morton insisted that the cousins come over for a nice glass of wine. Since the county car in which they'd be traveling couldn't leave for some time, Judith and Renie reluctantly gave in.

The Morton living room was still in disarray, with piles of laundry all over the floor, a spilled bowl of chili covering an easy chair, and a small pig sitting on top of the TV.

"Dang!" exclaimed Carrie May, searching frantically for a place to put her guests. "Thor! Rafe! Get Omar out of here! The TV's no place for him—put that pig in the kitchen, where he belongs. Better yet, take him outside."

Thor and Rafe didn't budge. They were too busy putting the dog's fur up in curlers. Omar the Pig toddled down from the TV, waded through the laundry, and climbed up onto the only vacant chair. Carrie Mae snatched him up.

"Come on, I'll put him out back. We can sit on the patio."

The patio was five square feet of plywood, adorned with coffee cans containing almost-dead plants. The little area overlooked the small shed that served as a barn and the backyard that sheltered the family livestock. The smell was dreadful. Judith grimaced; Renie squirmed. Carrie Mae carted the pig out through the gate and let out a shriek:

"Oh, no! Look what them kids did now! They glued the goat to their trampoline!"

Trying not to gag, the cousins gingerly approached the sagging wire fence. Sure enough, a weary-looking billy goat stood in the middle of a large piece of canvas that was stretched between four pegs. Setting Omar down, Carrie Mae picked up a trowel from a rusting oil can and started to pry the goat loose.

"Need some help?" Judith offered, hoping to speed up the process and retreat from the odoriferous patio as quickly as possible.

"Naw, I can manage." Sure enough, Carrie Mae had already freed the goat's front hooves. With an angry kick, he freed his back legs and raced off toward the shed.

Judith was about to suggest they go back inside the house when she glanced at the makeshift trampoline for the first time. She gasped. Renie stared at her cousin, then followed Judith's wide, astounded eyes.

"Egad!" cried Renie. "It's 'Spring River'!"

"Egad!" echoed Judith in horror. "It's ruined!"

Renie, however, burst into laughter. "How," she asked between guffaws, "can you tell?"

SEVENTEEN

"STOP!" JUDITH SHRIEKED. "I can't stand it! How could you?" She rolled over on the bed, buried her face in the white-and-yellow-flowered counterpane, and covered her ears.

Joe switched off the VCR. "I didn't *mean* to record it," he said, though there was not a touch of repentance in his voice. "I forgot to turn off the Kevin Costner movie I was recording for you, and I taped the news by accident."

"Like fun," Judith muttered, raising her head. "And Mother! Wouldn't you know she'd watch the channel that would have the full, unexpurgated coverage! And for the first time in ten years, Aunt Deb watches the news, too, all because her handyman's son-in-law was appearing before the city council to protest a bounty on possums!"

Joe made no response, but removed his terry-cloth robe, dumped it on the floor, and turned off the bedside lamp. It was almost 2 A.M. The exhaustion that Judith had fought off in the county sheriff's office thirty miles north of the city had now been replaced by restlessness. She was wide awake. Too many cups of coffee during the hour it had taken for her and Renie to give their statements, too heavy a meal too late at a coffee shop a block from the sheriff's headquarters, and too much of a reaction setting in during the escorted drive home had resulted in wakefulness. The final blow had come when Judith had found Joe lazing on their bed, watching a rerun of the eleven o'clock news.

"I liked the part where Renie jumped on that floorboard and knocked Iris flat," Joe remarked as he got into bed. "The camera angle wasn't very good and the lighting was fuzzy, but you were great going for the gun. It was better than the movies."

"Shut up."

"Your little speech to that Costello fellow was a gem." Joe chuckled as he arranged the pillow behind his head. "His eyes really bugged out when you got to the part about the Tin Hat and the tin cup. Still, he was right. You had no evidence."

"Shut up."

"I suppose that's why you had to confront Iris with nobody else around. Poor Renie couldn't understand why you let Clive drive off and you didn't alert the Kimballs when they came to retrieve Lark's other paintings. It was damned risky, but I can see why you had to get Iris alone. If you couldn't force her to either confess or try to put you two away, she would have gotten off scot-free."

"Shut up."

"What really put you on Iris's trail?" Joe propped himself up on one elbow. "That tape was only the clincher. How did Iris get hold of it?"

Resignedly, Judith crawled under the covers. "I'm not sure," she said in a vexed voice. "I think it was by accident. She may have gone snooping around Ward's studio, looking for the missing painting. Riley had inscribed the tape, from himself to Lark. Lark probably didn't realize that because her eyesight is so poor, but Renie and I saw the writing after we listened to it in the car."

"Was the rest of the tape blank?" Joe inquired, moving one leg just enough so that it touched Judith's thigh.

"Yes, as far as we could tell. The second time around, Riley actually sounded sort of phony, like an actor reading his lines. It was ironic that Lark was such a poor judge of men—but she was more on the mark with Iris. Lark said she was a rapacious conniver. But she was wrong about Iris not loving Riley enough—Iris loved him *too* much. She couldn't bear to lose him to another woman." Judith's voice had perked up as she warmed to her tale. And to Joe. "Iris saw that inscription on the cassette and couldn't resist playing it. She must have had a fit when she heard Riley make what amounted to a marriage proposal to Lark. Her jealously had already driven her to murder. But she didn't dare let anybody know that she had such a strong motive. That's why she made up that ridiculous story about Riley being Lark's father. Iris couldn't let anyone think she had a reason to kill Riley. So the tape had to disappear. Then there'd only be Lark's word for Riley's intentions, and that could be dismissed as the fantasy of an infatuated, impressionable young woman. Iris didn't know we'd heard the tape, too."

Joe flung an arm across Judith's pillow. "You didn't answer the original question."

"Oh. You mean about suspecting Iris?" Judith moved closer to Joe. "Well, there were a bunch of little things. When Renie and I first saw Iris, she had her groceries and a big shoulder bag. Then, when she came running over to tell us she heard a prowler, she claimed she was going back to the Green Mountain Inn to get her car. But she didn't have her shoulder bag. Now think about that. If she'd been telling the truth, she would have had it with her, because she would have expected to pay Gary Johanson if he'd fixed the car. If he hadn't, she'd need money for the pay phone to call for the tow truck."

"Good," Joe said, pulling Judith onto his shoulder. "Very good. But only suggestive."

Feeling the warmth of Joe's body, Judith relaxed. "Gary mentioned that the problem with Iris's car was negligible. The ignition was stuck, and all he had to do was turn the wheels to unlock it. Iris purposely jammed it as an excuse so that she could leave her car at the Green Mountain Inn and it wouldn't be seen at Riley's. She took the river route, walking along the trail, and she heard us at the cabin. Our presence might have surprised her, but it didn't deter her. In fact, it made us her stooges. She went from there to Riley's, got him drunk, strangled him, and then came over to give us her phony prowler story."

"And nobody saw her with Riley in the studio?" Joe rested his cheek on Judith's temple.

"Nobody would, ordinarily. The house is pretty well screened from the road, and there are all those trees between our cabin and Riley's. Nella wasn't home." Judith slipped her arms around Joe's chest. "But Iris *was* seen, and that was very unlucky for her."

Joe's free hand traced Judith's jawline, then touched the tip of her nose. "Who saw her? That agent, stumbling around? The art collector? The Hungarian dealer? Ward Kimball?"

Judith nipped at Joe's roving fingers. "They were all gone by then. Lark, too." She laughed, and realized her mood had definitely improved. "It was the Morton kiddies, being disobedient and crossing the road to play in Riley's yard."

Joe made an incredulous noise. "Now how do you figure that? Or did you ask them?"

"I did, eventually. Just to make sure." Judith pressed even closer and gave a little sigh before resuming her story. "Those kids kept yapping about Sweet-Stix. It dawned on me that they only did it when Iris was around. In fact, one of them said something about how Erica Dixon wouldn't give them candy of any kind and that she was mean. Then they tried to bribe me by saying they'd do anything for sweets. I realized that they'd learned that trick from experience. When I found a bag of Sweet-Stix at Riley's house, I knew for sure. Iris had handed the stuff out to the kids to keep them quiet about seeing her when she wasn't supposed to be there."

"Ah! Out of the mouths of babes!"

"In this case, *into* the mouths of babes."

"Getting kids to testify isn't easy," Joe remarked, brushing Judith's lips with his.

"That crew will love it." Judith laughed softly at the memory of the Morton offspring. "I should have figured some of this out sooner, frankly. Renie told me that Riley wasn't working in tempera—Lark used it, but he didn't. Maybe Iris purposely spilled the tempera to put suspicion on her rival. Or maybe, in her haste, she simply didn't think. Either way, I ought to have realized that the paint was there for a reason that had nothing to do with Riley's work. I'm still kicking myself for not realizing that Riley was dead when we saw him through the studio window."

Joe sniffed at the scent of soap on Judith's bare shoulder. "You see what you expect to see. People are like that. And Iris knew it."

But Judith wouldn't give herself a break. "Riley was propped up by that huge painting, the heavy easel, and that big box of paints. Still, he just had to look unnatural. But, of course, Renie and I were concentrating on finding a prowler. Looking back, I see that what really set me off was Iris's so-called revelation that Riley was Lark's father. When I stopped to figure dates and ages, like when Riley moved from San Francisco and how old Lark is, I realized there was a big discrepancy—at least six years. It just wasn't logical. And it wasn't logical for Iris to tell us such a lie unless she had a reason. There was no point in defaming the late Mrs. Kimball or even Riley. Why turn Ward into a cuckold? Why make Lark out to be illegitimate? It could only be a smoke screen to prove Iris wasn't—couldn't possibly be—jealous."

"Ah, men and women," Joe mused. "The eternal triangle. I sort of like an old-fashioned crime of passion now and then. It breaks the monotony of all those senseless killings where the only motive is dope—and the perps are all dopes, too. And then there are those con artists. I don't see much of them in my job, more's the pity. So Dewitt had figured out a way to get money from his tight-fisted wife. He knew she'd be willing to pay seventy grand for a Riley Tobias, but not a Lark Kimball. So what did he do? Connive with Clive?"

"Exactly. Dewitt had seen Lark working on that canvas. I'm guessing he confronted Riley and demanded a free painting. Otherwise, he would blow the whistle on Riley's deception. Riley had to agree—he'd already passed Lark's work off as his own once, and Erica had seen the picture in progress. But before he could retrieve Lark's 'Morning' from Nella's icehouse, he was killed. Clive knew Riley had given me a painting—he assumed it belonged to the Dixons. After he found it behind the Murphy bed, he gave it to Dewitt. But Dewitt discovered it wasn't the one Erica wanted. I doubt that at this point Clive knew what Riley had been pulling. But Dewitt had to tell him, so they got together the next morning at the Green Mountain Inn and agreed to a pact. Dewitt would 'buy' the real Tobias with Erica's money; then he and Clive would split the proceeds. Later, they'd sell the real 'Spring River' abroad and make even more money. But they had a problem—they didn't know where Lark's canvas was. Dewitt had nothing to show Erica when she returned from Europe. I suspect Clive and Dewitt practically had a falling-out before they even got started, each accusing the other of making off with Lark's painting. The Morton kiddies had swiped the Tobias from the Dixons' motel room, probably while Dewitt was picking Erica up at the airport. It got to be a real jumble." Judith kissed Joe back, then stiffened and pulled away. "Say! Speaking of con games, what kind of trick were you trying to play on me? Were you serious about another bed-and-breakfast?"

Joe's dancing green eyes studied Judith's face. "Were you?"

Mesmerized by his magic gaze, Judith hesitated in answering. "I don't think so. But I suppose I shouldn't dismiss the idea out of hand."

"No rush," Joe said, his voice very low. "Take one thing

at a time. That's what we're doing now. At the moment, it's bed." He kissed her again, holding her tight. "In the morning, it's breakfast."

Judith sighed happily. "It could be more bed."

Joe buried his face in her hair. "It could be both."

Gertrude was leaning on her walker, squinting at the restored Riley Tobias painting that rested against the door to the bathroom off the entry hall. She pulled a cigarette out of her housecoat pocket and flicked on her lighter.

"What does that lamebrained husband of yours think of this thing?" Gertrude asked in her raspy voice.

Judith paused, then answered truthfully. "He says it looks like sink sludge. He thought it was a waste of money to have it repaired after the goat sat on it."

Gertrude snorted loudly. "A lot he knows!" A cloud of smoke enveloped her small, wiry frame. "Tell you what—I've got room for it in the toolshed. You know, in my sitting room, where you hung my picture of the Sacred Heart. We can move Jesus into the bedroom. He won't mind, and I'd like to keep an eye on Him there. Get a hammer and a couple of nails and we'll go hang Riley Whazzisname."

"He's already been strangled," Judith murmured. "Hanging seems a bit much."

"What? Speak up. You know I'm deaf, you knothead." Gertrude expelled more smoke. Sweetums circled her ankles, then wove in and out of the walker's rubber-tipped legs. "Of course I know Riley was strangled," Gertrude went on heatedly, giving the lie to her hearing deficiency. "Didn't I have to see it all on television? *My* daughter, a *Grover,* and *my* niece, another *Grover,* acting as if they were in a wrestling match! It's a wonder the whole world couldn't see your underwear!"

"Our . . . ?" Judith was aghast. She was also strangely reluctant to part with Riley Tobias's last landscape. If that was indeed what it was. Never mind that it was plug-ugly, never mind that Joe hated it, never mind that Sweetums was now swishing his plumelike tail and showing signs of critical disdain. "Spring River," or so Judith had dubbed the work, since that had been Riley's title if only by default, was the work of a once-great artist. On the other hand, it had looked like hell on the staircase landing.

"Okay," Judith agreed. "Let's put this sucker up." She struggled with the painting and headed for the kitchen to get a hammer and nails. Gertrude clumped along behind her. Sweetums beat both of them to the back door.

"One thing," Gertrude called as they went outside. "You got it upside down."

Halfway down the back-porch steps, Judith turned. "Huh? How do you know?"

"Easy." Gertrude carefully made the descent to the concrete walk. "It's a picture of an appendix. The little pink squiggly thing goes the other way." She stopped and banged the walker. "Arlene! Hey! Stop weeding and come take a look!"

Arlene Rankers's red-gold curls bobbed up from behind the laurel hedge. "Hi! A look at what?"

Gertrude wore a smug expression. "Come on over and see my new masterpiece. It cost seventy grand. Of course, I didn't pay for it." Her small eyes sparkled as Arlene hurried into the backyard of Hillside Manor. Pointing to the canvas that Judith was trying to get through the door of the remodeled toolshed, Gertrude simpered. "Only a sap would pay money for something that looks like that. But my late husband always said I had good taste. And I like it. Beauty's in the eye of the beholder, right?"

Arlene studied the painting while Judith stood patiently on the threshold. "It's wonderful," she enthused. "I never knew cole slaw could be so beautiful."

Briefly, Judith debated with herself about hanging the picture, her mother—or Arlene.

Judith wore a jonquil crepe de chine silk suit with a jewel neck and a short, straight skirt. Renie was in coffee-colored palazzo pajamas and a matching drop-shouldered tunic top. Joe Flynn and Bill Jones wore two-piece suits. They said they felt like a pair of pallbearers.

"You look wonderful," Judith whispered to Joe as they accepted glasses of white wine and potted prawns from attentive wait-persons. "You and Bill should dress up more often."

"I wear a tie every day at work," Joe grumbled. "That's more than I can say for the professor over there. He could teach classes in a barrel at the university."

"With what they pay, he may have to." Judith glanced at Bill and Renie, who were engaged in conversation with Dewitt Dixon and Clive Silvanus. "I'm glad Dewitt confessed everything to Erica. Still, it might teach her a lesson. Maybe she'll loosen the purse strings a little. I don't think Dewitt likes being a leech."

"Probably not." Joe nodded a greeting at an official he recognized from city hall. "I suppose it was smart of the Dixons to hire Clive to run the gallery. He may not act like it, but everybody says he knows what he's doing. Let's face it, Riley was the one who tried to pull a fast one in the first place. In a sense, he set everybody else up."

"True," Judith agreed, sampling a raw oyster. "But that was typical of Riley. He liked putting other people on the spot. He could manage it even after he was dead."

"That's real clout," Joe declared. "I'm not excusing Dewitt and Clive, but they were presented with a temptation that was too hard to overcome. Entrapment, I'd call it. Now, with Lark Kimball as a client, they've got an investment instead."

Judith smiled over the rim of her wineglass. "Lark may end up doing as well as Riley did. Look at this crowd! Erica certainly knows how to bring people out."

Erica Dixon was at the center of a large group, exuding charm and pressing the flesh. The opening of her new gallery featured several Pacific Northwest artists and sculptors. Riley Tobias was represented by his "Unfinished Nerd," and, more happily, by a half-dozen works from his early and middle periods that had been released from his foundation by the imprisoned Iris Takisaki. The center of attention, however, was Lark Kimball's "Dawn" and "Morning." The former had been donated by Lazlo Gamm; the latter was dedicated to Riley Tobias.

"Well? What do you think?" Lark, in a pleated, sheer navy silk georgette dinner dress, sounded nervous yet exhilarated. "Did I do the right thing?"

Judith grasped her by the hand. "You've done wonderfully well. The critics and the collectors are enchanted, Lark. Erica might have beaten the drums, but they're dancing to your tune."

At Lark's side, Ward Kimball beamed. So did Lazlo Gamm, who was hovering at Lark's other elbow. His usual hangdog expression had been replaced by a rapt look of puppylike devotion. "I'm so proud," Ward Kimball announced. "Lark has found her niche in life. I couldn't be happier."

Studying Ward's joyful face, Judith decided that Lark's newly found confidence and success definitely agreed with her father. He looked ten years younger. "I see that Erica managed to coax a couple of paintings out of you, too. I heard one critic say he was forecasting a revival for your work. Any chance of you painting again?"

Ward's brow furrowed. "I doubt it. I've had my hour in the sun. It's time for the younger generation to take over. I passed the mantle on to Riley." His arm went around Lark's slim shoulders. "Now it's up to Lark." He smiled down on his daughter. "Do you want it?"

Lark's face glowed, and her eyes seemed to shimmer. "I must. I do. I will."

Judith smiled. The torch had been passed. Riley Tobias had been burned, so had Iris Takisaki, but Lark Kimball had risen from the ashes like a phoenix. The flame leaped in her breast. And in her eyes, which saw so little, though her soul had a vision of its own.

* * *

"Damn!" Judith tossed the official county document aside and stomped over to the coffeepot. "The taxes have gone up again on the cabin!"

It was a Saturday in October, and the third-quarter property tax statement had just arrived in the morning mail. Joe was perusing the sports section of the daily newspaper.

"How much?"

"Only twenty-three bucks. But that's still a lot, considering. We've never even put the new gutters in." She poured out more coffee for both of them.

Joe looked up from a story on the World Series. "You divvy that up with Renie and the rest of the clan, don't you?"

"Oh, yeah, right. Still . . ." Judith sipped from her coffee mug with its official NFL emblem. "It's been over five months since Renie and I went up there to clean out. The only members of the family who have used the cabin since are Cousin Sue's oldest and Mike and Kristin when they took their gang to celebrate their graduation. What's the point of keeping the place just for ourselves if we don't use it?"

Carefully, Joe folded the sports section and set it aside. "We flew to San Francisco in June. Then the summer tourist season set in and you couldn't get away. In late August, you went to Idaho for three days to help Mike get settled in on his new job with the Forest Service. Aunt Ellen and Uncle Win were out here from Nebraska in September. I just got back from that conference in San Diego. We lead busy lives, Jude-girl. Do you want to take on even more, or . . . ?" He let the rest of the question dangle.

Judith sighed. She reached into the sheep-shaped cookie jar and found only a single stale brownie. "I don't even have time to bake these days," she grumbled.

"And?" Joe's green eyes fixed on Judith's face.

Judith lowered her gaze. "And I'm bone-tired by this time of year. I don't see how I could possibly convert the cabin into a B & B, even if we had the money and didn't have to worry about what the rest of the relatives would think."

Joe gave a slight nod, then pushed away from the kitchen table and smoothed his graying red hair. "So how about a little R & R away from the B & B? We could do it ASAP."

Judith's jaw dropped. "You mean—today? But we've got guests coming in from California and Arizona and Alberta tonight!"

Joe seemed unaffected by his wife's objections. "We've also got Arlene and Carl Rankers." He stood up. "Throw something in a suitcase. I'll go next door and see if the Rankerses can bail us out for tonight and tomorrow morning."

"But . . ."

"But what?" Joe was wearing his most ingenuous expression. "Your mother? Uncle Al is taking her and Aunt Deb to dinner this evening, remember? Tomorrow, Auntie Vance and Uncle Vince are hauling the old girls up to the mountains to see the fall foliage." Joe came back to the kitchen table and leaned over Judith. "You're not chained to this place. Or to your mother. You're my wife. I want to go to the cabin. With you. Got it?"

Slowly, Judith's head came up. Her black eyes gazed at Joe's round, engaging face. She smiled. "I've got it." She rested her head against his slightly budding paunch. "It took almost twenty-five years," she said on a sigh, "but I finally got it."

Joe patted her shoulder. "Good. Then let's get gone." He went over to the Rankerses'. Judith went upstairs. A suitcase went into the back of Joe's MG. A bottle of vintage port went, too. And, half an hour later, Judith and Joe went to the cabin.

The world and Hillside Manor went on without them.